WITHDRAWN

MAGIC
HAS
NO
BORDERS

MAGIC
HAS NO
BORDERS

EDITED BY
SONA CHARAIPOTRA
& SAMIRA AHMED

HARPER TEEN

An Imprint of HarperCollinsPublishers

HarperTeen is an imprint of HarperCollins Publishers.

Magic Has No Borders copyright © 2023 by Samira Ahmed
and Sona Charaipotra
"Kiss Me Goodbye" copyright © 2023 by Tracey Baptiste
"Chudail" copyright © 2023 by Nikita Gill
"A Goddess of Fire and Blood" copyright © 2023 by Tanaz Bhathena
"Infinite Drift" copyright © 2023 by Olivia Chadha
"Dismantle the Sun" copyright © 2023 by Sangu Mandanna
"Shamsuddin-Jalal" copyright © 2023 by Tahir Abrar
"The Collector" copyright © 2023 by Sona Charaipotra
"Unraveled" copyright © 2023 by Preeti Chhibber
"She Who Answers" copyright © 2023 by Shreya Ila Anasuya
"The Hawk's Reason" copyright © 2023 by Naz Kutub
"Poetry of Earth" copyright © 2023 by Swati Teerdhala
"Mirch, Masala, and Magic" copyright © 2023 by Nafiza Azad
"Daughter of the Sun" copyright © 2023 by Sayantani DasGupta
"What the Winds Stole" copyright © 2023 by Sabaa Tahir
Illustrations copyright © 2023 by Tara Anand, Neha Kapil, Mira F. Malhotra,
Nimali, Cynthia Paul, Chaaya Prabhat, Neha Shetty, and Sibu T.P.
All rights reserved. Printed in the United States of America.
No part of this book may be used or reproduced in any manner whatsoever
without written permission except in the case of brief quotations embodied in
critical articles and reviews. For information address HarperCollins Children's
Books, a division of HarperCollins Publishers,
195 Broadway, New York, NY 10007.
www.epicreads.com

Library of Congress Control Number: 2022949056
ISBN 978-0-06-320826-1

Typography by Joel Tippie
23 24 25 26 27 LBC 5 4 3 2 1

First Edition

To the ancestors who fought for us to be free, to the ones who marched to the sea, and to the ones who fashioned us wings and told us we could fly. اِنقلاب زِنده باد

And to T, L, & N. Always and forever.
—Samira Ahmed

To those who came before, crossing borders and oceans. May your stories come to light. And to those who came after, lifting their voices to share our kahaanis.

And to Shaiyar, Kavya, and all the brown kids who finally get to write themselves into the narrative. —Sona Charaipotra

TABLE OF

CONTENTS

Dear Reader,

It is not lost on me that as I write this note for this gorgeous anthology that Sona Charaipotra and I dreamed up years ago, one of South Asia's greatest writers, Salman Rushdie, is lying in a hospital after being brutally attacked for his words. I remember meeting Rushdie in New York and hearing him talk about how poetry and stories cannot stop bullets or bombs, but they can tell the truth.

I am also thinking about how I write this on the eve of the 75th anniversary of Indian and Pakistani independence, when the yoke of British tyranny over the subcontinent was at last thrown off. Not peacefully, as so many textbooks wrongly claim, but through the violence of Partition—a violence deeply shaped and cultivated by British colonial policies—ones that sought to divide, to sow sectarian conflict, in order to ease an exit for the British. Conquerors always want to get off scot-free, don't they? The British hastily drew up articles of separation, a haphazard division of nations that ripped families apart. We still deeply feel those fissures today.

Despite Muslims mostly being forced to migrate to Pakistan, my own immediate family chose to stay in India. My Nani, my mother's mother, firmly planted her feet on Bombay soil, refusing to leave. She was born in India, she said, and so she would die in India. And she did, stubborn to the end. However, that decision also came with a high cost— half our Muslim family migrated to Pakistan, and with the ongoing hostilities between the newly formed nations, my grandmother was never able to see some of her family again.

My dad's side of the family lived in Hyderabad—an independent princely state that was never formally under British rule (about one-third of India prior to 1947 was never ruled by the British—this includes the area of Jammu and Kashmir, an area of continued, heartbreaking conflict). Hyderabad briefly maintained its independence during and after Partition, so my family stayed. My Dada, my father's father, had to go into hiding to escape first British troops and then Indian ones as India's new government forcibly annexed Hyderabad under Operation Polo.

Why am I referencing so much personal, sectarian, and state violence and colonialism as I speak to what inspired this anthology of diverse voices from across the subcontinent? Simply put, those divisive forces unfortunately shaped and shifted much of the post-1947 diaspora experience; but they do not define who we are. Those hostile dynamics don't speak to the subcontinent's brilliant and beautiful diversity—often erased by colonial rulers and political parties that seek to foment division and rancor where none need exist.

Like my Nani, I was born in India to a Muslim family that has been there for countless generations, and I won't let anyone take that away from me. Nor will I let any exclusionary power decide how "desi" is defined. A term rooted in the word for country, nation. I believe that word should be inclusive—regardless of religion or tribe, ethnicity or class or caste or gender. As individuals whose ancestors share a common geography, if not always a language or tradition, we get to define ourselves. That's the spirit behind this anthology. We are a people, unified, without borders, but filled with the songs and tales that hum in our bones. We are a global family that lives not merely in harmony but in melody.

For this anthology, Sona and I brought together a diverse group of desi authors who represent different regions and cultures and experiences to breathe new life into stories handed down through generations, to add a unique spin to characters both familiar and new. I'm so proud of the work of our contributors, each one of them a shining jewel not in the crown of an oppressor but in the endless treasure trove that is the South Asian diaspora experience.

Salaam, Shanti, Peace.
Samira Ahmed

Dear Reader,

As a small brown girl growing up in the heart of central New Jersey in the 1990s, I was an avid reader. I was absolutely shattered by the loss of my new friend on the way to Terabithia. I started a babysitter's club with my neighborhood pals. I reveled in creating stories out in Idlewild with Anne and Diana. I suffered through long, brutal New England winters with the March sisters. I even swooned over a pair of brooding vampire brothers from Fell's Church. But as much as I read—voraciously, delightedly—I rarely ever found myself or anyone who looked like me in the pages of my favorite books. And it was not until I was much older—in college, actually—that I even realized I was missing from the stories I loved so dearly.

But once I noticed it, I couldn't unsee it. Brown kids like me—the ones who wore sneakers with their salwar kameez and felt just as awkward at the eighth-grade dance as they did at the gurdwara on Sundays—were nowhere to be found on the page or the screen. And we certainly weren't out there saving the world like Ms. Marvel (who's from Jersey, like me).

Nearly twenty years later, as a new parent, I was shocked to realize that things remained so much the same. And that if writers like me didn't do something about it, my own little readers would live through that same shock. The hurt that brought was deep and profound. In fact, when my coeditor, Samira Ahmed, and I first dreamed up this anthology five years ago, we could still count the number of South Asian voices in YA publishing on two hands.

Now, with efforts from We Need Diverse Books and other organizations, things have finally begun to change. There are more of us writing and telling stories—and my kids do finally get to see reflections of themselves on the page. And in this anthology featuring some truly amazing voices, readers will get to dive headfirst into South Asian myth and legend and lore, reimagined by writers from across the breadth and depth of the South Asian diaspora—stories a kid like me could never even have begun to imagine growing up. I hope you love them as much as I do.

Thank you for reading.
Sona Charaipotra

MAGIC HAS NO BORDERS

ART BY NIMALI

KISS ME GOODBYE
By Tracey Baptiste

A goddess should not have to do her own assassinations. But if you want something done correctly, better do it yourself. So here we are again, for maybe the thousandth time. I say "maybe" because I stopped counting after about the three-hundredth reincarnation—a lot of them are a blur. But it always plays out pretty much the same. I awake into a new life and a new body, just in time to figure out who the target is, find all the traps that have been laid, foil them, kill the guy, and then go back to sleep until the next time the world forgets who I am.

It's the forgetting I can't stand. The whole point of being a goddess is the active worship. People need to remember and pay me my due respect. Sometimes that means I need to

3

remind them by taking a life. It's honor me or be killed. Simple. If people didn't forget, we wouldn't have to play this out over and over again, would we? So whose fault is that, huh? I refuse to be forgotten, to fall into the undignified realm of myth and legend or worse . . . superhero action movies.

Shudder.

Meanwhile, this host body is a little . . . let's say, feisty. I can feel her fighting me, trying to regain control. Frankly, it's sapping my energy and hella irritating. But it's also what made her a good host in the first place.

Don't worry, little host. You'll have your body back as soon as I'm done with my mission. It'll ruin your life, sure, but what's one human life when we're talking about the needs of a goddess? Shh.

"Kala? Kala! Are you listening?"

It's my mother. This girl's mother. It always takes a few hours to get used to the host's name.

"Yes, Ma," I say.

"I asked what time I'm picking you up today."

I catch a glimpse of myself in the sun shield mirror. I've clearly just rolled out of bed. My dark curls are a mess and my eyes are still puffy.

"Don't you have rehearsal?"

"Right," I tell Kala's—my—mother. "That."

"So?"

I squeeze the memory out of the host. "Six thirty. We'll be done by then."

And with any luck, so will I.

It's great when things are smooth. I figure out which host body has Lakhindar. I find the best and most efficient way to execute him. I'm out of the host before anyone realizes what's happened. I'm usually long gone before the confusion sets in and the questions begin. *Why did this happen? Why would they do this? They were always so quiet. So friendly. No one saw this coming.*

But sometimes I stick around long enough for someone to remember my name. They say *Manasa*, and suddenly they all know who I am, and they understand that these deaths are a consequence of their forgetfulness. They promise to always remember. And then . . .

"Well, get going, then," my mother says. "You'll be late."

I get out of the car, pull my backpack on, and head into the school building. I have never been a high school student before. In New Jersey, no less. Once, I was in New Orleans during Prohibition. Now *that* was a good time. America in the 1920s was also great for fashion. I look down at the ripped jeans and crop top I'm wearing. It's no beaded flapper dress, but a lot more comfortable than most things I've had to put on. I lose myself in the stream of students headed to class. They are mostly much taller than me. Every single time, I hope I'll find myself in the body of someone tall. But I'm an Indian woman. We're on the shorter side. Facts.

At the lockers, a girl with a bright orange stripe of hair waves at me.

"Hey Nikole." I pull at the combination lock and fiddle with it.

Nikole rolls her eyes. "Seriously? You're going to stand there like everybody isn't waiting to hear what happened yesterday?"

I look around the hallway. Nobody seems to be waiting for anything.

"What?"

"The hell happened with Marcus?"

As I pull out my stuff for chemistry, math, and world literature, I evaluate potential weapons: binder rings, a clicky pen, a dull pencil. Not stellar choices. "Nothing," I say.

She shoves her phone in my face. It takes me a second to adjust my eyes so I can read all the text messages. The one next to her perfectly manicured thumb reads *she kicked his ass*.

I snort. "I don't kick, and he doesn't have much of an ass."

"You're saying there wasn't a whole fight?"

I show her my hand. "I didn't even bruise myself. It was one hit. Heel of my hand to his nose. He went down. It was over."

Her laugh surprises the kids closest to us, but only for a moment. "Want me to do damage control?"

"The damage has been controlled already," I say, and hold up both fists.

My hosts tend to be a little on the violent side. Hot-tempered, quick to react. It makes things easier for me to have a little rage to draw from, but also to have someone who already knows how to land a blow. But I've never had a host who was so thoroughly nonchalant about it. There's usually some adrenaline. A rush of dopamine. But not this girl. I could not have picked a better host.

"Damn," Nikole says. "You are cold."

I shrug.

She grins. "So what does this mean now, for the two of you?"

I slam my locker closed. "It means I'm done."

Through the whole chem period, I look around waiting for Lakhindar to show up. I'm anxious to get this over with. Killing Lakhindar is rarely the problem. It's Behula who makes everything a nightmare. Her never-ending attempts to save him are infuriating. She hasn't made an appearance, either. As soon as I sit in my second-period world literature class, I feel him arrive. It's just like all the other times. An electrical current coats my skin and my head turns like a compass. Before I even spot him, I'm thinking about how this idiot only has a few hours left to live.

Lakhindar walks in. Tall. Bronze. A jawline of cut granite. One of those smiles that can melt ice. He is an actual god. My body temperature rises. My pulse quickens. Everything about me feels suddenly soggy and rigid at the same time. He slips into the desk behind me.

"Hey."

Fuck his fucking deep beautiful voice. Fuck.

"Kala." He whispers it like his tongue is heavy with honey. Like he is wrapping me in something soft.

"Yes." It is more of a sigh than a word.

"I heard about what happened with you and Marcus." He

is leaning so close, the hairs on my neck strain toward him. "Did that have something to do with me?"

I turn around. It's like looking directly at the sun. "You are not the center of the universe, you know." Except, he might be.

"Okay. I just thought that maybe because you and I . . ."

"At the moment, you and I aren't anything, remember? We agreed."

He frowns. He seems hurt by this. I feel an actual stab of pain. "I thought . . . never mind."

I cannot stop looking at his mouth, at the rise and fall of his shoulders as he breathes, at the way the bit of sunlight from the windows plays on his dark hair.

It looks like Lakhindar hasn't fully arrived in the body of this kid yet. I can sense him beneath the surface, but why he's not emerging, I can't tell. In the meantime, this kid is playing out a life I just don't have the time for. Still, I lean in a little because he smells a bit spicy. I want to inhale him more deeply, when I should be focused on how exactly I am going to kill him. Because the moment Behula arrives, whatever this is between his breath and my own is not going to matter.

"I know we agreed, but you went ahead and punched Marcus in the face. So that means you two are done, right? And that also means that you and I . . ."

"I already said, this is not about you."

He pulls back, and I focus on the front of the room. What are the available weapons in a literature class? Death by a million paper cuts? Inefficient. There's the possibility of slamming his head into the corner of a desk, landing right at the temple. I gauge his height and the leverage I would need to execute this. The physics are against me. I have to wait for Behula, anyway. She has to see it.

The kid, who will very soon become Lakhindar—though I wish he would hurry up already—gives me a side-eye at the end of class. Even his side-eye is hot. I adjust my hair a little so it's slightly over my face and fiddle with my notebooks so he's way ahead by the time I get out into the hallway. He looks great from the back, too. Like a swimmer. All muscle sloping down to a V and a really, really tight—

"Dammit!" My books are all over the hallway, and someone hops over my chem lab notes and continues walking rather than helping me. I stoop to grab everything and look his way again, but Lakhindar is gone.

"You could say 'excuse me,'" a girl says. She's standing over me with something of a haughty look on her face.

"Why should I? It's my stuff all over the floor."

"If you were paying attention to where you were going instead of staring at Jay Hassan's ass, it wouldn't have happened."

I grab at my lab notes, pinned under the heel of her sneaker. As I pull, she rocks back so the paper rips.

"Oops!"

It's then I catch the scent of her, like poison in the air. Sweet, cloying, covering something that would burn you from the inside out. Like floral-scented air freshener in a gas station toilet.

I bristle. "Behula."

She smiles. No matter how many times we've done this, or how many bodies she's occupied, that smile—that smug, irritating, vicious smile—remains the same. It's the kind of smile that makes you want to slap the teeth out of some-body's face.

"Manasa." She says my name as if there are shards of glass in her mouth.

"It's Kala, actually." I straighten up with the pieces of my lab notes.

"Get this," she says. "My name's Ronnie. Short for Veronica. Cute, huh?"

"Adorable," I say. "Enjoy your little fun, because it's not going to last."

"Not this time," she says. She looks back to where Lakhin-dar was before he turned the corner and applies some lipstick to her smirky mouth. "I think I might really enjoy this one."

I could get this over with. I could run down the hallway, grab Lakhindar by the hair, and drag him back in front of her as I bludgeon him with a binder. I could stab him in the eye with a dull pencil and hold him down while he bleeds out. Behula will see it happen. But neither of these are efficient. Someone in one of these classrooms will stop me. Call for help before he's good and dead. Plus, there are rules. Lakhindar has to be here, too. All the way in the body of his host. I have no choice but to wait. At least it gives me the opportunity to plan.

Meanwhile, the real Kala is trying so hard to assert herself.

She does not want me to do this. I've never had a host fight me so hard.

"It'll be quick. I promise," I whisper to her.

"Ha, I don't think so," Behula says.

I guess I wasn't as quiet as I thought.

"I think this time, you fail," Behula continues. "Then nobody will remember who you are. Forever."

As I turn to my next class, Behula runs a streak of her purple lipstick down my top.

"What. The actual. Fuck."

"Just for fun," she says.

"Oh, is it fun we're trying to have?" I say. "All right, then. Let's have fun."

I watch Behula leave, then, instead of going to my next class, I return to the chemistry lab.

"Did you forget something, Kala?" the chemistry teacher asks.

I hold up my ripped lab notes.

"Need tape?" she asks.

"There's some kind of gunk on the back of it, too," I say. "I'm just going to write out a fresh one."

"I need to go to the office," she says. "You'll be okay here by yourself?"

I nod.

"Lock the door when you leave."

Poison is an efficient way to kill a person. Simple. Bloodless. Doesn't require brute force. Elegant. But no one ever calls

11

me elegant. They hate me. They fear me. But if that means respect, I'll take it. Plus, I understand poison. Venom, really. It's one of the advantages of being birthed as a divine snake.

Another advantage is Kala's relationship with her chemistry teacher. I can't imagine most kids would be trusted enough to be left alone in a lab. Once again, I'm thrilled at my host selection, even as she fights against me. She actually stopped my hand when I reached for the 2,4-dinitrophenol. Which is why we're going subtler. Less explosive. More in my wheelhouse.

I like whipping up a good poison. It's all about creativity. Kind of like making a meal. There are plenty of combinations with potential. I could burn his skin off or make him puke until he bleeds . . . lots of ways to go. Kala hates each of these options. She makes the process painfully slow. I slip and spill all over the place. But I'm stronger. I'm in charge. And ultimately, it's my decision, though it's Behula who seals Lakhindar's fate.

Behula, the dutiful wife from the stories, sworn to save her poor helpless husband Lakhindar from me, the vengeful snake goddess. Why vengeance? Because Lakhindar's death was sealed by his family's disrespect to me. Imagine, not giving a goddess her due—well, they paid for that. In the beginning, I almost felt bad for them, suffering for other people's mistakes. But over the millennia, we sank into our roles, and a heated hatred grew between Behula and me.

This time, my vengeance is poetry, because she inspires the method of delivery.

At lunch, Nikole slides in next to me at the table. "He's here, you know," she says. "Marcus."

"I do not give a shit about Marcus." It is both me, Manasa, and host Kala who says this. The unison feels good. It feels right to be on the same side, to not fight each other.

"He's your boyfriend," Nikole says.

I roll my eyes. I don't have time for the distraction. I need to get the job done.

Wait.

It's Kala. Shit. That moment of working together let her break through to the surface somehow, and now I can hear her clearly.

Please.

I feel her fear. Her desperation. Her wild despair over why this is happening to her. I feel sorry for her. Actually sorry. It's not her fault. It's none of the hosts' faults. It's just . . . this is bigger than three people. This is divine. Cosmic. Still . . .

I'm sorry, I tell her.

Marcus sits next to me and looks me in the eye. His are bruised from my hit. I turn away quickly. This is not like me, not facing up to someone. Kala is distracting me, making this whole ordeal harder than it needs to be. "Is this really about you and me, or is it about you and Jay?" he asks.

I sigh. I do not want to be distracted by teenage love triangle drama. I don't want to know about this kid's feelings. Or what is going to happen after Lakhindar is dead, and Jay Hassan with him. I am not supposed to care that Kala is going to pay for my actions. I need to focus on my honor. I am only supposed to care about what I'm owed: respect, reverence, supplication.

"Tell me, Kala," he continues. "What's going on with you and Jay?"

I've had enough. It's time to end this. I search the cafeteria, but Lakhindar and Behula are nowhere around. I wonder what they're playing at. Things never take this long once everyone's found their host. Anger rises in me.

I am tired. I want to be done already.

I want to make my kill.

I look Marcus in the face. A kill is a kill, is it not? I wonder how deep a plastic spork could go into his carotid.

I hold it securely in my hand, ready to sink it into his flesh. I feel the desire to exact someone's death rising through my body, thrilling me.

He looks startled. A little afraid of what he sees in my face.

I like it.

My hand tightens around the handle of the spork so hard, it snaps. And with it, my rage breaks a little.

"You're lucky," I say. I am close, and my voice is a whisper. "If I were you, I would back off."

He does, but now that I'm wound up, I know no one is safe.

The cafeteria is a veritable cornucopia of killing objects. They don't even realize. A slippery patch where some asshole dropped their greasy burger could fell one of those big football guys, bringing him down on the hard floor with a crack to the skull. Concussion for sure. Potential brain bleed, maybe. But if he's nudged at the right angle and comes down on the wheel of one of the foldaway tables, it's instant death. Behind the salad buffet, a pair of metal tongs could gouge out an eye—both, if I squeeze the sides to the appropriate wideness. In the kitchen are knives, hot oil, heavy pans . . . less accessible, but I'm quick, and they are wholly unprepared.

I glance around the room. I could inflict serious pain in a matter of minutes. I get excited. This is when things get messy. This is when there is too much collateral damage. I need to calm down, focus. Poison is more me—a precision instrument, not a blunt object—and I have picked my path. It's time to get it done.

I step over the bench and stride to the nearest bathroom just to get away. I open the door, and there's Behula, in Ronnie's body, leaning toward the mirror, reapplying her purple lipstick. She caps it and sticks it in her front jeans pocket as I walk in. As the door slams behind me, she starts to clap.

"That was super entertaining," she says.

I pull some paper towels from the dispenser and swipe roughly at my face. I am crying. Why am I crying? I hate that my host is so close to the surface.

"In a thousand years, I don't think I've ever seen you so emotional. Cold, sure. Angry. But what's this? Regret?" She tilts her head like she's taking in the details of a specimen. "Could you actually be feeling sorry?" She shakes her head. "Nah. Never."

I get close to her. I can feel her rage coming at me in waves of heat. This is my moment. "Imagine thinking I care about any of these people, or you and your insipid little love."

"You don't get to insult love when you don't even know what it is," Behula says.

"People love me," I say.

"People fear you," she says. "When you squeeze adoration out of people like a boa constrictor, that isn't love. Ever think there might be a different way?"

This stops me, and she sees me waver.

"What you do isn't right," she says. "Someone has to stop you." She cocks a perfectly threaded eyebrow. "Imagine me, a regular lowly human being, stopping a goddess. A daughter of Shiva."

I will not be insulted. "If everyone remembered who I am as well as you do, we wouldn't have to keep doing this."

"Sad how everyone keeps forgetting you, though, isn't it, Manasa?"

I let her enjoy her moment, because it won't last long. "I don't mind reminding them," I say as I grab her arm and dig into it. "As a matter of fact, I enjoy it. Do you enjoy your part? Constantly having to save a man who can't save himself?"

Her smirk dissolves. I've hit a nerve. I let go of her shoulder and she pushes her way outside.

Nikole catches the door. "You okay?"

I toss Ronnie's lipstick into the air and catch it. "Yup."

Backstage, the school auditorium smells like dust and moth-eaten costumes from the last century. Shadowy, and full of hidden pockets of space behind equipment, it's as good a place as any for the scene of the crime. This time, I might even be able to get it done and save Kala from any of the consequences. Why I'm even considering saving the host . . .

Still, Kala begs. She wants none of this. *What if there's another way?* she pleads.

It's the same thing Behula said earlier. *There isn't,* I tell Kala. *There has to be!*

Behula arrives backstage and drops her bag off. She searches through her pockets. I know what she's looking for. They're about to rehearse the scene in *Little Shop of Horrors* where Seymour meets Audrey's boyfriend for the first time. Ronnie is Audrey, Jay is Dr. Scrivello, and the director has worked in a kiss. Ronnie is going to want her lipstick. Which . . . of course . . . she doesn't have.

Please, Kala says. *I don't want to kill anyone.*

"Will you just shut up!"

Behula and several other people backstage turn to me. I cover my mouth quickly so she won't see that my mouth is Ronnie purple. I can't tip my hand. Not yet. Nikole raises her eyebrows at me before returning to painting a backdrop. Behula and the others move away. I am not their concern.

"What is it with you the last few days?" Jay asks.

I startle. I had no idea he was there. I turn to look up into that face. That perfect, lovely face. I feel the real Kala's

17

stomach flip. I know how much she wants to touch him. How much she wants to kiss him. How much she will break if anything happens to him.

She fights me for control. "Just go," she makes me say.

But I need him here. This is exactly what I had planned. "Wait," I say.

"Which is it?" He looks exasperated.

I grab his wrist. The throb of his pulse makes me pull back as if I've touched a live wire.

Do not do it, Kala pleads.

I don't have a choice, I tell her.

I'll do anything, she says.

"Wait," I say again. Softer this time. He steps closer. I can smell the spicy scent coming off his body. I'm consumed by . . . something I don't recognize.

Is this . . . love?

There has to be another way, Kala begs.

I can't think. I can barely move. Kala's feelings are overwhelming.

"I get that this has been tough," Jay says. "Ending things with Marcus . . . realizing that you and I . . . have . . ." He can't finish.

I want him to say it, though. I want to hear his voice. I want him to tell me what we have. I need him to describe it, because I don't know what it is. I have never felt this before.

"I want this to be right," he says. "I'll talk to Marcus."

He is so close. I know that this is my moment. Everything

is set up. But Lakhindar is still not at the surface. And I am pulled in. Pulled into his skin, his breath, his scent, the way his larynx moves when he swallows. I just want him to touch me. Maybe Lakhindar is there enough. Maybe I can feel this boy's touch and dispatch Lakhindar in the same moment. Maybe I can enjoy this two ways. I finger the lipstick in my pocket. I feel the stickiness of it on my mouth. I can kiss him now. End this.

No, please! Kala begs. *Not like this.*

I turn my face up, inhale his breath, close my eyes.

I can't.

I won't.

I will not kill this boy.

I begin to pull back and open my eyes, but when I meet Jay's, it's not him I see. It's Lakhindar, finally. His eyes are narrowed to slits, and his face is etched steel contorted into a sneer.

He despises me.

"I can't believe you would kill this kid, after all this." He pushes me away.

His disgust shreds me. "No," I say. "I wasn't going to."

"I'm right here, Manasa," he says. "I saw what you were going to do."

"I changed my mind," I say.

I am in tatters, and inside me, Kala is similarly shattered. To watch her love turn on her like that. To be the object of his disgust. Her pain is explosive.

Whatever fight she had in her has turned to shrapnel. It is only me now.

"What was the plan?" he asks. "Poison?" He grabs at my hand and wrenches the lipstick out of it.

That was exactly the plan. I would have kissed Lakhindar with Behula's lipstick on. Then, when she kissed him onstage, he would have passed it to her, and that would've been the end of both of them. But Kala would have lived, because I made sure to put sealant on her mouth first.

The plan was clean. Good. And this time, Behula would not be alive to save her love.

"I wasn't going to do it," I say. "You have to believe me."

Sadness rises inside me like a tide. I purse my lips, pouting poison as I try to stop myself from crying.

There are certain defeats I will accept. Tears are not included.

"We really thought this time you would have some compassion," Lakhindar says.

Something cools in me.

"You thought?"

Behula steps up next to him. "Is that mine?" She points to the lipstick. "As soon as you took it from me in the bathroom, I knew we had you beat," she says. "But I really didn't think you would get this far."

"You planned this whole thing," I say. "Pretending to look for your lipstick just now, too?"

"Kala was a good candidate," Behula says. "She had

everything going for her. Rage, a love triangle, this play. It's an excellent setup."

"I chose her," I say. "Not you."

Behula laughs.

I have to admit, she got me, and I respect her for it. I chuckle and shake my head.

"I'm surprised you didn't see it coming," she says. "You're usually better than this. I've never actually been able to fool you."

I see that she respects me as well. "You've come close a couple of times," I admit.

"But this time . . ." She smacks a chef's kiss.

Lakhindar seems disconcerted at Behula's and my sudden camaraderie. "You weren't entirely right," he says. "You thought Kala's feelings would stop Manasa much sooner, but they didn't."

Behula snorts. "Believe me, if she wanted you dead, you would be."

"I told you I changed my mind," I say.

I carefully peel the sealant with the poisoned lipstick on it off my mouth and toss it in the trash.

"What did you use?" she asks.

"It's a compound that mimics copperhead venom."

"Classic," Behula says.

I sink down until I'm sitting on the floor between some of the props. A large leaf from Audrey II looms over me. Behula sits next. Lakhindar is still standing, looking confused.

"You wanna clue in your dear husband?"

Behula rolls her eyes. "I'm a little tired of explaining, to be honest." She looks at Lakhindar. "Sit."

He does.

The three of us are a triangle of folded legs and tired bodies facing each other. We have been locked in this position for seconds. Years. Millennia.

"Maybe you're right and there is another way," I say.

"I was hoping," Behula said. "I'm tired. Aren't you tired?"

I rest my head back on the dentist's chair prop. "Exhausted," I say.

"We weren't sure it would work," Behula says.

"'We'?" I ask.

She laughs. "Well, me. But I did explain it to Lakhindar. All he had to do was hang back from Jay for a while and give you a chance—"

"To fall in love with Lakhindar's host." Now I know why I could sense Lakhindar beneath Jay's surface. I look at the streak of purple lipstick on my cropped sweatshirt. "And this?"

"That was a risk, but I was hoping you'd take the bait," Behula says.

"Well played."

"You're good with weaponry," she says. "But like a true snake, you prefer poisons."

I nod. "I had no control of any of it, then."

"You could have ignored all of it and killed me anyway," Lakhindar says. He seems a bit sour.

22

"Then we'd have to start all over again," Behula added.

"What if it all resets anyway?" I say.

"At least we tried," Lakhindar says.

"There's that we again," I say.

Behula chuckles. Her hand falls on my knee. That heat returns. Different this time. Softer, somehow. More of a low burn than a roaring fire.

"I have a question."

Behula nods at me, encouraging.

"How Kala feels about Jay. The way she would do anything for him. She would have done anything to stop me. Is that love?"

"Yeah," she says. "It's like that."

"For the two of you, too?" I ask.

She arches an eyebrow. "I mean."

This catches Lakhindar's attention. "What? Don't you love me? You're my wife! You save me . . . have been saving me for all this time."

"Yes," Behula says. "I have. And what have you been doing?"

Lakhindar is surprised. His jaw is tight and his muscles tense.

My hand finds Behula's. I squeeze her fingers in my own. There's the slightest jolt. It feels good, like magnetic poles clicking together. "I knew that had to be irritating. So now what?"

"Now we leave," Behula says. "We leave and we see what happens."

I shake my head. "I don't know. That's too . . . passive for me. I don't want to see what happens. I want to decide for myself." There's something in the way she looks at me. Like something I recognized in Jay's face as he searched Kala's. I lean toward her. Her flowery scent overwhelms me. But this time, I don't hate it. I don't think it's covering something. It's just . . . her. "What do you think?"

She only nods.

I reach out with my other hand on her shoulder.

Her kiss is soft and light. I feel it thrum through every cell in my body and all the way through time and space. All this while, this was what I had been looking for. This kind of love. All these years, it didn't have to be the way we'd been doing it.

Behula and I pull apart. Lakhindar's mouth is open. We realize there are a few people backstage and the crew all have their mouths open as well. Nikole is texting. And behind her, Marcus stands rigid. He's shocked. Upset. Angry.

"Time to go," I say. I have never left a mess quite like this one.

Behula nods.

We begin to evacuate from our hosts. We leave like mist rolling away from sunlight, half occupying them and half out of their bodies. I feel Kala return. She reaches for Jay. He presses toward her and pulls her mouth to his.

There are actual gasps backstage now. From the front of the house, the director yells, "What is going on back there?"

"What was that?" Jay asks. He is almost fully himself again.

"I don't know," Kala tells him.

"That was . . . wild," Ronnie says.

All three of them are holding hands, looking at each other, wanting each other as all six of us are still intertwined. But as Behula, Lakhindar, and I exit their bodies, some small piece of us lingers. Kala, Jay, and Ronnie are uneasy. In uncharted territory. But they are excited, too. I can see it in the way they lean into each other.

Now, I sense Lakhindar's worry about Behula and me. This is new for us, too. We will think about that later. For now, we are free of this and they are free of us.

Things are going to be different. I don't know exactly how, but I am excited to find out. Worship, it seems, doesn't have to come with a whiff of venom.

But damn. I am going to miss killing people.

I can't lie. That part was fun.

AUTHOR'S NOTE

There are a few versions of the story of ill-fated lovers Behula and Lakhindar. In one, Behula is selected to wed Lakhindar not knowing he will be killed by the snake goddess Manasa. After his death, Behula travels to the heavens and begs for his life. I wanted to upend the women's roles of duped, suffering wife and perpetual villain. And I wanted it to be sexy.

ART BY CYNTHIA PAUL

CHUDAIL
By Nikita Gill

Every three years, a girl disappears from our hill station. For three hundred years, this has always happened in the strange, nameless season between monsoon and winter. The signs are all there. The mountain river runs red for a day. A massive deodar withers, and we all know cedar trees are near invincible, especially up here where our oldest trees are centuries old. And just before she disappears, the girl sees *her* at the window. The chudail in the forest who we speak of in hushed tones. Three days after she sees the witch, the girl is gone, never to be seen again.

In the nameless season of my fifteenth year, the chudail came for me.

It had been such a beautiful, normal day. I was sitting

on the garden swing after school, drinking nimbu pani and reading a book. Our house overlooks the valley, as so many houses on this side of the hill station do. The sky was slowly melting into an indigo blue from the soft orange of sunset. My mother had already called me inside three times, but my rebellious streak had put me in the habit of disobeying her until she would literally march out to get me. Everything was still and peaceful, the sound of the birds and crickets chirping their soft songs, the distant bubble of the river rushing down the side of the hill.

And then, all at once, everything fell silent.

At first, I was so engrossed in my book, I didn't notice it. But soon, the uneasy quiet caught in my throat. A feeling of wrongness that was so strong, a shudder ran up my spine.

I put my book down, my fingers cold despite the warmth of a summer day still in the air.

Snap.

I looked up, panicking, the air suddenly stifling. There in the bright, flower-rich garden I had grown up in stood a woman who looked less woman, more corpse. Her wild long white hair fell in tangles about her face and her empty eye sockets glared back at me with malice. She wore an old ragged white nightgown, but it was her feet that truly gave away what she truly was.

Her feet were facing backward.

My body went rigid. She was so close, I could smell the musty, rotten smell of death wafting from her. My heart raced, my mind screaming at me to run. And yet I stayed sitting there. It was as though every part of me had suddenly recognized its fight-or-flight mode and despite choosing flight, I was unable to move. She stepped closer until her face mirrored mine. I felt sweat begin to form on my back, my hands, and my forehead, and my mouth opened in a silent scream. Something began to pull me, like the dark root of an invisible tree, toward her—a deep devouring etched into her long-dead features.

Bile rose in my throat as she opened her mangled mouth to say, "If not her, then you."

I squeezed my eyes shut in terror, expecting the worst. And—

Nothing happened. Slowly, I opened my eyes . . . and she was gone. Vanished as though she had never been there at all.

As if being broken out of a trance, I fell to my knees from the swing, threw up, and then screamed until every one of the hills around me echoed my terror back to me.

When I opened my eyes, I was lying on my bed in my room. The feeling of a cool towel being pressed against my burning forehead was the first sensation. Shaking, I turned to see my mother's worried face and my father pacing. Both my brothers sat quietly, watching me. It was deeply disconcerting, since they rarely took any interest in anything other than themselves.

"Beti!" My mother was the first to properly notice my open eyes, despite my two brothers sitting there like guardians.

I squinted slightly to ease the blur that turned everything around me into a soft oil painting. My mother touched my cheek with a cool hand, telling my father, "Mohan, she's awake!"

"Asha, what happened? Your mother and I were worried sick!" My father kneeled by my bedside, shooing Shiv out of the way. My brother moved grouchily, muttering under his breath.

I opened my mouth to speak, and a single word escaped my lips: "Pani."

My mother immediately handed me a glass of water and I sat up slowly, the movement making me realize I had a horrible headache. What happened came back to me in pieces. I didn't want to tell my family. There would be our life before the sighting and then our life after, and I didn't know if I was ready for what would happen to our family after this.

I had seen the haunted faces of the parents who had lost their daughters. I had seen the gouges of pain they carried like welts across their souls. When the chudail took Seema's older sister six years ago, her father walked around the woods like a ghost, calling for his child for almost a year. He stopped speaking after that. Jamal's older sister was taken three years ago; he and his mother still wept every time she was mentioned. I didn't know the others who had been taken well, but I knew that dozens of girls had gone missing over the years.

And the police did nothing, *nothing*. The parents got no help and slowly wilted in their pain. The people of the hill station continued as though we weren't losing daughters and sisters at an abnormal rate. I didn't want that to be my parents.

But my father was waiting impatiently, and my older brother Karan was now visibly annoyed at the fact that I hadn't answered anyone. The little vein in his temple throbbed, as it always did when he was frustrated. "Asha, answer our parents. They've had to call the doctor."

I wanted to protect my family, but lying to them would mean that when the chudail came for me in earnest, it would leave them possibly more shattered than it would if they knew she was coming.

I took a deep breath. "I saw her."

For a moment, no one spoke or did anything, the shock gripping my parents. Even my brothers stopped their muttering and stared at me, wide-eyed. Then the glass I had given back to my mother fell from her hand and shattered on the floor. My father sat heavily on the chair and covered his face with his hands. Karan held a hand over his mouth and Shiv backed away into a corner slowly, as though I was condemned.

And I sat there, head throbbing, not knowing what would happen next, a terrible anticipation holding my body and mind hostage.

My mother couldn't speak. The blood had drained from her face.

My father's voice was thin and quiet as he said, "I think . . .

I think we need to call your mother, Pragati."

My mother's whole body stiffened. My mother, who was the most cheerful woman I had ever met, suddenly had a glint of anger in her eyes. My mother, who was the most beautiful woman I knew, had a mouth twisted with rage. She turned to my father, who she never disagreed with, and said, "No."

A single word fell like a chasm between them, opening cracks in what was a perfect marriage.

"Yes." My father's voice was firmer now. "If she saved you, she can save Asha."

I frowned. What on earth was my father talking about?

My mother, still radiating with rage, responded to him coldly, "She destroyed my childhood with her secrets. I will not call her now to have her destroy my daughter's—"

"Pragati. She saved your life. You're the only girl who saw her and—"

My mother held up her hand, her eyes flashing with fury. "Don't."

I started at this, as did both my brothers. My tired brain went into overdrive as I pieced together exactly what my parents were saying. My whole body went rigid as I demanded, "Wait . . . Ma? *What does that mean?*"

Shiv asked the question more elegantly than I could manage. "You *saw* her? And you're still here?"

A terrible silence engulfed our family. My mother sat in thought for a moment, and then defeat turned down the corners of her mouth. "Yes. I'll . . . I'll call my mother."

"You saw her," I repeated, trying to prompt her to respond.

She looked up sharply. "That's enough. You need rest. Everyone out." She looked at Shiv, Karan, and my father. "All of you out."

"But Ma—" Karan complained as she got up and began to herd them all out of the room.

"No," she said firmly. "Out."

I shivered as she shooed them out of the room, leaving my bedroom door open so she could keep an eye on me.

For as long as I can remember, my mother has had a difficult relationship with her mother. It's the kind of thing you pick up on as a child. There were few visits between either of them when I was growing up, though I would visit Nani ma secretly after school often. It's a strange thing to say, that my form of rebellion was visiting my grandmother. But out of Shiv, Karan, and I, I was her favorite, probably because I visited her the most, and I savored being superior to my brothers in at least one house on this hill station.

Half an hour later, my grandmother's tall, regal frame filled my room. She sat across from me with her yellow woolen shawl wrapped around her shoulders, the pleats of her indigo blue sari falling around her feet like the twilight sky. As time went on, her hair had grayed but her face remained as sharp and angular as ever, eyes still dark as midnight. My mother hovered in the doorway, wringing her hands so much that in happier times I would have joked that they would fall off.

"Asha." Krishnaa Devi's voice held the echoes of centuries. "Tell me what you saw."

In painful and excruciating detail, I described to my grandmother the socketless eyes, the backward-facing feet, the corpselike appearance of the chudail. Finally, I said, "And then she said, 'If not her, then you.'"

At this, my grandmother sat up.

"She spoke to you?"

I nodded.

My mother started. "You didn't tell me that." She looked like she was going to crumble. "Why didn't you tell me she spoke to you?!" Then, to my horror, she burst into tears.

"Pragati," my grandmother snapped at her. "Get a hold of yourself."

Instantly, as if a switch had gone off inside her, my mother turned to my grandmother, eyes still streaming, and snarled, "Why do you have to be so cruel?!"

"It's not cruelty, girl, it's survival. Do you think I would have been able to raise you as a single mother in this small town full of rumors and gossip if I had burst into tears at every small thing?" my grandmother retorted, an impatient frown across her face.

"No version of survival requires you to be so aloof with your own child." My mother's rage had returned. I watched the two of them helplessly, not knowing what to do or say.

"If I hadn't been so 'aloof,' as you describe it, I wouldn't have been rational enough to save you from what came for you." My grandmother's icy tone was clipped and blunt. And my mother, who clearly did not have a response for this, shrank back slightly.

The silence that filled the room was so awful, I had to will myself to speak. "What am I going to do?"

My grandmother looked at me, a glint of steel in those midnight eyes. "You are going to live with me for the rest of the year."

"No!" My mother protested, her voice furious and shaking all at once. "You can't just walk in here and take my daughter. I—"

Nani ma raised her hand to stop her. "If you don't want to lose her, you will allow her to come and live with me. I was able to keep you safe. And I can do the same for Asha." She looked my mother right in the eye and something unspoken passed between them.

Then my mother did something that surprised me.

She nodded.

Nani ma's house was full of books, herbs, and music. She played the sitar and sang beautiful songs that were so old, we barely heard them anymore. I had loved coming here as a girl, and now, living here, it felt like a different kind of paradise. My grandmother loved her own company. My brothers found it difficult to stay in silence for long as they sought to fill in the quiet with conversation. But I loved the peace those silences gave us, just as my grandmother did. And after my encounter with the chudail, the solitude was exactly what I needed to process the constant pull I was feeling toward the forest. It was like an invisible rope was attached to me, yanking me toward the darkness between the trees.

After two weeks, I finally grew the courage to ask, "What happened between you and Ma?"

My grandmother, busy making aloo paranthas for us to eat with mango pickle and yogurt, didn't bother to look at me. "Sometimes people are just different."

I watched her carefully melt the ghee before cooking the parantha in it. "What does that mean? For you and Ma?"

She dusted the flour off her hands. "She never told you what happened after she survived the chudail, did she?"

I shook my head. "She never told us that she saw the chudail at all."

My grandmother looked out the kitchen window to the winding hill station built into the hillside, cottages rising out of the slopes.

"What do you know about this town?"

I recounted what I knew as if I were in school: "It was built by the British colonizers so they could escape the heat of the plains in the summer months and—"

My grandmother shook her head. "Not that. What do you really know about this town."

I looked at the pattern of the floral tablecloth before me, focusing on it hard. "That for three hundred years, girls have gone missing, and no one does anything about it. That it is the chudail who takes them." I stopped, hesitating on my next words.

"And?" my grandmother prompted me.

"And they say that is why this town is paradise. Why almost nothing goes wrong here. Why death only visits rarely, and the abundance here defies everything. That people move here and never move away," I finished, and stared at her. She had this faraway look in her eyes as she gazed out to that spill of cottages framed by the verdant hillside and the blue, blue sky.

"The only girl who saw her and got away was your mother," Nani ma said, not looking at me, her hands busily rolling out the dough. "Because I did not let her take her. But those years . . . in those years, famine came. Everything withered. The three big businesses went bankrupt. The winters lasted longer than the summers. Death was particularly unkind, leaving cracks within almost every family."

She turned to look at me, that same hard gleam in her eyes, one that reminded me of the clash of ancient swords. "A less superstitious place would blame something else. Statistically, nowhere could stay so lucky for so long. But it was much too easy to hold someone responsible for the pain. It's what humans do, isn't it? Hold other humans responsible for things they cannot control. So they blamed your mother. They tormented her in school. She lost all of her friends. And she blamed me for refusing to leave this place."

I stared at her. "But why didn't you leave?"

My grandmother shrugged and turned back to the paranthas, carrying a plateful to the table. I caught a flash of defiance in her stormy eyes as she set the food down.

"This is my home. Why would I ever leave?"

Even in this peaceful place, the nightmares came. I saw myself drowning in the river after trying to run away from the chudail in the forest. The fury of her face, the malice of her existence stifled me. One night, I woke up in a cold sweat and found Nani ma sitting on the old emerald-green armchair, watching me.

"Fifteen nights you have woken up screaming, child," she said quietly. "This can't go on."

I winced, thinking I had interrupted her sleep. "So sorry, Nani ma, I just . . ." I trailed off, realizing Nani ma was shaking her head.

"Hush. I'm here to tell you a story. Something that may chase the nightmares away and make you brave."

I took a deep breath. Nani ma was a woman of few words. For her to tell a story was simply unheard of.

Her eyes gleamed, reflecting the moon over the mountain as she sat back in the armchair. There was something otherworldly about her, although I couldn't decide just what it was. Was it the way her long hair was wild and open when she usually kept it neatly plaited? The way the moonlight danced across her face? I focused instead on her words, a tale woven so carefully that the fabric of time itself seemed to disappear.

Many, many years ago, in an ancient forest not far from here, two boys decided that they were brothers, even if they came from vastly different households. This was the kind of friendship, they said, as they hunted and grew up together, that the bards and poets would write stories about. And they were right. However, not in the way they thought.

You see, although the two boys were the same age and studying under the same warrior guru, one of the boys was the son of a king and the other was the son of their teacher himself. And although teachers bring wisdom and value beyond material wealth to this world, the guru was not a rich man. While kings' sons and warriors came to his ashram to study, he treated them the same as he treated his own. Everyone would sit together on the floor to eat, and food was distributed equally. Everyone slept under the stars during the summer and inside the hut in winter. But when the young men finished their learning, the guru's sons would remain with the guru. The others would return home to their princely kingdoms, their warrior homes, to fulfill their destinies as princes and kings.

And so it went that the two boys known as Prince Draupad of Panchaal and Dronacharya would also part this way. Draupad, for his part, was distraught, and promised Drona that he would always be his kin. And to prove his loyalty to his friend, he made a blood oath with him, promising Drona half his kingdom if he ever desired it.

Draupad returned to his kingdom and Drona learned from his father how to teach the next generation of young men. Both boys grew into established young men in their destinies. Draupad was a fair king, and Drona soon grew a reputation as the best teacher in all of Bharat.

The trouble came with milk. One day, Drona's wife watched from their modest little hut as a group of young boys had gathered around her son, laughing at him because he had never drunk milk in his life. They were too poor to afford it. So when the child came crying back home, his mother mixed some flour with water and added some jaggery to it. The boy proudly drank the mixture and declared to all his friends, "I too now know what milk tastes like."

And the mother, who had never wept for anything, cried her first tears that day.

Drona, upon hearing the story, was devastated, and took the two of them to Draupad, asking him to honor his promise.

But years of being around opulence had changed Draupad. He had Drona and his family thrown out of his kingdom, calling them paupers and thieves.

Drona's revenge was brutal. He trained a group of warrior princes—a hundred Kauravas and five Pandavas, cousins from the same royal family—to avenge him.

The princes were successful, and soon, Draupad found himself in chains before the very man he had once called brother, then thrown out of his kingdom of Panchaal.

Drona was fair. He took from Draupad what he had been promised. Half of Panchaal. Then he released his old friend in a show of generosity.

But by now, the love between them had curdled to a deep bitter hatred, and Draupad was hungry to avenge this humiliation. So he had every priest in the land create a sacrificial fire in prayer to the gods. For thirty days, all manner of creatures were given to the fire. Rumor had it that in desperation, the king even sacrificed infants. All this in the hope that he would be granted a son to avenge him. For thirty days, the king starved himself, growing so thin that his people were afraid he would die.

Fortunately for Draupad, a boy finally emerged from the flames, making the whole assembly around the fire gasp. He carried himself with the wisdom of God and the nobility of an emperor, and a voice followed him into the room: "Here is the son who will avenge you, but your quest for vengeance will destroy you."

And then, in the blink of an eye, followed a girl. A girl the fires proclaimed "A gift from the heavens who will change the course of history."

The girl is our story. Draupadi, as she was named, grew up to be an empress in her own right, the wife of the five Pandava princes, and the architect of the splendor that was the Palace of Illusions.

But pain followed Draupadi wherever she went. Widely known as the most beautiful woman in Bharat, she was coveted by kings and princes alike, not for her courage or her intelligence, but as a possession.

You must understand, things were different then. But also very much the same. Women did not hold power; we took it by stealth where we could. To be principled and fair was also to be subservient. Draupadi's husbands were good, kind men who built a kingdom, Indraprastha, from a barren land. Its crown jewel was the Palace of Illusions, which Draupadi designed. It was a mirage within a forest built of mirrors, glass, and fountains, so intricate that it was equal parts diamond and maze.

But even good men have vices, and unfortunately for Draupadi, the eldest of her husbands, Yudhishthira, was a gambler. For years the rivalry between the Pandava princes and the Kaurava princes had grown, until an incident at the palace, where Duryodhana, de facto leader of the Kauravas, fell prey to one of the mirages and found himself soaked in a pool of water. Draupadi and her maids saw this from her balcony and their laughter sent Duryodhana mad with rage.

This humiliation, coupled with the jealousy and rivalry between the cousins, led him to devise a plan to rob the Pandavas of Indraprastha, the beautiful kingdom they had built.

Yudhishthira was an easy mark. The man never passed up a chance to gamble, and Duryodhana selected a game that he knew Yudhishthira would lose. And so the emperor gambled away everything. His horses, his chariots, his army, his home, his brothers—and finally, he bet and lost Draupadi.

Draupadi did not take this news lightly. She fought with the men assembled, asked what right Yudhishthira had to gamble her, a queen, away. The Kauravas piled on humiliation after humiliation until finally they attempted to do the unspeakable and strip her of her sari. Draupadi's prayers saved her, as the sari became endless, and the Kauravas pulled at the fabric until they *fell exhausted on the floor. It was Draupadi in the end who won the Pandavas back their freedom and weapons. It was Draupadi to whom they owed their lives, and the fact that they were not enslaved to their cousins.*

As the Pandavas left the palace penniless paupers, Draupadi said to her husbands, "I will not wash my hair until I am able to wash it in the blood of Duryodhana."

She was blamed, then, for the war that took place next. She was held responsible, the match that lit the fire. It was easier to blame a woman for what went wrong with the choices of men than it was for men to take responsibility for the harm they caused.

But I'll tell you now, child. The war was not Draupadi's fault. Even after Draupadi lost all her sons to the flames, she remained fire. Even after her husbands died, she remained fire. And she took her only daughter and ran into the forests of time. To make something new. Something better.

Silence fell after Nani ma said these words. The moonlight still gleaming off her skin, my grandmother's eyes were a thousand miles away.

"Nani ma," I said very quietly, "what does Draupadi have to do with the chudail?"

She looked me directly in the eye and suddenly, I saw it. The fire, the story, the secrets she was hiding. "There is a reason the spirit in the woods will not touch you or your mother. You have an ancient war in your blood, child. It recognizes that."

My hands were shaking. "Are you saying that—that—"

My Nani ma smiled. "Your mother should have taught you more about the Mahabharata."

"Why are you telling me this story now?" I asked her.

She was silent again for a few moments, deep in thought.

"Asha, I was the woman blamed for a war. Your mother was a woman blamed for famine and pain. It is the legacy of the women in this family to face unfairness and find a way to survive and thrive within it."

I swallowed hard, my heart thudding. I had a strange feeling I knew where this conversation was heading, like a pull inside my heart.

"Do you know what a chudail is, Asha?"

"A demonic spirit?" I asked, balling my hands into fists to stop them from shaking.

Nani ma shook her head. "No. She is a woman who has been wronged so deeply that her spirit returns for revenge. She feeds on the males of the family that wronged her."

I frowned then, because this didn't explain the chudail that was haunting our hill station at all. Girls went missing here, not boys. And this place was thriving. Had for centuries. Unless . . .

"What lives in that forest is not a chudail at all."

My grandmother nodded. "This land thrives. Despite everything around it burning. It is the twenty-first century and forest fires have never touched this hill station. No earthquakes have broken through these hills. No police raids have ruined the peace here. There is barely a government, and yet . . . it is like . . ."

"Like it's held together by magic," I finished for her. My grandmother wanted me to see something, and slowly my eyes were opening to it. As the moonlight spilled into the room, I recognized the wounds that had spread like cracks throughout this town, how they had been hidden by layers of surface abundance. We were so obsessed with the material, we did not even notice what we were giving up.

"It's the girls, isn't it?" My voice broke slightly, the full horror laid before my eyes in Technicolor. "Someone is sacrificing the girls of this town the same way Draupad sacrificed flesh to get what he wanted."

Nani ma's expression set, and for a moment, I could see every one of her years etched into her ageless face. "It took me some time to read the land. But I have finally learned what it is. This is where I was born. This is where the sacrificial fire was created. People think it was Panchaal, but it wasn't. It was here on this sacred land in the hills that we lit a celestial flame that burns even today. But sacrificial flames like that need feeding. And its nourishment must come from the living. I don't think my father knew what he created from his bitterness, nor what it would cost even years after. Hatred that deep and powerful is always hungry, and leaves nothing but chaos in its wake."

The full weight of what she was saying hit me. A fire. Thousands of years old. Devouring girl after girl, like the girl it gave to the world.

Nani ma got up. "It is time to confront what started with me."

It was as if the room began to spin. Everything shook and moved in a way I was not ready for. I understood now what my grandmother was saying. It would take the girl who started the fire to end the flames. Only then would the hungry rift in time close.

My eyes filled with tears. "Nani ma, you can't!"

She smiled. "Oh, but I can, dear child. I should have done this years ago, once your mother was married. I wanted to see at least one of my children grow up safe and away from war, and I received that. It's all the forest promised me. If I don't go now, it will take you. Just like it tried to take your mother."

She looked back out into the forest, and I followed her line of sight across the vast valleys of lush green deodars, proudly swaying in the breeze. Was it my imagination, or could I see a blue flame dancing across the treetops?

When Nani ma looked to me, I saw the flames dancing in her eyes. "Tell your mother I have loved watching her grow up. She and you are everything I ever wanted from a daughter and a granddaughter. I am so proud of the woman she has become and the woman you will be, Asha."

I tried to stop her. But something had gripped me tight and wasn't letting me go. So I stayed rooted to the bed, watching her as she rose, her sari rustling softly.

She held my face in her hands and kissed my forehead.

Then she opened the front door of the little cottage and walked into the dark, dark wood, the moonlight highlighting her tall, serene form until I could not see her anymore.

For centuries, every three years, a girl used to disappear from our hill station. It used to always happen in that nameless season between monsoon and winter. People still talk about the signs. How the mountain river would turn red. How a massive deodar would wither. How the chudail would visit.

But that is a story from long ago. A legend that is slowly becoming a myth, which will soon be forgotten in the ashes of time.

It has been thirty years since my grandmother left us.

Not a single girl has disappeared since.

ART BY MIRA F. MALHOTRA

A GODDESS OF FIRE AND BLOOD

By Tanaz Bhathena

"You're the girl who injured the warden, aren't you?"

The woman's voice was like wind rustling through the neem trees, her words so quiet that for a second, Amira thought she was dreaming. Not of home or the safflower fields or the emerald glow of earth magic on her baba's dirt-filled hands, but of a woman she'd never seen before. An apparition with glowing, deep brown skin, bedecked in jewels and silks so rich that Amira could hardly differentiate sari from shawl.

"Ji, Rani Juhi," demurred the guards at the labor camp when the woman ordered them to step back and give her some air.

"As if the heat tonight isn't suffocating enough!" The woman's stern voice prickled across Amira's skin. "I can't imagine how these young girls tolerate it, locked up as they are like hens in a coop. How old is this one?" She gestured at Amira. "Twelve? Thirteen?"

Fifteen, Amira mentally corrected her.

Though clearly she didn't look it. Ever since she'd been ripped away from her old life, Amira had felt like she'd been hollowed out, grown smaller somehow. She held her breath as the woman turned to face her again.

No. This wasn't a ghost. Nor a dream. This was one of King Lohar's three queens.

Witch, Amira had heard the guards call this queen in private. *Demon,* for her black eyes and the streaks of blue in her midnight hair. Yet from what Amira had heard the other girls say, Balram-putri Juhi, a former princess of Samudra, was really King Lohar's prize—the spoils in Ambar's brutal three-year war with the southern kingdom, which had ended with a peace treaty that had made Juhi its living, breathing collateral.

"She may live at the palace, but Rani Juhi is also the king's prisoner," the girls had told Amira. "Like us."

Now the queen leaned closer to the bars containing Amira and whispered something else. Something that made the girl look at her in astonishment and then spin around to see if anyone else was listening. By the time she looked at Rani Juhi again, the woman had already turned away, the jadai nagam ornamenting her long braid glinting gold in the light of a lone yellow moon, leaving behind nothing more than a trail of jasmine-scented air.

"Was she an incarnation of the sky goddess?" a voice asked. "Do you think she will return?"

Big gray eyes peered up at Amira from the cage next to hers. The girl, Kali, was about Amira's age, as delicate as the flower bud she'd been named after. Amira had ignored Kali since the girl had arrived at the camp. Flowers never lasted long in this place.

Yet for some reason, Kali had. Not only that, but last night, as the guards were beating Amira for biting the head warden's thigh, she'd screamed herself hoarse, calling them all sorts of filthy names, until their attention turned to her.

Amira wanted to tell Kali that there were no goddesses. That there was no way they'd see Rani Juhi again. But the bruises under the girl's eyes stilled Amira's tongue. It was difficult to be unkind to or ignore someone who'd taken a beating for her.

"Maybe she is," Amira lied.

She did not tell Kali about the queen's final words. Words that kept Amira up in the nights that followed. That gave her hope even as they terrified her.

"Be ready to run on the night of the moon festival," Rani Juhi had said. "The goddess in the camp's temple will show you the way."

Amira was born to run. Pulse ticking at her neck and behind her ears. Feet pounding the earth behind the zamindar's bajra and safflower fields, her dupatta tied around her waist, the air billowing her ghagra and filling her lungs as she sped past the bullock carts and tongue-clicking goatherds, nearly keeping pace with the black-and-white-tailed shvetpanchhi that crested the air above.

"Goddess be praised, she's faster than any child in the village," her baba had declared to a tall, bearded man who came to visit the year Amira turned fourteen. "Look at her. Strong legs, strong back. She was made to plow the fields, sow magic in them, and sprout every seed."

The last bit was a lie. Amira had no earth magic in her; she could swallow a pound of dirt before she could grow a single blade of grass. In Ambar, children born with magic in their veins could be trained to do different things, depending on aptitude and skill. Most students at the village school specialized in earth magic like Amira's parents and became farmers. Some magically healed people, becoming vaids. A few became astrologers, who predicted the future with magic and cowrie shells, or truth seekers, who gleaned lies by touching a person.

In her village, Amira's power was even rarer—the sort that made bullies in her schoolyard cower. Death magic: A power that flowed through the blood of warriors. A magic that could be used to kill a person—not that Amira had. With a simple paring knife, she could channel her magic to project shields and burn holes in trees. Outside the controlled environment of schools, the use of death magic was prohibited to all except the Sky Warriors, an elite force of soldiers who'd protected every monarch since Ambar's first queen.

When she was little, Amira had dreamed of using her magic in battle.

"I'm going to be a Sky Warrior!" she'd declare to anyone who would listen. *She* wouldn't be like her mother, worn out from working the fields and doing house spells, all while raising five children. As Amira grew older, though, she learned to hold her tongue—if only to avoid Mai's beatings.

"Fool girl!" Mai had said more than once. "Do you think your father and I have the coin to send you to the Sky Warrior academy? We barely scraped enough to send you to the village school!"

Yet what worried Mai even more than Amira's death magic was the diagonal black streak that marked the smooth brown skin of her daughter's left shoulder blade—and the prophecy attached to it.

Revealed to King Lohar by his astrologers when he first took the throne, the prophecy spoke of a girl with a star-shaped birthmark, a girl with magic foretold to kill their king.

The sky will fall, a star will rise
Ambar changed by the king's demise
Her magic untouched and unknown by all
Marked with a star, she'll bring his downfall

The power of the girl referred to in the prophecy was unclear. It *could* be death magic, the astrologers told the king.

But it could also be something else—a magic no one had seen before. Only one thing was certain: the first prophecy made for a new monarch by the royal astrologers always came true.

King Lohar didn't want to take any chances. He decreed that every girl in the kingdom born with a star-shaped birthmark and magic in her blood—*any* magic—was to be arrested. Citizens were awarded ten swarnas in exchange for information about such girls, who were then captured and taken to labor camps where their magic was drained from them by the Sky Warriors. The draining was said to render the girls harmless without killing them, destroying their "dangerous magic" forever—along with any possibility of it being used to kill the king.

Amira did not understand how magic could be drained from a person, or even destroyed.

But she understood her mother's worry. Ten swarnas was a lot of gold—enough for a family of four to live comfortably for a year or two. Enough for people to report neighbors, friends, even family. Amira was grateful that her own birthmark was easy to hide, even though she thought it looked more like a smudge than anything. Mai, however, insisted it looked like a falling star.

Amira had never seen a star fall, a rare astrological event when priests charged silvers for prayers instead of coppers at the sky goddess's temple, a time when wishes supposedly came true. If she *did* see a falling star, Amira had decided, she would wish for a way out of the village she'd been born in, this drudgery of a life interminably bound to the land.

She had watched as her father held out his hands for a sack of coin that the bearded man placed in them. Baba had turned to Amira and nodded. It was time for her to leave—to go to this man's home and till his safflower fields until the harvest. Back then, she had not understood the greed in the bearded man's eyes and the guilt in her father's. She had not known that wishes, especially those carelessly made, had the tendency to come true in cruel and unusual ways—that once inside the stranger's cart, she would never see her parents again.

Truths found Kali long before she understood what they were. Or what they could be to her father, whose heart she had broken at age five by asking him about the woman she'd seen her mother kissing. Papa had not been able to forgive Ma her deception. And Ma had never forgiven Kali for her truth.

"Useless wretch of a girl," Ma had said before leaving the village in sobs. "You'll amount to nothing, I tell you. Nothing."

Ten years later, Ma's curse finally took effect.

The magic Kali had inherited from Papa—knowing truths from lies by touching a person—had been leeched from her by a pair of Sky Warriors at a labor camp. She had been shackled to the wall in her cell while two masked soldiers had shot strange weblike red spells at her with their atashbans, the powerful magical crossbows carving glowing lines into her skin in a way that had felt like they were repeatedly scraping her skin with a blunt knife. Ten times, a hundred times. Enough times that Kali was howling by the end of it, begging them to stop.

They hadn't, of course. They bled drop after glowing drop from what felt like a thousand cuts in Kali's skin, and then directed her magic in a beam through a block of Prithvi Stone, a substance that destroyed it for good. Or so Kali was expected to believe.

"Only the gods can destroy magic," someone in a neighboring cage had whispered to Kali. "The king and his Sky Warriors are but human. If our magic was truly gone, wouldn't they send us home? Why keep us here?"

Goddess help her—Kali *wanted* to believe the girl. In rare moments of optimism, she even did. But most days, she still felt the absence of her magic like a lost limb.

Had it been Kali's father who'd revealed the diamond-shaped birthmark on her right calf to the thanedars? Who'd stood by quietly as they'd dragged her away? Or was it Kali's mother, whom he'd thrown out after learning of her affair with the other woman? Her mother, who'd informed the authorities about Kali's birthmark and finally taken her revenge. It was a truth Kali still did not know—a truth she wasn't sure she wanted to learn, even if she got her magic back.

"Save me, goddess," she whispered at the end of each nightly prayer at the temple in the labor camp.

Built with stone brick around the pillars of four large neem trees, the sky goddess's temple was older than the girls and their guards, older than any other building inside the camp. A fear of the goddess's rage, or perhaps some form of lingering conscience, had prevented the king from knocking it down or converting it into more barracks for his guards. Temple prayers were the one concession the girls were allowed after their mornings of grinding flour for the capital's largest mill, before being locked up in their cages again.

Kali found comfort in these prayers and in the goddess's serene face. Her features were soft, Kali thought, despite being carved of stone, and the garland of starry honeyweed flowers was always fresh, replaced by someone each morning.

Even Amira came to the prayers, though she never moved her lips to the hymns. Kali could feel the girl watching her at times—especially when Kali closed her eyes and whispered the words engraved at the base of the sky goddess's statue: *Freedom lies at her feet.*

A few days after Rani Juhi visited them at the camp, Amira spoke to Kali at the temple: "Blood lies at her feet, too, you know."

Kali winced—not so much at the mockery in Amira's tone but the reminder of the blood. Old and red, staining the letters at the goddess's feet no matter how much they'd tried to scrub it clean. A few months ago, a girl had snuck into the temple and slammed her head over and over against the stone, screaming at the goddess to set her free. The girl had been withdrawn from the camp—though where she was taken, Kali still didn't know.

She forced herself to look into Amira's hard brown eyes. Kali liked the girl, despite her coldness, and admired her more for her courage. Kali might no longer have her magic, but she didn't have to touch Amira to know her truths. Amira rarely refrained from speaking her mind or fighting, even when she was afraid—even against the warden. That was why, a week earlier, when the guards were beating Amira in her cage, Kali had found herself rising up. Screaming. Taking on Amira's punishment herself.

"I know you don't believe in it," Kali told her now. "But I've always felt that prayer was a way to reach the goddess. That what the world takes from us unjustly, the goddess always returns."

She expected Amira to snort or shake her head in disbelief.

But the other girl simply stared at the goddess and the single oil lamp flickering in her sanctum, a furrow between her brows.

Two full moons rose on the night of the moon festival. It was Chandni Raat, the only time each year when both orbs appeared in the sky. Tonight Sunheri glowed bright and golden like her namesake—like a lover who'd finally spotted her heart's desire. The sight of the blue moon, Neel, wasn't one Sunheri alone pined for. Thousands across Ambar celebrated the sighting of the two moons, hoping that the goddesses for whom they were named would gift them with new love or a binding.

Yet Amira knew there was another reason for the celebration. It was likely the reason Rani Juhi had thought of while advising Amira to run away on Chandni Raat.

"Long before Sunheri and Neel granted wishes of love, they were charting stars and changing fortunes," Mai had told a four-year-old Amira. "They were bestowing luck on those who needed it the most."

"Will they bestow luck on us, too, Mai?" Amira had asked with awe.

"I hope so, my little love." Unexpected sadness had flickered over Mai's face. "I think this year, they might."

They hadn't. Not that year, nor the next.

Unlike Mai, though, Amira had not persisted in her worship. She'd understood—even if her mother hadn't—that there was no point in depending on the gods for anything.

Now, while the other girls silently trickled outside the temple for the sighting of the moons, Amira hung back. Carefully picked up one of the many oil lamps lining the sanctum.

"What are you doing?" a voice asked.

It was Kali, wide gray eyes full of curiosity.

Amira hesitated. Had it been another girl, she might've responded with a retort that would have sunk in like a blade. But Kali wasn't as fragile as she looked. Amira suspected that insults would not make her wither. Also, Kali had taken a beating for Amira when she didn't need to, when no one else would have. A strange emotion bubbled inside Amira when she looked at the girl. Trust.

"Let me show you," Amira said.

Ignoring Kali's gasp, she leaped up over the ledge separating the goddess's inner sanctum from the worship area. Then, with a deep breath, she threw her weight against the statue and pushed hard.

The high squeal made Amira look up, stop in fear. But no one else had been drawn to the temple. Sweating, her heart aflutter, she turned to Kali and said, "Look."

The statue hadn't moved much. Maybe an inch or so. But it was enough to see a gap between the stone floor and the statue, a hole in the ground that made Kali's gray eyes bulge.

"How did you know—?" Kali began.

"A hunch," Amira said truthfully. One based off what Rani Juhi had told her: *The goddess in the camp's temple will show you the way.*

"I heard that old temples had secret passages built into them. To help priests escape in times of war. I thought since this temple looked really old, there may be something like this here, and . . ." Amira's voice trailed off.

And then what?

She hadn't given much thought to what she would do beyond moving the statue itself. To be fair, she hadn't expected it to move at all. But now that it *had*, her heart slowly began to sink. How could she have been so foolish? A guard could come in to check on them. A guard *would* come in, and—

No. Amira severed the thought. In a place like this, a chance at escape was akin to glimpsing a god or a falling star. Amira would not lose that chance.

"Do you want to help?" she asked Kali. "We can escape from here, but I don't think I can do this on my own."

Kali frowned, saying nothing.

"What is it?" Amira asked.

"What about the other girls?" Kali said. "It doesn't seem fair to leave them behind."

Amira's stomach twisted. She hadn't been thinking about the other girls at all. By Svapnalok, she hadn't thought of taking *Kali* along until a moment earlier.

She exhaled sharply, hating the words that spilled from her mouth next. "There are forty-eight girls in this camp, apart from us. I don't know how we can save them, too, without getting caught."

There was a long silence as Kali stared at the bloodstained words etched into the base of the statue. Outside, voices began to sing a hymn:

> *There were two goddesses born of the sky*
> *Friends first, then lovers,*
> *Destined to die . . .*

Kali looked up at Amira again. "What do you want me to do?" she asked.

Wood, Kali's papa had told her once, caught fire easiest when doused in grassoil. But there had to be a lot of it.

Certainly not the amount that existed in the tiny oil lamps before them. When Kali pointed this out to Amira, the other girl scowled.

"Where in Svapnalok are we supposed to find a *whole tin* of grassoil?" Amira demanded.

"In the head warden's quarters," Kali said. Inside the room where he took the girls who caught his fancy, keeping them there until he tired of them.

Amira's hard jaw trembled at the mention of the man. "The . . . the head warden?"

"I'll go," Kali said, ignoring the quaking in her own limbs. "I know where he keeps the key."

"No," Amira said, shaking her head. "We'll forget this idea. Come up with another plan."

"There isn't time," Kali pointed out. They were alone in the temple now, but they had an hour, maybe less, before the guards began rounding everyone up in their cages for the night. "You'll need a distraction while you move that statue. I can give it to you."

The memory of her mother's eyes flashed before Kali. Dark brown like Amira's. Full of rage. *Useless wretch,* her mother had called her.

Well, even wretches could be useful at times.

"I'll come with you," Amira said. "I can't let you do this alone."

"No!" Kali said, her voice so fierce that Amira stepped back. "The statue is heavy. You need time to move it. When

I set fire to the barracks, you'll get it. Then I can join you here."

"Can you? What if you're seen—or worse, caught in the act?"

I'll be killed. Of this, Kali was sure.

"So be it," she told Amira.

Death or not, Kali didn't plan on stopping tonight.

Tonight, goddess willing, both she and Amira would leave this hell—one way or another.

The head warden's room was exactly how Kali remembered it: a large four-poster bed at its center with a shadowlynx's spiraling horns mounted overhead on a plaque. On the small night table next to the bed, he kept a fanas burning, the flame within its glass walls constant, no matter what time of the day. A man afraid of little—except the dark.

Kali tried holding her breath, but it was impossible to avoid the scents that still filled her nightmares: the tobacco and sweet paan the warden always chewed, the champa ittar that scented his clothes.

"You're quiet, aren't you?" he'd told Kali once, as she lay mute next to him on the bed. "I like my girls fiery."

Not as fiery as Amira, though. According to the stories Kali had heard from the other girls, Amira had lasted maybe an hour in that room, maybe less, fighting the warden the whole time.

"She bit him where it counted the most," the other girls

had said spitefully. "He won't be heading to our cages any-time soon."

And he hadn't. At least not for the past week. Some suggested that the head warden now went to a brothel to find new girls. That he wasn't in his room right now was a blessing, as far as Kali was concerned—a temporary one that could be taken away at any moment.

She froze as someone walked outside the window she'd climbed through minutes earlier. The familiar tap of a guard's stick sounded against the rock.

Yet when Kali risked a glance outside, she only saw Sunheri and Neel, shifting silvery patterns marking their orbs. According to legend, when the two moon goddesses still roamed the earth, they wore the same patterns as birthmarks on their skin. Kali did not know how true the story was, but remembering it always calmed her.

The moon goddesses were powerful, she told herself. *They had birthmarks, too.*

Exhaling, Kali headed to the almarih next to the bed and eased open the wooden door. From within, with a grunt, she slowly began removing a heavy container of grassoil.

"Gray Eyes?"

The tin of oil slipped from Kali's grasp and fell to the floor. She turned slowly, oil pooling around her feet, and found the head warden staring at her with surprise.

His beady brown eyes narrowed, deepening an old hunting scar on his cheek. "What are you doing here?" he demanded.

He wore his sky-blue uniform, a dagger sheathed at one hip, a ring of brass keys strung at the other.

Kali's gaze lingered on the keys for a brief moment—keys that gave the warden access to every cage in the camp.

"Your fanas was low on oil," she whispered, allowing a tremor to enter her voice. She lowered her lashes, the way she knew he liked. "I . . . I've been thinking about you."

The soft tone of her voice turned the suspicion on his face to a leer.

"I thought you liked girls, Gray Eyes." His words curled around her like smoke. "Did I change your mind?"

Had she the strength, Kali would have crushed his skull. Bitten him like Amira or the shadowlynx whose horns he'd taken. But Kali wasn't like Amira. She was quiet like her father. Deceptive like her mother. Brimming with a rage kept hidden for far too long.

"I suppose," she told the warden, her voice as cloying as the floral ittar that now scented the air in the room. She turned around, as if shy.

On the side table, the flame within the fanas flickered. Still alive.

Slowly, Kali approached the bed. Heard the warden move closer.

Save me, goddess.

Kali watched the warden's mouth open in a snarl as he ducked to avoid the fanas that flew over his head and crashed onto the floor, setting the patch of grassoil alight.

By Svapnalok, the cursed sky goddess's statue felt like it weighed a ton!

No, *ten* tons.

She was heavier than a plow, heavier that anything Amira had ever attempted to move. The screech of stone against stone made Amira's heart stop at regular intervals, wondering each time if she'd finally been caught.

Then the screams began. Shouts for the girls to return to their cages. A guard's voice, magnified with magic, boomed across the camp and filled the walls of the temple: *"Fire in the barracks."*

The sound made Amira's head hurt.

Seconds went by.

Minutes.

What felt like an hour.

Where is Kali? Amira wondered with each passing moment.

"It's done."

The soft voice made Amira jump. She hadn't even heard Kali come in.

She took in the gray-eyed girl, the blood seeping down her bone-white face, matting the neckline of her choli, her long black braid.

"The warden won't hurt anyone else," Kali whispered. She held up a piece of bloodied broken glass—the sort that came from a fanas. "I gave his keys to one of the girls and freed her. Hopefully, she can free the others, too."

Amira didn't know if she wanted to admire Kali for her courage or shake her for unilaterally modifying their plan. Gently, she extracted the glass from Kali's trembling hand and tossed it aside.

"You were very brave," she said, meaning it. "You did what everyone in this camp wanted to do—and more. Now, come on. We need to get moving."

Her words seemed to clear the strange glaze over Kali's eyes.

With Amira's help, she climbed into the sanctum and they both began to push hard against the statue. Together, they managed to move the goddess faster than Amira had alone, creating a gap large enough for half an adult to pass through. Or two skinny fifteen-year-old girls.

"Prisoners on the loose."

The voice pounded Amira's head. "Quickly!" she told Kali.

Kali nodded and slid down through the gap as easily as water. Amira went next and found a set of stairs leading into the dark.

A scream somewhere above. For a change, it belonged to a man, not a girl.

Amira's insides fluttered. Were the other girls fighting the guards? Would they make it out as well?

"Come!" Kali tugged at Amira's arm, but Amira shook her head.

"The statue," she said. "We have to make sure it's moved back. They'll find us otherwise."

She didn't have to see Kali to feel the fear in the cold hand gripping her arm.

"Goddess of the sky and the air, let your hand guide mine," Kali whispered. "Let me find strength—"

"Curse your goddess!" Amira exclaimed. "She's never here when we really need her!"

Her voice echoed through the dark, vibrating the stone under her bare feet.

She looked around wildly and, under the faint light streaming from the lamps overhead, saw a shadow jutting from the wall. Shaped like a trident, it was a lever made of metal, grown tough with rust. It cut Amira's bruised hands when she touched it, stung her like a hundred bees.

"I wish you'd do what you're supposed to," she muttered. "Just this once."

Amira didn't know whom she was addressing: the lever, the sky goddess, or her own worn-out body. But for a second, she felt a flare of emotion. Anger. And underneath, something else. Something that glowed bright and hot like the magic she'd lost, bringing down the trident with a crack.

The statue moved, almost in silence, sealing them within the tunnel seconds before indecipherable voices began hammering above. Amira's heart hammered in turn. *Was that—was that really my magic?*

But the glow—or whatever it had been—was gone now. The spaces inside Amira were still empty. Disappointed, her heart slowed, calmed to a steady beat. She allowed Kali to take her hand and followed the smaller girl through the darkness, through a tunnel that stank of rust and urine, that sounded of rats and other foul things.

Amira hardly expected to find light at the end of it, let alone a tree.

A large peepul, hollowed from within, its branches laden with roosting shvetpanchhi, their white feathers gleaming gold and blue under the light of the two moons.

Amira and Kali climbed out of the tree trunk and collapsed underneath it.

Amira stared at the stars dotting the sky and at the pond before them, golden lotuses budded shut over its surface.

She wasn't dreaming again, was she?

No. Pain bloomed over her skin as Amira pinched it. She wasn't dreaming. She was *free*. And so was Kali.

Cheeks aching from what might have been her first grin in years, Amira turned to face Kali, who was also looking at the stars. And crying.

"What happened?" Amira cried out, all lightness fading.

"N-nothing!" Kali wiped her eyes. "I . . . I'm grateful that you got me out, Amira. Truly. But I can't help thinking of the other girls—whether they escaped or if the guards locked them back in their cages. I'm sorry. I'm being foolish. I know we couldn't have saved everyone. I was lucky you decided to help *me*."

Guilt swelled in Amira's belly. She wasn't selfless—never had been. But somehow, it felt bad—*wrong*, even—to hear this confirmed by Kali.

"You're not foolish," she told Kali. "And you weren't the only lucky one. I had help, too." From Rani Juhi. From Kali herself.

Kali, who was far better than Amira could hope to be.

"Maybe we *can* help the others," Amira said, her mind racing. "Not tonight, with the guards on high alert. But maybe later . . ." Her voice faltered as Kali turned to stare at her. "Between the two of us, I thought we could figure out the details?"

Kali's smile was brighter than the two moons. "That's a great idea," she said.

A pleasant warmth rushed through Amira's cheeks. Flooded through her veins.

And that was when she felt it again. That strange, familiar flare of heat. A surge of *something* in her diaphragm that faded in the blink of an eye.

"Kali," she said after a moment, "do you really think we can get our magic back?"

"I don't know. I mean, there were rumors at camp that the Sky Warriors could never *truly* destroy the parts of us that produce magic. I'm not sure." Kali sighed. "Then again, I didn't know I'd be setting our camp on fire tonight, did I? I didn't know we'd be out *here*. Who knows? With the goddess's help, we might even regain our powers."

The sky goddess didn't help us tonight. We helped ourselves.

But Amira didn't speak the words out loud. Something

about what Kali said gave her pause, reviving an emotion that Amira hadn't felt for years. Not since Mai had told her the story of the two moon goddesses. A time when Amira was still her mother's little love.

Foolish, Amira thought now, *to have hopes that would never be fulfilled.*

But for a few seconds, she couldn't help it.

She let herself hope. Wish for impossible things.

She didn't look up. Nor did she see the streak of light in the sky—one associated with a falling star.

ART BY CHAAYA PRABHAT

INFINITE DRIFT

By Olivia Chadha

It begins like most strange and wonderful things, with sound.

An E-flat major chord, to be exact, just a question, barely audible. The sound of a flower opening its petals. Then, a pinprick of light. Heat. An awakening of life from the primordial dust. Sometimes it fails and then begins again, again, again. But when it's time, the Drift opens wide, sound pulsing, light illuminating, like a shimmering gap in time and space, a bridge to Everywhen.

And so, it begins.

EVERYWHEN 575

When Archana's boots hit the ground as she fell out of the Drift and into a timeline, the earth moaned. She wanted to apologize for landing so hard, for dislocating so much sand and red dust. But the ground knocked the breath right out of her lungs and there were no words to be had. She was new at this; in the service for only a few hundred years, the others considered her green. But the Drift had sent her here through the Everywhen for a reason. A reason she suspected but couldn't confirm yet.

This locale reminded her of a high-desert region from a previous Drift ride, but there was more sand here, less fauna. She coughed. Why did the ride make her so thirsty? Teacher Wen once told her that it was the splitting of the molecules through the wormhole that dehydrated their bodies. Or was it the stretching of them? She couldn't remember. She wiped her eyes and took a swift drink from her water pouch, then tucked it back into her pack. Her hand grazed her favorite katar, a blade named Stick. When she looked out across the landscape with her Earthen Glass, a spyglass anchored to a sextant that only Drift Riders could read, she saw a structure rising from the hill in the distance. That was why she headed west. High desert. Nothing around but red dust. Outpost. Must be the place. She wasn't into overthinking things.

All she knew was this: she had been sent here by the Drift, and the Everywhen didn't make mistakes on where and when to send the Riders. There was work to do here with a boundary, and she would enter the fight without question, support those who needed her help to keep the timeline on track. The timeline was most vital.

But this episode seemed different. As she walked across

the hilly land, she didn't hear swords clashing, rifles firing, electro-guns stunning, or drones dropping bombs. Weapons usually gave away the When and Where. The silence here kept the time a secret, and she scowled, impatient at having to wait to learn more. Boring Drift Rides were for Level Ones, or even Level Zeros, those newer to this whole immortal task. And she was a Two on the verge of Three, which, if she remembered correctly, was the equivalent of the age when some cultures sent their young to university or the like. Though the Drift was eternal. Her boots sank into the hot, sun-washed soil. And for a second, she felt the soil push back, lift her up. She made a note in her records under "Location 575." Time wasn't linear, so it was always difficult for her to pinpoint where on the spiral she was. Numbers helped.

She took in her surroundings. The outpost was not distinct. Not tall or wide or gleaming with magic or a fusion power core. She had skittered across time. Seen armories surrounding smaller posts in the twelfth century during the Hundred Years' War. Once the Drift dropped her on the front lines in the year 2335, when the Water Wars ended and a resolution was agreed upon at the Algae Flats Space Station.

But it was eerily quiet. Either no one was here, or so few that they didn't make much noise. The structure rising out of the ground was a simple rectangular shape, walls fifteen or so feet high. Loophole bastions in the four corners, probably to offer basic shooting defense. She assumed there was a walled inner courtyard as well. This was no major fort. Not the front lines of a war or skirmish or even a virtual battle with drones and synths. Archana was not impressed. This would not be a story to add to the urn, to share with the others. A minor border or boundary disagreement, perhaps. An easy out-and-back, nothing to it. Better to get it over with, find out which linchpin moment she'd entered, keep it on track, and return to the Drift.

Archana wondered if Earth had two suns in this timeline, as she was accustomed to. Only one sun was visible, subtle but generous in size. Archana was intrigued. If not a major battle, perhaps this would be a story anyway. She'd never been able to share something new with the others before. It could elevate her to the next level, earn respect.

The stone parapet glowed white in the sun's gentle rays, and she felt like she was being watched. Which was odd, since she should have been invisible under her Drifter's cloak. She froze. Fast as lightning, she withdrew her chakram from her waist belt and spun around to defend herself. But only a small hoofed creature blinked at her; its tan body and the broad horns twisting from its forehead made it seem like the offspring of a sheep and a gazelle. Animals could always sense Riders. They saw with their souls, not their eyes. Its bleat gave it away. Definitely a type of goat. Its rectangular pupils and pushy muzzle said something like, *what the heck are you doing here?* And also, as it nudged Archana's pack, *surely, you have a scrap of food in there to share.*

She gave it a scratch and then pushed it off her pack, but when she started walking, the goat creature followed. So she named it Bakari, which wasn't very creative at all. During the

Holy Wars, she named the horse she rode Ghora. Once she met a rabbit on a mission and named it Bun Bun. Naming was not her strong suit. Fighting was. Which was why, she assumed, she was here.

Approaching the fort, a familiar scent caught her by surprise. Something she hadn't smelled in hundreds of years. Bakari apparently also smelled it and trotted ahead to stuff its face into whatever the wonderful thing was.

"Onions and cumin," Archana whispered. Her mouth salivated, and other sensations arrived along with it; like a breeze carrying seed parachutes, each one brought her closer to lost things. One by one, each triggered a memory that whispered about her home. Her first one. In her real life.

A few feet from the stone walls, a glint of light caught her eye. Not a laser or a fire, but a flash like a multifaceted stone caught in a momentary blaze of sunlight.

"Heliograph? Very clever." Another time clue, perhaps the late nineteenth century or around there. The sand told her high desert. The smell of onions and those particular spices, though, was the most definitive clue: this was near where she had been born, a very long time ago. Even if it was a different timeline, it was familiar enough. Her breath caught at the thought. It had been too long. She'd been taken abruptly when she was sixteen. And her death had been so violent that the elder Drift Riders had cleansed her mind of memories and left only her last few thoughts of love before her final breath.

She slipped inside the outpost as silently as she could. It wasn't battleworthy, just a supply station of some kind. A halfway point, perhaps? She had a moment to spare to investigate the food, the scent promising to lead her closer to her real memories of who she'd been when she was alive. Images flickered in her mind like flashes of reflections on a pool of water: a dhaba, a child's laugh, the warm sun, a dusty road. And then as soon as they arrived, they dissolved.

In the inner courtyard, a man crouched over the fire stirring a few large pots. Maybe rice, a stew of some kind. He wore a turban but the sides of his face were shaved clean. Simple clothes, not a soldier's uniform. He was probably an assistant, a helper in the fort. She moved closer, and he shivered. Of course, he couldn't see her; that's what the cloak was for. But humans still felt things beyond their senses. In the pot was daal; the fragrance caressed her like a familiar blanket. There were voices of other young men waking. She let her guard down.

And just as she did, the air tightened around her. A thrum broke the silence and a delicate release of G-major chords peeked through, too subtle to hear, more likely felt deep inside her chest. The sound was a question of hope.

Then a voice came from behind her. Another man. *"Tusi ki ho? Tusi bhoot te nahi ho?"*

She ignored the voice at first. He couldn't be speaking to her. She was an invisible observer, a silent assistant, the Ghost Hand of Justice.

"Hey? Wait . . . ," the person spoke again, this time in English, a whisper. The voice came from behind her. "Are you a ghost?"

When she turned, her cloak still covering her, Archana came face-to-face with a young man not much older than she'd been herself when she left the world. His scraggly beard wasn't full yet. It must have been a mistake. His gaze locked on hers, eyes wide. There was a curious flash of pain in his eyes; something she could not place, a darker recognition that gave her pause. Could he really see her?

The cook said, "What'sa matter with you, Gurmukh? Do I look like a ghost to you, ullu?"

"Sorry, Khudaji. My eyes play tricks on me in the morning." He never looked away from Archana as he spoke. But when the older man he called Khuda stood, Archana rushed into the shadows, away from the rich scent of her childhood, away from the boy who might have noticed her. She'd have to go memory hunting another time, when her anonymity wasn't on the line.

Her heart pounded in her chest as she dashed away. *That was close. Too close.* It was a rule in the Everywhen to move invisibly through time and space. She'd learned that terrible things could happen to Drift Riders who were seen. Some changed the timeline too much, and the elders had to spend years remedying the ripples they created. She climbed the stone steps to the top of the parapet that surrounded the courtyard and found a corner from which she could observe. In the distance, the land woke with a red-and-gold sun over a mountain range. Soldiers stirred in the post below, set out for morning prayers, breakfast.

On the horizon, a massive dust cloud appeared at the base of the peaks in the distance. Soon it became clear that it wasn't a cloud at all; rather, line after line of bodies marching in the outpost's direction. She sharpened her katar with a whetstone. War wasn't strange to her. It's what she did. But these fellows in the fort, they might have seen it before once, maybe twice for the older ones. The younger ones seemed softer. This wasn't a major fortress; it was an outpost manned by a few brave souls. It wouldn't protect them long.

This would be a bloodbath.

Archana scanned the area with the Earthen Glass. She had learned how to read the strain of the earth, how the tension of soil reacted to human manipulation. The mountains and soil rippled, shifted, trembled angrily. A border war was coming, and the land was not pleased. Earth didn't approve of human wars over lines and boundaries. As if drawing a new line would change the ground beneath, the old ground, which had been in existence for millions of years before and would continue long after the last human ants marched on its crust. Each time people renamed a land, Earth roared, but they never heard it. When their blood spilled on the surface, it churned. Whatever was coming would be a major shift. No one ever considered what the land wanted. Whether it desired a new border, or to be divided here or there arbitrarily. But if they had, they'd have learned one of the world's greatest secrets: if only they would listen to the land itself, it would tell them how to live peacefully upon it.

Footsteps rushed the stairs, and Gurmukh clambered to the heliograph on the opposite parapet. Had it been an accident? Could he really see her? She made herself as small as possible and waited. The stand of the heliograph had four thin wooden legs that held the mirror upright. He used binoculars to gaze into the distance. He'd see what she'd seen growing on the horizon and then he'd alert the others. The signalman turned the mirror to the light, flashed a series of flashes. She could read the Morse code from where she sat. *Under attack.*

When he was done, he wiped sweat from his forehead with a handkerchief and waited.

And then his eyes fell on Archana. A flash of pain. "You. No, it can't be. What are you?"

She was curious. "I'm just passing through."

"You must be a demon." He ran to her with his kirpan drawn.

She easily stopped his attack by blocking his arm and then pushing him down to sitting. "Yaar, I mean you no harm. Please, I don't want to fight you."

"You can't be here. What do you want?" He spit his words.

She didn't want to hurt him. But she couldn't leave this timeline until her job was fulfilled. His eyes were scared more than anything. He was a young signalman, not a gunner. He needed to finish his task. Get the message of the approaching enemy to the other fort in the distance. She pushed him back firmly. "Please." She held her fist blade in his direction. "I'm not an enemy. Truthfully, I wasn't supposed to be seen."

"What do you mean?" He must have looked at her dress, the strange and foreign warrior clothes worn by Drift Riders. A long cloak tied at the waist with a belt that held weapons and treasures from her journeys. Her necklace, a chain of tokens from her many battles across the ages. Coins from Alexander's time, a twist of iron from the Middle Ages, a nanobot's chip from the Drone Wars. The thin tattoos across her brown skin from fingers to face that marked her path through time and space in lines and dashes, maps only the Riders could read.

"What. Are. You?" He separated each word with a period.

"I'm . . . just passing through." Her life depended on her secret; her whole society did. Without the cloak, she was corporeal. If she didn't complete her mission, a pinprick hole in the fabric of time would open. The elders would have to come through and mend it. But if this boy could truly see her, the elders would already have to come back to erase the impression she had made on his mind. And anyway, it would sound like a lie if she told him the truth. It would be easier if he thought she was just a poor girl, stranded. "I escaped a bad place and was just making my way south. I was cold. And hungry. I didn't mean to interfere."

The young man lowered his hands and his weapon. He didn't seem to believe her; his grin almost humored her. "This place isn't safe. You'd be better off in the wild. Head south as fast as you can. Don't stop until you get to the next fort."

She listened to Gurmukh, not intending to do anything of

the sort. But she had to stay out of his way, Ghost of Justice and Balance and all. "Thank you." She bowed her head. Some ghost, though. She needed to know why he could see her. She'd taken all the necessary precautions.

Glints of light flashed in their direction, a response from a fort off in the east. Archana counted the dashes and dots and knew what it said: *Lt. Col. Haughton will send troops if possible.*

A roar of wind seemed to startle Gurmukh, and he fumbled with the heliograph's mirror. It fell, and Archana caught it just before it shattered.

There was chaos below, about twenty men rushing this way and that. Most ascended the stairs to the rooftop. One, taller than most, barked out orders to the others. But only a few against ten thousand approaching? This would be an outright slaughter.

"Have you fought before?" Archana ventured. Perhaps Gurmukh's history would tell her something about why he could see her.

"We are all warriors, regardless of our experience." He smiled. He seemed so young, his turban too large for his face and shoulders. Surely that's why he was the lamplighter, the heliographer in the bastion, and not polishing his rifle with the others below. Archana saw something in his eyes, a confidence overriding the tears.

As Gurmukh walked to the opposite side of the parapet, where a few soldiers were gathering to take in the approaching tribesmen, the news from Colonel Haughton seemed to weigh on his gait. The tallest of them all, the leader, stood with a looking glass, taking in the horizon. Not one of them noticed Archana. At least she had made only one mistake on this Drift Ride.

"Havildar, sir," Gurmukh saluted the tall man with the bright orange turban.

"Say what you came to say, Gurmukh." The havildar spoke to the young signalman as he might to a child, with kindness and patience.

"Sir, Colonel Haughton will send support troops."

"Right. Keep your rifle close. Stay at your post, soldier. Don't leave the lamplight unless you have something to report."

"Sir." Gurmukh saluted again.

When he returned to his heliograph, he calmed his shaking hands and squatted where he could receive another message if it came from the distant fort.

"They'll be here soon," Archana said. "The tribesmen."

"They've been attacking other forts along the Samana Range all week. It's their land. Tribesmen don't like the British. Think the British will order us to cross the Durand Line. Don't trust them."

"Can you trust them?"

"The British? We've sworn our allegiance. We are honored to be soldiers of the Thirty-Sixth Sikh Regiment."

"Of course. I see." But she didn't see. Mortal ideologies became more confusing the longer Drifters were away from the coil. Some things became clearer, and other things fell away like layers of sediment covering a fossil of a fern. It was strange what stayed. Allegiances, empires, borders all changed. But honor, that was unique. That never lessened in importance.

"It's who you are." Archana wasn't sure if she was speaking to herself or to Gurmukh.

His turban was neatly wrapped. The belt around the waist of his khaki uniform was polished. Gurmukh seemed proud of his position. There was something familiar about this boy, though. Something she couldn't place. She thought he felt it, too, speaking so openly to her; a strange girl wearing odd clothes who showed up in an isolated outpost on a border to nowhere wasn't usually welcomed so easily.

"Where are you from?" He appeared to search Archana's face, hidden still by the shadows of her cloak—a cloak that apparently didn't matter to him.

"Not far from here. South. Punjab," she lied. She couldn't remember. But the name came to her effortlessly.

He smiled. "What village?"

The loud commotion drowned out her honest words, that she didn't know, that she'd left home one day and didn't return. But that it had been hundreds, or possibly thousands, of years. That she'd moved from this realm to the Drift some time ago.

"You?"

"Garhshankar." He observed a flash of light from afar.

The other fort repeated a message denying support. They wouldn't come in time, couldn't break through the wall of men approaching, their troops were too far away. Archana's heart plummeted. Gurmukh stared at the repeating message with a trembling hand, holding the heliograph mirror.

"Why haven't you left yet?" she asked. "Surely it would be best to escape while you can. All of you can leave and join the other fort."

Gurmukh faced her. "It's better to stand here and finish this than to run. We aren't cowards." He even laughed. "We either fight or die fighting. It's a part of our culture, our history."

"That's why the British assigned your regiment to this fort. They knew."

"Yes, they knew. They put Sikhs along this border because we won't retreat. Whatever the cost."

And the cost would be their lives.

It's all a game for those in power, she thought. *Just like always.*

He replied to the message with flashes of light, his observations. How many were marching toward them, how many were in the fort ready to defend it. This was a relay station between two others. The approaching tribesmen were going to cut off communication between the two larger forts.

Gurmukh ran to speak with the leader, who was at the ground level, encouraging his troops with a speech, and Archana followed. The signalman stopped in front of the tall man, Havildar Ishar Singh.

"Sir, Colonel Haughton and Colonel Munn attempted to

send a diversion. But they've been overrun," Gurmukh said. "We are on our own."

The havildar nodded. His stern brow deepened. Archana and Gurmukh took in the men all standing at attention. A fine group, yes young, not battle hardened, but they stood tall, unwavering. A few couldn't hide the terror in their tears. Gurmukh took his place between a man with broad shoulders and a boy whose uniform was two sizes too big.

The havildar continued his speech: "We will do this for ourselves. For our ancestors who died on this land. Not for the British. This is a battle of honor. We will give the wounded water. Until the last man standing."

Each soldier saluted the havildar, even Kudha the cook, who was not wearing a uniform and was holding a large water bladder, probably to offer a drink to soldiers on the battlefield.

Then the havildar spoke only to Gurmukh. "You communicate with them every detail that transpires here today. Every bullet and skirmish, every name of our fallen. You will let the world know what happened here. But for now, you just respond with one word and one word only: understood."

"Yes, sir." He saluted the havildar.

As Gurmukh went back up to the heliograph on the parapet, Archana thought about her early memories on the Drift. For decades she hadn't even been allowed to fight. Here these young men were brave enough to stand tall and salute their commanding officer without doubt. Would they shoot when necessary? They should leave this place. Surely they could make it to the next fort. What had they called it? Lockhart, or Gulistan? They could run on foot; it would be faster than a backup battalion could arrive. Why weren't they leaving? They'd at least survive to fight another day. For the first time in her journey on the Drift, she wished she could stop what was coming, change the path. But she had to trust the spiral. Archana hadn't heard of odds like these since Thermopylae, but even then, the numbers weren't so wild. She knew—she'd been there, too.

Then it was time. A rumble poured from the earth and vibrated through Archana's bones. A Prometheus chord in the voice of ten thousand violins all striking the strings simultaneously reverberated across the land, blocking out everything aside from her breath. The approaching tribesmen's footsteps were the thump of a dhol drum matched to the pace of her heartbeat, growing louder and louder. It was the sound of war, of sweat on soldiers' brows, of the last prayers they whispered to the wind, of goodbyes. The Sikh soldiers loaded their rifles as the approaching men came into range, just beyond the thicket of branches and thorns that surrounded the fort, a moat of natural barbed wire.

She returned to the parapet, near Gurmukh's station. Archana's Earthen Glass told her the land was defiant, that both groups were like a sea of fleas on its back and it was itching to kick them all off. This must be one of the Untamable Territories. Archana had learned about these places in her training. For some reason, humans fought on these hot spots, but never won. The land wanted to be free of people, and so it returned to that state again and again. But humans continued to try to march across it again, and again, and again.

Why was she here? If the battle was so unbalanced, and the land was so defiant, what was her purpose? The elders had told her it would reveal itself in every situation in time. She would be the power to turn the tide. She'd fight.

The first rifle blast shattered the countryside with a violent crack. Then another, and another. A symphony of discord enveloped the land as war descended. The tribesmen's weapons were jezails and Martini-Henry rifles. She could tell by their explosive sound. Archana left Gurmukh at his post, ran down the steps, and slipped outside the walls of the fort to stand guard. The thousands of tribesmen lingered back from the natural barrier of branches and briars. But one by one, they slipped through it, and as they did, she silently ended them. After hours of fighting, the soldiers inside the fort had killed hundreds of men by shooting from the parapets. Only two of their own were dead.

Khuda brought the soldiers water. All reloaded their rifles. The second assault arrived with the power of a tsunami. The Sikh soldiers fought with their rifles and bayonets through the bastions and doorways. Archana moved among the tribesmen in the field outside the fort to deter them. Hundreds of the attackers fell. And suddenly, Archana heard a low rumble like an approaching herd of elephants, a song of deception, and the tribesmen lifted a white flag. They wanted the outpost, or were pretending to offer safe passage. Said they would allow the few within Saragarhi to go unharmed. A man from the approaching group yelled to the soldiers.

"Surrender. Surrender and we will let you pass!"

One of the men inside the fort said, "Could it be? Should we surrender?"

Havildar Ishar Singh said, "They are liars. Don't trust them. Either way, we die. We fight to the end." He pushed his remaining men into the inner courtyard. *"Bole so nihal!"* he chanted, and all his men responded, *"Sat sri akal."* Then he locked his soldiers in the courtyard and stood outside to fight alone.

Archana climbed atop the fort to Gurmukh, who had never left his heliograph. Half a day had passed. He sent a narrative of the battle to the other fort every minute of the six hours that the battle went on. He signaled each name of his brothers who died over the day. Songs rose from the fallen soldiers, every song they wouldn't sing, their lives cut short. Gurmukh recounted every brother who fell, in flashes of light across the soil to Colonel Haughton. He wiped his tears with a dusty hand. He signaled when the approaching tribesmen burned the briar fencing. When they began to throw their bodies at the stone walls and, hours later, when they opened a hole. When his brothers in arms used bayonets against them. He was the historian. He crouched along the wall of the parapet; Archana covered him from the oncoming rifle bullets. And then, in the inner courtyard below, the hole in the wall widened under the weight of the men pushing through, and they were overrun.

"Are you scared?" Archana asked.

Gurmukh took a small photograph from his shirt pocket. It

was so worn, it appeared to have been there for years. He held it lovingly by the edges. "It is God's will."

Archana's heart turned to lead. She scanned their surroundings, this impossible battle, and her mind heaved with questions. So much death. And why? She'd seen life leave hundreds, no, thousands of bodies, but she'd never interacted with a person on a mission before. She could take up arms and rush into the battle and kill a few more men. But she couldn't kill a thousand, not even her. And even if she could, there would be nine thousand left and the blood of those men on her hands. It didn't seem right. A pain in her mind refracted as she turned back to Gurmukh, who was still staring at his photograph.

"Is that your family?" she asked.

He looked at Archana and laughed. "Of course." Like she should have known. "Don't ghosts know everything?"

And then she took in Gurmukh. She was much more than a ghost. Perhaps others saw her as such. To him, she wasn't fully real. "I'll be here until the end," she said gently to him.

There were only three men left alive: the havildar, a soldier, and Gurmukh. The solider made it to an interior room in the post. When the tribesmen broke through the central walls, they overran the havildar, and then the soldier. They lit a fire and the smoke rose like a demon through the fort. She knew that would be it. Gurmukh was the last survivor. She sat beside him as he sent his signal, the name of his leader who had fallen.

We are being overrun. Request permission to close down and join the fight. He flashed the words to the fort and waited.

The response was swift. *Permission granted.* Gurmukh opened his heliograph case and gently dismantled the tool, locking it when he was done. Such tender care for the inanimate object drew a surprised tear from Archana. Gurmukh saluted the fort in the distance and picked up his rifle. It was clear to her that he'd never killed anyone before, but he used the weapon properly as any trained soldier might.

The smoke and fire rose around them. Then a stray bullet hit Gurmukh in the chest. He locked eyes with Archana, who lowered her cloak. His gaze widened into the forever. She reached out and touched his shoulder as an old friend might. The photograph fell from his fingers. When she saw the image, her breath caught. Gurmukh, standing in a black-and-white family photo beside elderly women and men sitting in chairs. A girl stood beside him. The eyes, the smile, the way she stood favoring her right leg. It was her, before the tattoos and charms and millennia of traveling the Infinite Drift. Archana.

And then the sound arrived, and she knew what her purpose was at last. The greatest honor for all Drift Riders. She would be the escort of a new Rider. He would join them.

E-flat, a hum that sang the song of all beginnings. Then a spark of light brighter than any star and full of every color. They watched it together as the flames grew higher and hotter around them. As Gurmukh's spirit left his body, the Drift opened wide, and she held his hand as together they walked into the Infinite.

His spirit stood above his mortal body and followed Archana into the sound.

"I knew you'd come one day, sister," he said, as they walked into the burgeoning light.

AUTHOR'S NOTE

"Infinite Drift" is a sci-fi historical reimagining of the Battle of Saragarhi (September 12, 1897). This battle took place during British colonial rule of India, when they began to expand their empire north toward Afghanistan in order to block Russian advancement into India during the conflict known as the Great Game. Two forts, Lockhart and Gulistan (also called Cavagnari), were the main outposts along the Samana Range in the Hindu Kush along the Durand Line. The Durand Line was a border agreed upon by the British Indian government and the amir of Afghanistan. This line is the present-day border between Pakistan and Afghanistan. Between these two well-supported forts stood Saragarhi, a modest outpost that acted as a hub for communications between Lockhart and Gulistan. It was staffed at the time of the battle with only twenty soldiers and one assistant from the 36th Sikh Regiment; most of them were very young.

ART BY TARA ANAND

DISMANTLE THE SUN

By Sangu Mandanna

I

The warrior's first breath was smoke and grief. Her heart stuttered out its first uncertain beats. Each beat became rage, each thump a battle cry.

She uncurled and rose to her feet. Her legs were new, but they already knew how to hold her up. Her limbs were strong and supple. Her neck was graceful. There was a sword in each of her clenched fists.

She had been the earth beneath their feet, watered with the ashes of a princess and the tears of a god, and now she was born.

"Look at me," said the god.

He had a stern face and angry eyes. Bronze skin, like hers.

Black hair, like hers. A furious heart, like hers. He was the Destroyer, a beautiful and terrible god, but he was also her creator.

"Do you know what you must do?" asked the god.

She did. She had his memories. And the princess's, too. Their memories were mirrors, distorted. His were like broken glass, jagged with fury: a princess, a king, a ceremony, a fire. Hers were like winter flowers, soft with love and sorrow: a god, a father, a ceremony, a hand at her back—

—and a white-hot blaze as she was pushed into the flames, burned, and was gone.

The warrior felt nearly mad with fury. "Yes," she said, carefully forming the new syllables. "I know what I must do."

He nodded. "Then go. Go where I cannot. Do what I cannot."

The fire ceremony, a rite the kingdom practiced every year for a prosperous harvest, hadn't ended. It should have, the warrior thought savagely. It was a rite of flames and prayer, not a rite of sacrifice. No one was supposed to *die*. So why, then, hadn't those in attendance cried out in protest? Where was the justice in this terrible place? It had scarcely been an hour since the princess had been murdered and yet they carried on with their rituals, tended the flames, and drank their wine as if she had never been there.

So the warrior ended their ceremony for them. She had come to restore justice and balance to that wretched place, and she did it without pity, without mercy, and without hesitation. For she, too, was a destroyer.

Her twin swords cut the cruel king in two. They killed the queen, who had refilled her cup of wine while her eldest daughter burned. Her blades took the heads clean off the shoulders of the pious priests who had not batted an eye at cold-blooded murder on supposedly holy ground. When the princes seized their weapons and came at her, she cut them down.

There were a few gods at the ceremony, there to bear witness to the kingdom's rite. They stood frozen at first, stunned and whispering among themselves in the wake of the princess's murder. Then, as the princes died one by one, the gods finally intervened. They tried to stop the warrior, and it cost them dearly. She could not kill them, for they were gods, but they could be wounded and humiliated. Their blades and arrows came for her, but the warrior did not stop. She cut the hand off one god and took out the eye of another, slicing and swinging until they retreated and begged the Destroyer to restore order to the chaos. He refused.

It was a mistake to assume there was no order here. That the warrior did not know exactly what she was doing. Out of the corner of her eye, she saw the wide, terrified gazes of servants and young children—and she made sure her swords did not touch a single one of them. She had not come to this wicked place to harm the powerless or the innocent.

The warrior went back to the last prince, who lay dying, and quenched the fire with his blood.

When it was over, she returned to her creator.

"You did well," he said. "Now you must return to dirt and ashes and tears."

She bowed her head and waited to fall apart.

But she did not.

The warrior looked up in surprise. The god had raised his palm to undo the alchemy that had transformed her from the earth, but now he paused. He searched her face, and something softened very slightly in his.

He lowered his hand. "No," he said at last. "You need not go."

And so she was born. And drenched in blood and tears, she lived.

Having decided rather to his own surprise to keep the warrior he'd made, the god found himself dealing with a conundrum. What was he supposed to do with her? He was the Destroyer, restorer of justice and balance; he was not the Creator, tender nurturer of the living. What little softness there had been in him, he had given over to the mortal princess he had loved and lost.

In the madness of his fury, he had intended only to conjure a warrior, had not given any thought to the gender, age, or form of that warrior and had not expected the one that had materialized. She was a girl, and a *young* girl at that. She looked like she was possibly seventeen or eighteen in mortal years, and he was unnerved to see his own dark, fathomless, flashing eyes in her elfin face. If he looked at her too long, he saw tiny jigsaw pieces of the lost princess in her, too, and it crossed his mind that perhaps he had subconsciously created the child he and the princess might have had, in another universe.

After *that* thought had crossed his mind, it had been impossible to scatter her back to the earth.

Now she was here, and he, for the first time in many millennia, was at a loss.

Unexpectedly, it was the warrior herself who gave him an answer. "You made me because gods are forbidden to directly strike humankind, are they not?" she said. "So let me do as I did today. I will deliver your justice in places you are not permitted. I will be your hand in places you cannot strike."

The god agreed, but he had a warning. He touched the side of her cheek, where another god's arrow had grazed her. "You are not human, but you are not a god, either. You will always look like this. You will never age. But you can be killed."

"We'll see," said the warrior, and a tiny smile tipped up one corner of her mouth. It reminded him so much of the princess that he had to look away.

"You may do as you please, and go anywhere you wish," said the god. "Just as long as you come when I call, and wield your swords for me when I command."

"I would be honored."

"And you will need a name."

The warrior waited, her large, dark eyes steady and expectant.

"Vira," said the god at last. "You will be called Vira."

It was a bloody, peculiar beginning, but Vira did not bewail her lot in life. She embraced her duty to serve the god who had made her, for the world seemed to be constantly in need of his justice, and she felt her strongest, most familiar self when she held her beloved twin swords in her hands.

It was not unexpected, then, that as the years passed, the sight of Vira in the doorway of a throne room, descending from a chariot, or climbing off the back of an enormous wolf filled even the bravest of hearts with terror. As the hand of a god, Vira was above kings and queens, governments and armies, and she was free to go anywhere she pleased and dispense the Destroyer's justice anywhere it was called for. There were those who tried to fight back, of course, and she had the scars to show for it; still, even bleeding, even broken, she did not leave until her swords were red and her duty done.

It was a bitter, glorious kind of power in a world where power was a difficult thing to come by. It made up for the days when all she felt was a quiet emptiness that she later learned to recognize as loneliness. She did not belong with the gods, but she did not belong with mortals, either. She did not know friendship, family, or love. There was no space in the world for her that she did not carve out and cleave for herself.

But she accepted this, and all the rest, because to do otherwise was inconceivable. To lay down her swords and turn her back on her duty would be an unthinkable betrayal of her purpose.

She was Vira, warrior and wielder of the twin swords, and for ten years she painted the world in blood.

II

A young, frightened face edged around the library door. The new maid. "Shall I fetch you a hot cup of tea, lady?" she asked in little more than a whisper.

Vira lowered her book and saw that she'd been so absorbed, her tea had gone completely cold. "Please do, Masha."

The maid let out a faint squeak of assent and started to edge into the room to retrieve the tea tray. Vira suspected poor Masha wouldn't last a week before she, like countless others before her, decided the generous wage was not worth the terror of life in the household of a god's blackhearted assassin.

Out of the corner of her eye, Vira caught sight of a distortion at the edge of the library, a place the light avoided.

"Actually, Masha," Vira said quickly, "I'll have my tea later. Please just clear the tray, thank you."

Masha did as she was told, seizing the tray and fleeing from the room as quickly as she could. The moment her footsteps faded away, the distortion rippled—and a god stepped into the room.

"Thank you for waiting," Vira said. "Masha would have packed her bags and left before nightfall if she'd seen you."

The Destroyer shrugged, unsurprised. He knew he was as feared as he was revered. He stood at the edge of the library for a moment, preternaturally still, studying her with flashing dark eyes set in a severe, implacable face. He often looked at her like that, as if he were trying to find the answer to a riddle, and she never knew what to make of it. Any moment now, he'd snap out of whatever reverie he was in and give her the name of her next target—

Vira blinked as the Destroyer crossed the room and took the chair across from hers. He glanced at her, hesitating, and then looked away.

"Father?" she said uncertainly.

They took tea together sometimes, but always at his invitation, and always in his home. *This* was unprecedented.

"Who do you want me to—"

"I have no name for you today," her father interrupted her.

Vira tried not to stare.

"Of late, I have had doubts," he said slowly, and now Vira *did* stare. "For centuries, I have delivered justice in the heavens, protecting humans from the power and wrath of gods, monsters, and other otherworldly creatures. I did not notice the power imbalances and injustices of the mortal world, not until . . ." He trailed off, leaving the princess's name unsaid. Always, *always* unsaid. "I created you so that this world would have the justice the heavens have enjoyed for so long, but I also created you at a moment of rage, of near madness."

Anger bloomed white across Vira's vision. "As you said," she replied tightly, "the mortal world needed justice. How can what we're doing be wrong?"

"Not wrong," the Destroyer replied. "Just, perhaps, limited. I've been thinking lately of what *she* would have wanted, and I know she would have asked these questions. Have *you* never considered them, Vira?"

Vira's mind flashed, unbidden, to memories she'd tried to forget over the years: the terrified eyes of bystanders, the sick and swooping sensation in her belly every time she walked away from yet another scene of carnage, not allowing herself to give a second thought to the survivors. She had never *dared* to ask herself these questions.

"How dare you, Father?" Vira said out loud, her anger slipping through the cracks in her control. "How can I *possibly* ask such questions when to do so is to undermine my very existence? For ten years, my purpose has been the foundation of everything I am. If I question it, if I doubt myself, I am *nothing*."

"Or maybe you would be something more. Something better."

The word *better* echoed in her head, as noisy and dissonant as a klaxon. She knew she should not be hurt by it, yet she was. "So what you're really saying, Father, is I am not enough as I am."

"That is not what I'm saying," the Destroyer said sharply. "Not *you*, Vira. Your purpose. If there is one thing gods and mortals have in common, it is our prejudices. We are unwelcoming and intolerant, suspicious of anyone who is different. *You* are proof of that, Vira. You are an outsider who does not belong anywhere, who has never been *accepted* anywhere. So was . . ."

Again, the name hung between them. "Sati." Vira said it out loud, her voice cracking, and watched her father flinch. "Her name was *Sati*."

"I know her name," the Destroyer growled. "You have no idea—"

"I know her better than you did."

Silence rang between them. Vira watched fury and pain crackle like lightning in her father's eyes, remembered his unfathomable power, and almost wished she could take the words back.

Almost.

Instead, she held her chin up and did not look away. "I have her memories, Father," she went on. "I thought you knew that, but maybe you didn't. Maybe you never realized I grew out of her ashes, too. And you've never asked. You never talk about her. Do you even know what her life was like before she met you? She was born without the ability to speak, and her family never forgave her for it. They didn't care that she was funny, whimsical, and kind. They didn't care that she made her voice heard anyway. No, they saw her only as a flaw in their perfect family portrait. And she, instead of trying to twist herself into knots to please them, leaned *into* being different. She was not meek and biddable. She insisted on having the same education as her brothers and stole that education when it was denied her. She refused to marry the man her father chose for her and fell in love with *you* instead. She left her home to be with you."

"I know all that because she told me, in writing and with gestures," said the Destroyer, his voice jagged with pain. "I do not have her memories, Vira, but I have the story she *chose* to tell me. I do not say her name because it breaks my heart. I do not speak of her because it is agony to do so. Not just because I lost her, but because of *how* I lost her. I could have stopped her from going to that fire ceremony."

"Why didn't you?"

"Because she wanted to, and it was not my place to stop her from doing something she wanted. Too many people had done that already." His eyes were dark and far away. "Years after fleeing her home, she discovered she had a young sister. A child of just six years old. She went to the ceremony to meet her sister, in spite of knowing her presence would infuriate her parents. She wanted to make sure her sister was safe and well." The Destroyer let out a slow breath. "We both know what happened after that."

There was a long, heavy silence, a silence scored through with years of grief and hurt and too little healing.

"I'm sorry," Vira said at last. "I want to talk about her, but not like this. I lashed out. I shouldn't have."

"You're angry because I asked questions that frighten you."

"You created me in a moment of grief and fury, Father. Ten years on, you see things differently. That is not a luxury I have."

"Why not? You can evolve. Sati died because she was different, Vira. Because her father, enraged and embarrassed by her existence, thought he could push her into the flames and get away with it, instead of celebrating her for her kindness and intelligence. And her story isn't unique."

"That's why we do what we do—"

"This is not about your twin swords coming in to offer justice *after* the fact," said the Destroyer. "What if that's not enough? What if, instead, we reshaped the world so that everyone is accepted? So that no one is dismissed, belittled, or killed for being different?"

"Oh, is that all?" Vira asked. "Why don't you shatter the moon, dismantle the sun, and start the world from scratch while you're at it?"

"Changing the world is not impossible. It starts with changing our purpose."

Vira shook her head and stared at the floor of her library, feeling betrayed. The one thing she had been able to count on all these years was that they were on the same side. Now he wanted her to ask questions, to doubt, and he did not seem to understand that if the foundation beneath her feet cracked, she would have *nothing*. She had sacrificed friendship, love, companionship, laughter, and joy for the sheer rightness of her purpose. It was sacred to her. She could not bear to consider that after all that, her purpose might be flawed.

Perhaps seeing the anguish in her face, the Destroyer's own face softened slightly. He rose. "Think on it."

By the time Vira looked up, he was gone.

III

Weeks passed. A sickness swept the lands, leaving corpses in its wake. Kings feasted while orphans starved. Harvests were reaped, babies were born, and the season turned.

In the warrior's home, her swords were sharp as she waited to be called on. Miraculously, the maid Masha had stayed on, frightened squeaks and all. The Destroyer did not visit again, and Vira did her best to put their argument out of her mind.

When her summons arrived, it came as it always did: without warning. She woke from dark, restless dreams of swords and blood to the presence of a shadow on her balcony. He waited patiently for her to get up.

"Vira."

"Father."

His steady, sharp stare sized her up in an instant. "You haven't been sleeping well."

Vira shrugged. Tentatively, she asked, "How have you been?"

"The gods have been unruly lately. It's kept me busy."

Vira's mouth flattened. After the fire ceremony, when the gods had intervened to stop *her* instead of stepping in to save Sati in the first place, she only ever expected the worst from them.

Her father's dark eyes searched her face, seeing too much. She wondered if he could see all the way to the small, secret loneliness she'd tucked away in a dark corner of her heart.

But if he did, he said nothing about it. Instead, he told her of the wrong he wanted her to right and gave her a name.

"I'll see it done," she said, as she always did.

On the table beside her bed, gleaming silver, her twin swords sang.

"Masha," Vira said to the wide-eyed young maid the following morning, "I am going to hunt down a monster. I will be gone a few days. Could you ask the stablemaster to ready my chariot, please?"

"Yes, Lady," Masha squeaked. "What weather do we expect to encounter? Just so I know what to pack."

"The mountains, so there might be snow." A beat passed before Vira picked out the oddity in Masha's sentence. "What do you mean, 'what weather do we expect to encounter'? You can't possibly be thinking of coming with me?"

"I am your maid, Lady," said Masha, looking so surprised that it seemed she had momentarily forgotten to be terrified. "I go where you go. That is how it works."

"This is a sacred mission for the Destroyer, Masha, not a tea party. I have never taken a maid with me before." Vira didn't add that this was at least partly because she had never had a maid stick around for more than a few days before. "You can't come."

"I'm very sorry, Lady, but I must insist. You hired me to be your maid, and that means I will *be* your maid, whether that be here in your home, at a tea party, or on a sacred mission."

"You insist," Vira repeated. This was unprecedented from

anyone, let alone from the skittish Masha, but Vira was so delighted by the novelty of the experience that she had no intention of being offended.

Masha's cheeks were flushed pink, but she didn't back down. "Again, I'm very sorry."

"There will be blood."

"I see blood every month, Lady," came the reply.

"That's not what I—" Vira gave up. "Very well. You may come with me. Thank you, I think?"

So for the first time, when Vira rode out in her gleaming golden chariot pulled by two magnificent white mares, bred by the horse god himself, she had a companion with her. She drove at a teeth-rattling speed, guiding the horses expertly while Masha sat white-knuckled on the seat beside her.

Beyond the gates of Vira's fortress, the horses took to the air with a powerful surge of strength and drew the chariot across the sky. Out of pity for poor Masha, Vira tugged on the reins to slow them down, and they crossed the skies at a more sedate pace than she would have, had she been alone.

"M-May I ask about the m-monster, Lady?" Masha asked timidly, her teeth chattering in the face of the icy winds.

"He's a high-ranking courtier in a mountain kingdom," Vira said quietly, repeating the Destroyer's own words from the previous night. "He's a widower with two young daughters and an illegitimate half sister he uses as little more than a nursemaid. He preys on women who are too afraid to refuse him. When he's done, he hands them over to his pack of soldiers. One of the women is now dead. Two are still alive, but will never wake up. The others, *dozens* of them, live in dread that he'll return."

"Oh," Masha whispered.

Vira's heart gave a vicious thump, a familiar battle cry of rage. "But I am going to make sure he never goes back."

Masha nodded.

"Why did you take this job, Masha?" It was a question Vira had wanted to ask every time a new maid, cook, or stable-master joined her household, but this was the first time she had actually asked it. Her second question was one she had never had cause to ask before: "Why are you still here?"

The maid looked down at her hands, and her voice was little more than a whisper. "I am safer in your household than I would be in most, Lady."

"I'm sorry that you have reason to know that."

"So am I."

The courtier was traveling through a cold, pale mountain pass, his carriage luxuriously sheltered from the weather, the wheels trundling over well-worn grooves in the winding road. His loyal pack of soldiers, a dozen of them in all, rode on horseback alongside the carriage, gleaming swords and spears at their waists as they laughed and mocked the huddled, flinching carriage driver.

Vira descended like a storm and left a trail of dark, bloody red in the pale frost beneath their feet. The horses bolted, untouched. The driver cowered, untouched.

The carriage door crumpled like paper. Vira caught a glimpse of a thin, frightened woman shielding two small girls before her blazing eyes settled on the courtier. Astonishment passed over his face, followed swiftly by confusion, outrage, and then, at last, terror.

"You!"

Vira dragged him out of the carriage by the collar of his expensive silk coat.

"But I am unarmed! I am helpless!"

She brought her teeth close to his ear. "So were they."

Then she cut his throat.

Vira watched him crumple to the ground, her heart an angry, savage, satisfied roar in her ears, and she waited, beat by beat, for it to go quiet again. It was the calm that came *after* the storm.

There was a crunch of footsteps in the frost a little way away, and Vira knew from the sound of the faint, sharp intake of breath that followed that Masha had left the safety of the chariot perched on an outcropping above them and come after her. Why? Had she wanted to see for herself what Vira really did to the monsters?

"It's time to go," Vira said, and made to turn.

"Wait!"

She froze, startled. The thin, frightened woman had emerged from the carriage, her hands clutched in front of her, her eyes fixed on Vira's face as if they were afraid to look at anything else.

"What about us?" said the woman. Her voice caught as

she glanced over her shoulder at the two little girls inside. "You can't leave us here. I'm his half sister, and they are his daughters. None of us can inherit. We'll be at the mercy of his uncle if we go back. Worse, if we return unharmed while he and his soldiers lie dead, the king and court will think *we* had a hand in this."

"Tell them what really happened," said Vira. "They know who I am. They know *what* I am."

"Please," said the woman. "We need help."

There it was again, that sick, swooping feeling in her belly. The ache in her heart. It took her breath away. "I'm sorry," she said mechanically, reciting it by rote. "My part has been played."

She turned and saw Masha's face for the first time. The girl was white as death. Her eyes were not on Vira, the blood, or the mangled remains of the courtiers and his soldiers, but were fixed instead on the woman trembling outside the carriage and the quiet, terrified faces of the little girls behind her.

"You can't," Masha said, her lips barely moving. "You can't."

"Masha—"

The instant her hand touched Masha's elbow, the girl jerked away and her eyes snapped like magnets to Vira's. "You can't just walk away," she whispered through her chattering teeth, her eyes dark with an old, old rage. "You can't just leave them. You can't do this again."

Quiet settled over Vira like snow. "Again?"

The girl's eyes were full of tears, but her gaze didn't waver. "You've seen this before." The warrior's world tilted, a kaleidoscope of sound, color, and blood. So, so much blood. "When? *When*, Masha?"

"I was there," said Masha. "Ten years ago, at the fire ceremony."

The kaleidoscope fragmented, splintering into pieces. Like shards of glass, each weighed down with the reflection of a face, a moment, a scream. And there, the memory distorted by the madness of rage and grief, was a face she'd glimpsed only briefly: a small girl, just six years old, white as death. Watching as one by one, her family died.

Vira staggered back a step. "You were the youngest princess. The sister she went back there to see."

"And you were the one who left me behind."

IV

They took the woman, the two little girls, and the trembling carriage driver to the port town on the other side of the mountains. There the driver fled to find his family while Vira paid for the woman and girls to travel by ship to a neighboring country. She gave them an emerald anklet she had once received as a gift, which would buy them weeks of food and shelter until they had a chance to settle into new lives, and she watched them go with a confused, stormy heart.

Then, when she and Masha had returned to the chariot and were high in the sky, Masha told her story.

After the fire ceremony, in the chaos, with her whole family dead and her kingdom up for anyone's taking, a loyal servant had snatched Masha up and spirited her away, afraid of what might become of her if she were found by enemies. She had been raised in the servants' quarters, making the best of the hand she had been dealt.

"By all accounts, my family was kinder to me than they were to my sister, but not by much," she said. "I didn't even know she existed until the day of the fire ceremony. When I saw her, I was hopeful for the first time. I thought she'd save me. So believe me when I tell you, Lady, that I did not mourn my family when you killed them. I was *glad* of it, even, after what they did."

"But then I walked away," Vira said.

"Then you walked away and didn't once look back." Masha nodded. Her knuckles were almost white as she sat with her hands clasped over her knees. "I hated you for that. And still, when the last household I worked in became unbearable, the only place I could think of to flee to was to *you*. I thought I would be safe with you, but more than that, I wondered if perhaps what had happened to me was a mistake. Perhaps you hadn't *meant* to leave me behind."

Vira looked ahead, where ribbons of clouds and stars pointed the way home. "You hoped I'd be the best parts of your sister. I'm sorry, Masha."

"You were going to walk away after you killed the courtier. It's what you do every time, isn't it? You do what you're supposed to, and then you walk away and don't look back."

There was a deep, keening cry inside Vira, fighting to get out, but she suppressed it and the pain from which it sprang.

"I'm a warrior," she said quietly. "I am the hand of a god. I can't be more or less than that."

"You were today," said Masha. "You gave those two little girls and their aunt something better than whatever fate awaited them back in their king's court. You fulfilled your sacred purpose, and then you did something more. You did what you should have done for me ten years ago." There was a pause, and a soft breath, as if Masha had at last released everything she had held close for ten long years. "We both had dark, bloody beginnings, Lady, but that isn't where our stories end."

It seemed to Vira, surrounded by the pure, cold clarity of the stars, that the Destroyer and Masha, god and mortal, had seen something that she, who was both and neither, had not. They had seen that her purpose was important but *limited*. Her justice came too late and left too early. Her life and purpose were not a lie, but they were not everything they could be, either.

Not yet.

The warrior found the Destroyer in the heavens' summer garden, on a balcony overlooking the Milky Way. She put one hand over his.

"All right, Father," she said. "Let's go dismantle the sun."

ART BY SIBU T.P.

SHAMSUDDIN-JALAL

By Tahir Abrar

The hakim asked Shamsuddin to catch a jinn.

"It is a vile creature," the hakim said, when Shamsuddin paid a visit to his shop after praying Asr at the masjid. "We must put a stop to its wicked ways."

The hakim was an older man, as old as Shamsuddin's abbu. He wore his gray-streaked hair short and his mehendi-dyed beard long. His body was frail beneath his white kurta and his right hand was covered with a large burn scar. He did not look capable of stopping a tire swing, much less a jinn.

"What will you do to it?" Shamsuddin asked.

"Kill it," the hakim said, as if it were obvious. "It resides in the kabristan. Catch it tonight and bring it back to me, and I will destroy it."

Shamsuddin could not say no to someone who had provided medicine to his abbu when everyone else had refused to help. He nodded.

Now he was here, following the narrow dirt path that led to the graveyard that lay in the forest outside town. Though it was almost midnight, the journey was not as eerie as Shamsuddin had expected. Crickets chirped, cicadas sang, frogs croaked, and the summer breeze felt as uplifting as it did during the day. Even the sight of the kabristan ahead of him did not bring with it any sense of doom; it was, simply, a place where dead people were buried.

All the same, Shamsuddin remained on his guard. He was young and healthy, with arms made strong from lifting crates at work and lifting his abbu at home, but it was no small matter to catch a jinn.

He entered the graveyard and looked at the rows of tombstones. The hakim had not specified the jinn's residence, but there was an enormous, sprawling tree at the far end of the graveyard, where the clearing returned to the wilderness, so that was the most likely spot.

Shamsuddin took a deep breath, lifted his chin, and approached the tree with a steady stride. When he was mere steps from the trunk, a figure dropped from the tree's densely packed leaves. It hung upside down, swinging slightly as if swayed by the breeze. Its back was facing Shamsuddin, so all he could make note of was its long black hair.

This must be the jinn, though it was not as dreadful as

Shamsuddin had envisioned. Perhaps when it turned around—

The figure spun to face Shamsuddin, though it remained upside down. He had a feeling that its feet must not have turned with it; wherever they were, concealed in the leaves, they had stayed in the opposite direction while the jinn turned its body.

Shamsuddin met the jinn's gaze. Still, it was not dreadful. It—he—looked quite human. The only indication of the jinn's true nature were his dark eyes, which glittered far too brightly.

Regardless of such an innocuous appearance, the jinn was still wicked, and Shamsuddin had still promised to catch him.

"Salam alaikum," Shamsuddin said.

The jinn cackled. The sound echoed through the graveyard, overwhelming the noise of the crickets and cicadas and frogs. It rang in Shamsuddin's ears, but he resisted the urge to cover them.

At length, the jinn's laugh faded. "Such politeness!" he teased. "Lagta hai koi khwaja aa gaya!"

Shamsuddin ignored this. He had heard enough qawwalis to know that no one would ever sincerely apply the title of khwaja to him. "I have come to capture you," he said.

The jinn cackled again. In a blink, he dropped from the branch, flipped himself upright, and stood beneath the tree. He seemed to be seventeen or eighteen like Shamsuddin. His hair fell to his waist in thick waves, and his long nose had a gold hoop in it, which glinted in the sliver of moonlight visible between the many clouds overhead. He wore a red churidar of a deeper shade than Shamsuddin's own red kurta. His bare feet were turned backward, as Shamsuddin had expected, though the sight did not horrify him. The jinn's backward feet were natural, and who was Shamsuddin to be horrified by anything that was natural to someone's being?

"And where will you take me?" the jinn asked, as if it were a joke.

"To hakim sahib," Shamsuddin said. "He will stop you from doing any more wicked things."

The jinn seemed amused by this statement. "Is that what I've been doing?" he asked. He grinned, and this, at last, was dreadful: it was too wild and too sudden, as if someone had taken hold of either side of his lips and forced them to stretch. "How delightful! Here I've just been living in this tree, and all this time I could have been doing wicked things! Why did I never think of that?" Some of his great mass of hair fell forward into his face; he tucked it behind his ears to reveal gold hoops in each earlobe. "Is it standard procedure to announce that you're going to capture one of us? This is my first time, you see, so I'm a little nervous. I'm behind on all the etiquette."

"I don't know," Shamsuddin said honestly. "I've never caught a jinn. But to announce my intentions is the honorable thing to do."

He waited for the jinn to laugh a third time—surely it would mock any mention of honor—but the jinn only tilted his head.

"Curious," he said, then straightened his back. "Well, I

can't make it too easy for you, can I? Catch me—if you can!"

With that, the jinn leaped into the air and disappeared into the tree. Shamsuddin gritted his teeth and ran toward the trunk. He grabbed a low branch and hoisted himself up, then grabbed another branch to climb farther up the tree. As he passed into the canopy of leaves, he heard another laugh, though this one was softer and harder to trace. It seemed to come from all around him at once, disorienting him in the darkness of the thick leaves. The tree seemed broader from within, never-ending, as Shamsuddin continued his ascent.

After what felt like an age, Shamsuddin emerged from the top of the tree. In one direction, he could see over the forest as far as the town, where a few lights sparkled; when he turned his head, he could see the rest of the forest behind him, looming long and vast. He held still, listening, then again heard that soft laugh.

He took a deep breath and dove back into the leaves. He thrust his arm out at random and his hand closed around something shaped distinctly like the limb of a human, not a tree. He tightened his grip, then was briefly blinded by a light illuminating the space.

He squeezed his eyes shut against the light, then opened them to see the jinn sitting on a branch with his legs stretched out in front of him. The jinn held a tiny orange flame in his right palm. Shamsuddin's hand gripped the jinn's left ankle.

Shamsuddin exhaled with relief. The corner of the jinn's mouth curled.

"You caught me," he said. He did not sound displeased.

The jinn closed his fist around the flame in his hand, casting them into darkness once more. Shamsuddin blinked, still seeing flecks of orange against his eyelids, then found himself and the jinn sitting on the ground in the same position. He let go of the jinn's ankle and scrambled to his feet, then pulled at the jinn's arms.

"This is very shoddy work," the jinn remarked as Shamsuddin hauled him to his feet. "Aren't you worried that I'll escape? You don't even have a rope."

Shamsuddin tugged the jinn's arm around his shoulder. The jinn obligingly wound his arms around Shamsuddin's neck and jumped onto his back. Shamsuddin staggered, then reached back and grasped the jinn's legs, bringing them forward around his waist to balance the weight. He turned away from the tree and began walking through the graveyard.

"Hey." The jinn poked the side of Shamsuddin's head, then yanked at one of his short curls. "I'm already bored and you haven't even left the kabristan yet. The least you can do is answer my question."

People had tried tying up Shamsuddin's abbu when he had had his first fit. Shamsuddin would cut off his own hand before he considered doing such a thing.

"It would be dishonorable to tie you up," he said. "If I catch you, you will come with me. You will keep your word."

The jinn cackled. The sound reverberated even more when it was so close to Shamsuddin's ear. "Honorable man!" he shouted. "You'll get cheated in two minutes by any half-brained con artist."

"Better to be cheated than to be dishonorable," Shamsuddin said staunchly.

"Hm." The jinn leaned closer, pressing his weight to Shamsuddin's back. "Aren't you going to ask me something, O Honorable Man?"

"Like what?"

"Like my name." The jinn leaned away. "It's Jalal."

Shamsuddin felt his face grow hot. How rude of him not to have considered that this jinn had a name, and that he ought to refer to him by it.

"Forgive me for not asking," he said. "I am Shamsuddin."

"Arrey." Jalal always sounded amused, but now he seemed especially so. Most people were amused when they heard Shamsuddin's name for the first time. "Kya naam hai."

Shamsuddin walked in silence for a few seconds. The journey to the hakim's shop was not too long, since he lived on the outskirts of town, and the night air was refreshing. It should be a straightforward trip, so long as Jalal kept his mouth shut.

This, however, was not possible.

"I told you, I'm *bored*," Jalal complained, before Shamsuddin had even left the graveyard. "Kahani sunoge?"

This must be a trick. "What kind of story?" Shamsuddin asked warily.

Jalal's voice brightened. "A fun story!" he said, "with a question at the end of it!"

"A question?"

"Yes," Jalal said. "We'll make a game out of it! If you answer it correctly, then I'll go back to my nice cozy tree. If you don't, then I'll stay with you, and you can take me wherever you like."

Shamsuddin considered these terms, then snorted. He had heard of these rules before.

"And what if I refuse to play?" he asked.

"Then I'll kill you," Jalal said cheerfully. "You can't stop me from talking, and you can't stop me from asking you questions, and you can't"—he tightened his arms around Shamsuddin's neck until they felt like a noose—"stop me from ripping your honorable head from your honorable neck."

Shamsuddin came to a stop. He was just inside the line of trees, surrounded by no living beings bigger than a frog. His only weapons were his pocketknife and his own two hands, while Jalal had already set his terms and had any number of magical tricks at his disposal. If Jalal wished to kill him, Shamsuddin stood no chance of victory.

"All right," Shamsuddin said finally. He resumed walking. "Tell me your story."

"Excellent!" Jalal said. "Here it is.

"There was once an imam's daughter who was renowned in five towns for her good character. She was pious, clever, accomplished, and beautiful. Despite this, her family despaired, for she rejected every rishta, no matter how well suited the suitor was. As the years passed, the townspeople began to gossip that she was too proud to accept any man who was less than perfect.

"The truth, however, was far more shocking: the imam's daughter had no interest in men at all, and was in love with her childhood friend, who was a woman."

Shamsuddin reflected on this, then decided that it was not so very shocking. Had he not admired the brown tint of his male classmate's hand or the curved line of his male coworker's shoulder? Had he not noticed that Jalal's long hair and large eyes were appealing on him, in a way that such features were not appealing on any woman, not for Shamsuddin?

"The imam's daughter's beloved returned her affections," Jalal went on, "but their happiness was ruined by the arrival of the daughter's twenty-sixth birthday. Her father, afraid of society's censure at having such an old daughter still at home, fixed her marriage against her will. The daughter and her beloved decided that their only recourse was to run away. They needed funds for their journey, so the imam's daughter waited for the wedding jewelry to arrive, then tucked it into a bag with her other belongings and went to meet her beloved at the edge of town.

"Her betrothed was out for a walk and spotted her escape. He was a handsome man, as handsome as yourself"—Jalal tugged on one of Shamsuddin's curls again—"but he was also an aggressive man, accustomed to getting his own way. When he saw what his intended was doing, he attacked her. The daughter's beloved was nearby, so she intervened and killed the man with one blow to his head.

"The women escaped. The daughter's beloved preferred to cross dress, so they passed as husband and wife in a faraway city and lived a long and happy life together. So I ask you, O Honorable Man," Jalal said, leaning forward to speak into Shamsuddin's ear, "who is responsible for the betrothed's death? The beloved, who struck the killing blow? Or the imam's daughter, who was the reason for this fight?"

Shamsuddin was quiet. His sandals made soft sounds on the dirt path.

"Remember," Jalal said, running a hand through Shamsuddin's curls, down to the nape of his exposed neck, "you must answer."

He could lie. He could say that he did not know the answer. But that would be unfair, and Shamsuddin knew too well how it felt for people to be unfair.

So he said, "It is the imam's fault."

"Oh? Why?"

"The women acted as they must," Shamsuddin reasoned. "The imam's daughter acted out of love and desperation, while her beloved acted out of love and protectiveness. The imam had no such excuse. He condemned his daughter to a life of misery because he feared society. A man should act only on what is right, not what is expected."

"Well said!" Jalal said approvingly. "So well said that I am afraid I must leave you now."

The weight on Shamsuddin's back suddenly lifted. He

turned to see Jalal sprinting away from the path.

Shamsuddin swore under his breath and chased after him. Jalal moved unnaturally fast, weaving through the trees rather than heading directly to the graveyard, so it was several minutes before Shamsuddin stumbled, gasping for breath, into the clearing.

Jalal was sitting on a tombstone. His legs were crossed at the knee and he was inspecting his fingernails.

"Back already?" he asked mildly. He was not out of breath at all.

"I promised that I would take you to the hakim," Shamsuddin said, when he could speak.

Jalal hopped off the tombstone. Shamsuddin jumped forward and grabbed his upper arm. He waited for Jalal to do something—surely it would not be this easy to catch him again—but Jalal merely shrugged and said, "Turn around."

Shamsuddin obeyed. Jalal climbed onto his back and they set off down the path once more.

"Do you always keep your promises?" Jalal asked, then, without waiting for a reply, added, "If so, then you'll like this story.

"There was once an old seamstress in a village next to a river. She had been widowed young and lost her only child to illness, so while she made a decent living as a seamstress, she was terribly lonely, and thought longingly of her death day.

"One day, a child came to her home. The seamstress thought this child was a boy, but she was a girl at heart. The girl had been told to leave her home and had walked along the river until she reached the village. The seamstress was a pious woman who did not believe in withholding kindness for any reason. She offered to take in the girl if the girl would help her around her home.

"The girl agreed. She assisted the seamstress with her chores, and in exchange, the seamstress made her a set of girl's clothes and protected her from society's scrutiny. The seamstress promised to never abandon the girl, and the girl promised to always honor the seamstress's wishes.

"The years passed, and the girl grew into a young woman, with plenty of friends and a village that had come to accept her. The seamstress taught her everything she knew, and so the day came for the young woman to take over her work. The seamstress said to her, 'Beti, you have always treated me dutifully, as a daughter treats a mother. I must ask a favor of you. Promise me that you will fulfill it.'

"The young woman promised, as she had promised years ago to always honor her mother's wishes. To her horror, the seamstress then asked the young woman to kill her.

"The seamstress explained that she had been ready to let go of life for decades, but suicide was not permissible, and then she had been blessed with this adopted child. But now the young woman was grown, and did not need her in any practical sense. Why should she continue living when each day was an ordeal? She wished to put an end to it.

"The young woman refused, despite the seamstress's pleas.

She lived with her mother for another ten years, keeping her company and doing her best to cheer her spirits, until the seamstress died of old age. So I ask you, O Honorable Man," Jalal said, "was the young woman wrong to break her promise?"

"No," Shamsuddin said immediately. "If the young woman had kept her promise, that would have meant the seamstress broke hers as well. The young woman had promised to honor her mother's wishes, but the seamstress had promised to never abandon her. If she had died a chosen death, then she would have done just that. One broken promise is better than two."

"Again you have spoken well," Jalal said, "and again I am afraid I must leave you now."

The weight on Shamsuddin's back vanished for the second time. He spun around, but Jalal was not on the path, nor among the trees. He heard a laugh and looked up to see Jalal perched on a branch high above his head.

Jalal waved. "Khuda hafiz!"

Shamsuddin resisted a groan of frustration. Jalal leaped to the branch of another tree, then another, then another. This time, Shamsuddin did not follow Jalal; instead, he ran along the path straight to the kabristan, then hid behind a tree and waited.

After a few minutes, Jalal appeared in a tree to Shamsuddin's right. Jalal leaped, aiming for the top of the tombstone upon which he had sat earlier. Shamsuddin hurried out from his hiding place and got in front of the tombstone just in time for Jalal to land in his arms.

Shamsuddin felt a rush in his chest, though it felt more like delight than triumph. "I've got you."

Jalal laughed. "Indeed you have!" he said. He did not sound dismayed at having been caught yet again. "How fun! I suppose I ought to get comfortable."

Shamsuddin let go of him. Jalal climbed onto his back for a third time.

"Aren't you tired of this?" Jalal asked as Shamsuddin set off down the path. "Why do you keep coming back?"

"The hakim has given medicine to my abbu for the past year."

Jalal made a dismissive noise. "Hakims are all quacks," he said. "They deal in things that are evil or useless or both."

"When someone is badly sick," Shamsuddin said, "then you will believe in anything."

"Hm." Jalal's voice sounded thoughtful. "Is your abbu all that you have left?"

"Yes," Shamsuddin said, then, without knowing why, added, "Everyone else has moved away or is dead, except for my ammi. She left when I was a child."

"An event that ostracizes all who are involved," Jalal said wryly. "No wonder you must rely on a quack. To take your mind off the difficulties that you must have faced from such a childhood, let me tell you another story. I will try to keep it short.

"There was once a pair of jinn who were master and servant. The men felt deeply for each other, so deeply that they would have died for each other without a thought and killed for each other without pausing for breath. The master's work involved the collection of human souls, a task with many complications.

"One evening, while disguised among humans, the servant heard a man insult his master. I will not repeat it, but it was a disgusting comment, disparaging of the master's mannerisms and affection for his male servant. The servant was enraged and challenged the human to a battle. The master was pleased by this, but he warned his servant to only injure the human enough to win the battle—if the servant killed the human, there would be dire consequences.

"The battle ensued. The servant was so incensed by the insult that he ignored his master's instructions and killed the human. He swore that he would take the full punishment for himself and would not let his master be harmed for his actions. So I ask you, O Honorable Man: Was the servant right or wrong for what he did?"

Shamsuddin hesitated, then said, "I don't know."

"You don't know?"

"Even if the servant wishes to take full punishment, the master may still suffer," Shamsuddin said. "The servant should have listened to him, both as his servant and his beloved. But he acted out of love. If someone harms a person who is dear to you, then it is difficult to stand by and do

131

nothing. Even if they tell you to leave it alone, it is sometimes better to act upon your anger. Your anger on their behalf is part of what forms your love for them."

Jalal was quiet for a moment.

"So you do not know?" he asked again.

"No."

"Then," Jalal said, "you may take me wherever you like."

Shamsuddin walked in silence. He did not feel triumphant, only weary. Jalal pressed against his back.

"You will be bored soon," Jalal said. "Kahani sunoge?"

"No more stories," Shamsuddin said sharply. He tightened his grip on Jalal's legs. "You set your terms."

"This is a different kind of story," Jalal said. "This is the story of a hakim who chained up a jinn."

The words hit Shamsuddin with a jolt. He halted.

"Why are you stopping?" Jalal asked. The smile in his voice was audible, though it sent a chill down Shamsuddin's spine. "Keep walking. I am eager to see hakim sahib again.

"There was once a jinn who met a hakim. This hakim was stupid, even by human standards. He made his living prescribing sham medicines and performing pointless exorcisms.

"The jinn thought of himself as clever and decided to play a trick on such a stupid man. But the jinn was careless, and the hakim ruthless. He captured the jinn and chained him up in his home, which lay above his shop.

"The hakim wished to cleanse society of its sins. He planned to do this through the sacrifice of both a jinn and a purehearted soul during a wicked ritual. He commanded the jinn to commit murder on his behalf for the sake of this ritual. The jinn refused. The hakim's power was enough to restrain the jinn, but not bend him to his will. For days, the jinn was trapped in the hakim's home, denied all food and drink and fire.

"One night, the hakim made a mistake. He brought a candle with him into the room where he kept the jinn. The jinn manipulated the flame to burn the hakim's right hand and refused to relent until the hakim released him.

"The hakim agreed, so the jinn escaped and hid in the kabristan. Still hoping to complete his ritual, the hakim made several attempts to recapture the jinn. Each time, the jinn outwitted him.

"But then," Jalal said, "the hakim thought of a new strategy. He sent someone else to do his work for him. Someone who was strong and purehearted, who faced society's censure for what his ammi had done, and who would have only a half-conscious abbu to miss him if he died without warning."

Shamsuddin slowed his steps, then stopped. Jalal leaned closer, until his lips were right at Shamsuddin's ear.

"O Honorable Man," he whispered, so low that the words nearly blended with the hum of the insects in the forest, "do you understand what I am saying?"

Shamsuddin turned his head to look at Jalal. He could smell sulfur on him; he wondered if all jinn smelled like this. "What should I do?"

Jalal smiled. It was not so wild this time, or perhaps familiarity had made it less dreadful.

"Trust in me," he said. "You have not mistreated me, and you have indulged my chatter tonight. Greater bonds have been forged on weaker foundations than this."

The rest of the journey passed in silence. As they emerged from the forest and approached the hakim's shop, Shamsuddin felt his heartbeat quicken. He spotted the hakim standing on the roof, with the faint glow of a lantern beside him. There was a way to access the roof from within the shop, but Shamsuddin did not want to take Jalal through the place where he had been held prisoner. Instead, he went to the back of the building, where a ladder leaned against the wall.

He let go of Jalal's legs and reached for the first rung of the ladder. Jalal unwound his arms from Shamsuddin's neck and floated up to the roof, landing gracefully upon it as Shamsuddin climbed. When Shamsuddin reached the roof, the hakim was already wrapping chains around Jalal's torso, wrists, and ankles. The lantern sat on a stool, with a small rug to its left and a low table and two chairs to its right. Upon the table stood a teakettle and two chai glasses.

The hakim finished chaining up Jalal and shoved him to sit cross-legged on the rug, then turned to face Shamsuddin.

"Salam alaikum, hakim sahib," Shamsuddin said.

"Shabaash!" the hakim exclaimed. "I knew that you could catch it." He took one of the chairs. "Sit, and we will drink to your success before I destroy this creature."

Shamsuddin sat down and looked at Jalal as the hakim poured tea into each of the glasses. Jalal winked and shook his head.

The hakim handed one of the glasses to Shamsuddin. "Here, beta."

Shamsuddin took it carefully. Both glasses had been filled with tea from the same kettle, so if Jalal was correct and something was suspicious here, it would be in the glass, not the drink.

"Your abbu will be proud of you for what you have done tonight," the hakim said with a benevolent smile.

Inwardly, Shamsuddin recoiled, but he nodded. They each lifted their glasses to their lips, though Shamsuddin moved more slowly, waiting—

Jalal shrieked. It was a dreadful sound, more dreadful than his laugh. It almost made Shamsuddin drop his glass.

The hakim set down his glass and turned to Jalal. Jalal held up his arm and shook it, rattling the chain.

"This is awfully loose," he remarked casually. "You might want to check it."

The hakim stood with a grumble. As he examined Jalal's chains, Shamsuddin swiftly swapped the glasses.

The hakim retook his seat. "Deceitful creature," he muttered.

Shamsuddin and the hakim lifted their glasses to their lips again. The hakim drank his tea first, then Shamsuddin followed.

The hakim observed this with a broad smile. "And now," he began, then broke off. Suddenly, his eyes widened.

"Aap teek hai?" Shamsuddin asked, with feigned innocence.

Jalal snickered. The hakim stood so abruptly that he knocked over his chair. His hand went to his chest, then his throat, then his forehead.

"You—?" he said, bewildered, then his expression contorted into one of fury. He whirled around to look at Jalal. "*You—!*"

Jalal gave an exaggerated yawn. "Does all poison work this slowly?"

The hakim collapsed.

"Ah, there it is," Jalal said. "Finally!"

Shamsuddin got up and undid Jalal's chains. Jalal stood and kicked the chains away from himself.

"Thank you," he said.

Shamsuddin glanced at the hakim's body. He had no sympathy for a man who had committed such violent acts, but it was wrong to disregard a corpse. "I should inform the masjid," he said. "They will arrange for his janaza."

Jalal waved a hand. "Leave it," he said. "Someone will find him when he starts to rot. He doesn't deserve a prayer."

"That is not for us to decide," Shamsuddin said.

"Fine, fine, O Honorable Man."

There was a pause. Jalal tucked his hair behind his ears. Shamsuddin looked out at the forest, thinking of the kabristan

136

within the forest, and the tree within the kabristan.

"What will you do now?" he asked.

"Oh, I don't know," Jalal replied. "I like my tree, but it's getting a bit tiresome seeing the same old leaves night after night. Maybe I'll find a new one."

Shamsuddin studied him for a long moment. The clouds had parted, revealing the moon. Jalal's eyes glittered even more in the added light.

"There is a tree," Shamsuddin said finally, "outside my house."

Jalal met his gaze. Then he laughed, and the laugh, like his smile, did not seem so dreadful anymore.

"O Honorable Man," he said. It sounded both more genuine and more playful than any of the previous ones had. "Qubool hai!"

ART BY CHAAYA PRABHAT

THE COLLECTOR

By Sona Charaipotra

The boy was a mere child of nine—in human years, at least—
when his father first brought the puppets home. They arrived
in a silk-lined bloodred velvet bag, tucked away among other
spoils of war from the far reaches of Regasthan, where the
empire had staked its newest claim.

His father told Aaryan that, for many millennia, the puppets had traveled the far reaches of the desert lands, carrying
with them the storied history of kings and common lok alike.
Regally inspired and royally patronized, the legendary kathputli were made of cloth and hand-carved wood by artisans
in the small tribal communities that traversed the Thar. And
ancient though they might be, these two were exceptionally
crafted, twin sides of the same sikka, perhaps, their strings

intertwining as his father made them jump this way and that. Their long, thin faces were painted in bright colors, their large eyes black and all-seeing, the crimson bandhani silks they wore woven through with gold-thread embroidery, the mirrorwork glinting like the bloodstained steel of his father's talwar.

"Jantar and Mantar, they are called, chote shahzada," his father had explained. "For, like the old instruments scattered across the land, they were the keepers of time itself."

In the years since their arrival in Asma Jahan, though, the kathputli sat untouched on a towering shelf in the grand library, frowning down at the boy as he grew, their all-knowing gaze surreptitiously stalking his every move. But Aaryan knew this was all in his head. That's what his beloved mai had told him from the time he was a small child—that his imagination was bigger than the entire world.

Though he now stood tall and sturdy, born of hardy Persian and Turkish stock, he knew that the nasha from the neel kamal root coursing through his veins made the delusions that much more potent. Another blistering winter had settled upon Asma Mahal, the crowning glory of the empire, carved of ice and stone right into the heart of the Himalaya. And for as long as Aaryan could remember, Mai had ensured he drank a ruby chalice full of the blue lotus tea as the sun dipped below the clouds, bringing necessary warmth deep into his very bones.

As dusk settled, he woke with a start, leaping up from

where he had lounged on a velvet-enrobed settee in front of a roaring fire, his limbs made heavy by both the weight of snow leopard furs and the neel kamal nasha. Mai hovered near as he veered close to the edge of the cliffside veranda, the mountain winds whipping his face, frost nipping at his nose and his fingers as he peered down into the still burning plains and red rivers of Punjab below. For days he'd felt it: the rumble of thunder, the heat of fire, as if the very root of war had seeded and burst, the tentacles clawing up, up, up, threatening to pluck him from the safety of his mountain-side perch.

For hundreds of years, the Asmani Empire had reigned from its throne in the sky, devouring everything below in a bloodthirsty quest, plundering tea from Darjeeling, cardamom from Idukki, diamonds from the mines in Panna, and the heady neel kamal root from Srinagar. The shahenshah's latest mission had taken his father's envoy to the far reaches of Regasthan, the desert promising treasures of gold, copper, and silver from within its hidden oases. His half brother heir-apparent Akashvir's agenda included the blood roses of Gulabi Bagh, and even the very light of the sun from the ruins of the temple in Multan across the river Neelam.

For a long time, the boy did not realize his father was the king. As a child, Aaryan's earliest memories with the emperor were small and tender, filled with songs and sweets, or the throwaway game of shatranj on the marbled black-and-white court in his father's courtyard, where an army of human Rukhs and Fils loomed, taller than the boy himself.

Mostly, though, it was evenings spent on this very veranda off the library, curled by the roaring fire. The boy was bedazzled not by the weight of his father's golden crown, made heavy with hard-won jewels, but rather by the stories the shahenshah regaled him with—tales of great kings, snow leopards, and elusive, seductive jinn, of conquering kingdoms and rivers red with blood. The stuff of myth and legend, false tales well told. Like the tomes that lined the shelves in the towering two-story library carved right into the side of the cliff, the marbled verandas overlooking the endless empire below.

But then, with each conquest, his father began to bring home a new trophy for his curious prince. Shawls woven of silks as light as air, elephants carved from the finest sandalwood and teak, a bulbul fashioned of rubies, emeralds, and sapphires that perched prettily on the boy's pinkie finger. And, of course, the truly marvelous kathputli from Regasthan, which haunted him even now.

Long before the rumble of marching soldiers shook the very mountain that cradled his palace, his father had brought him the grandest prize—a ruby the size of a child's fist. It was marked with Farsi and Arabic, promising a thousand and one stories in its bloodred depths. The stone, his father claimed, once sat at the center of the mythical Peacock Throne.

Legend told that the infamous ruby, nestled now into a bracelet wrought of gold, contained the beating heart of the long-lost city of Shalimar. And when Aaryan wore the bracelet his father gave him, he could feel the pulse of countless souls thrumming along with his own, its power compulsive as he worked. The whispers of all the lost souls of Shalimar filled his heart and his head.

More than the objects themselves, Aaryan coveted the stories they brought, the time he'd spend curled up with the shahenshah as his father spun fantasies of faraway lands to be discovered and won. Together, they'd scrawled the names and lines on parchment, spilling ink and blood, leaving a legacy that the world would long remember. A legacy, Aaryan soon learned, that he was meant to claim as his own.

But as the boy grew big and strong and tall, his father's pen paled in the shadow of the sword, which loomed large and bloody, felling and claiming kingdoms. Aaryan was unsure of his role in the game now, for his brother Akashvir was bigger, stronger, and taller still, a head that seemed far more worthy of his father's attention and, yes, the crown.

Never one to cower, Akashvir ensured that his baby brother knew his place, challenging the boy to daily duels, cliffside clashes that on more than one occasion left the young prince battling for breath and footing at the very edge of his stone-carved veranda, worried that he might fall to his death below.

For most of the kingdom and its keepers, it would have been no grave loss. His own mother, Begum Nazneen, had little use for the boy. Where Akashvir was decisive, Aaryan was thoughtful. Where Akashvir was bold, Aaryan was deliberate. And most important, perhaps, where Aaryan was content collecting dusty words and objects, Akashvir was brave, charging forth in the name of their father and the empire. His mother found in the older, stronger Akashvir an obvious heir, even if it meant forsaking her own. Thus, her allegiance—and perhaps his father's—was cast with the Akashvir the victor. Spare princes rarely survived past childhood, and Aaryan knew, as they all did, that he was destined to die young, his blood spilling in the lines that marked his brother's palms. It was only a matter of time.

When Aaryan was small, the pain of it pinched. But as he grew older, the boy learned to console himself with the truth of his fate. He didn't want to claim the mantle anyway. His pen was his sword, and with it he could slay jinn and snow leopards, as his father had long taught him. He'd spend his days tracking the spoils of his father's and brother's battles, noting their weight and value, reveling in the magic that pulsed within each object. He would be the keeper of the Shahnama, documenting the reign of the Sultan-e-Asmani, and his words would become history itself.

And as for the solace that came with a mother's love? That, too, came in the form of a gift from his father. A nursemaid he only ever knew as Mai, a woman so tender and sweet that it mended his history as a motherless child whose own mother was very much alive and, well, the queen.

Kuwarji, the mai called him, her little prince. Under her kind care he was remedied and flourished, the childhood nightmare long since passed and forgotten.

Mai tended his wounds with soothing words and a hot steel needle that wove golden thread, stitching up the holes his half brother Akashvir poked during their jousts, sealing the boy's scars with a skin-sizzling cautery and the salt of her own tears. The pain, livid and red, was only ever subdued with a dose of neel kamal doodh, the lotus root crushed with warm rose milk and honey to release its charms, warm and intoxicating.

As each new wound healed, Mai would follow the young prince around his father's towering library, letting Aaryan fill her head and heart with the stories the emperor had shared, cooing over invaluable stones and small mundane keepsakes alike. But Mai's mind always seemed slightly far away, unreachable, as if it were trapped in some life she hadn't yet forgotten, stuck on a memory she couldn't quite reach, a land unknown.

Aaryan, too, knew from his father's stories that there was only one real conquest left: the legendary Shalimar. Together, Aaryan and his father had pored over the Kabirnama a thousand times, the shahenshah polishing the details like the finest ruby. "There stands a palace unlike one seen before or since," Sultan Amir said, his voice booming in the boy's head still. "A black marble mahal, millennia old, endless and echoing and awaiting its begum. Within it sits the Peacock Throne, carved of the finest gold, studded with diamonds and rubies and sapphires and pearls." His father's eyes were always wet, far away when he spoke of it. "It wasn't just pretty to look at. It was more powerful and magical than anyone would ever know. It held the key to life itself."

But the throne had been dismantled, its stones scattered, destroying the city and all the souls it once held. That's what the Kabirnama claimed.

Aaryan knew, somewhere deep in his bones, that the legend of Shalimar was true. And if only he could make it real, bring those storied stones together, he'd be able to give his father the gift of time immortal, to make his empire complete.

It would all be over once Akashvir took the throne. Which would be soon enough, if the rumbles and roars that rose from deep within the earth were any indication. The Sultan-e-Asmani had won a million battles, yes, but the sands were slipping through his fingers fast. Empire was a young man's game, and many a king had been murdered by his very own kin. And Akashvir certainly was a bloodthirsty sort.

So Aaryan resigned himself to the books in the kitab khana, poring over old parchments and pages. An ink-tipped peacock pankh was constant company as he sipped the kanwal kakkari, at once sweet and bitter, ground and soaked in milk with rose petals and turmeric. It had gone from an occasional remedy to a daily necessity, the effect heady and intoxicating. Just enough of a softening, a blurring of the harsh, cold edges that every corner of his world presented.

Which was why he didn't react the first few times the puppets spoke.

For many moons, their voices had played in his head, childish laugher rattling his already brittle bones. Slowly, surely, he was losing his mind. The chatter remained a vague white noise, the frantic flutter of moth wings too close to a flame. But soon they began to call his name, growing louder, ever more insistent. Then one evening, as the sun and the moon shared the sky for a blazing moment, the voices beckoned again. Louder this time, sure and confident. An eerie mist had settled above him like the clouds themselves had descended upon the veranda, a blanket of smoke and snow.

Watching the flames, he'd dozed off on the settee, drunk on neel kamal and rose hip smoke, his thoughts slow and labored. At first, it seemed like a dream, perhaps a nightmare. He couldn't quite make out the words, except . . . *A prophecy, the prophecy, the one that would end it all.*

Using all his might to break free of the dream stupor, he sat up and shoved aside the furs, jolting himself awake just as the moon began to cast shadows. Limping, unsteady, unsure, he followed the whispers into the depths of the library, through the carved teakwood shelves, the endless almirahs filled with objects that beckoned—each with its own story to share, muted in their new role as the spoils of war. The words grew louder, clearer still, coming from on high as he wove through the endless aisles, peering into this corner and that. He raised his head, his jeweled crown tumbling onto the floor as his eyes met the puppets', peering back down, absorbing all of him.

Then they rose, terrifyingly alive, looming in and up as their chatter grew loud again, swooshing close like locusts buzzing in his ears, raspy and reedy, sending shivers down his spine.

A prophecy, the prophecy.

The pair of puppets pranced, leaping off the shelf and landing at his feet, reaching out to encircle him within their eerie dance. He stepped back as they spun, possessed, no strings attached—none that he could discern, in any case—and did a small raas, gleeful and free, their hands clasped, their eyes gleaming. And then he knew, deep in every aching muscle, that this wasn't the just the neel kamal nasha, nor simply another hallucination. This was real.

Ek tha raja, ek thi rani, dohno margeh, shuru kahaani.

The king must die, a queen will, too, the puppets warned in their maniacal singsong. But that was merely the beginning of the story. There would be more. *A prophecy. The prophecy. The one that will mean the beginning of the end. We see it in the stars.* Their words clanged and clashed together like their jangly limbs as they continued their dance, growing larger than life, towering over the prince. *A girl like a doll, with roses in her cheeks, the pinnacle of your collection, here in this library of souls. She will bring with her the end and the beginning, the destroyer of empires and the savior of worlds.*

Then, zooming in to close the circle, they knocked him out with a single crushing blow.

Sunlight seeped in as the mai pulled open the carved wooden doors of the veranda, and Aaryan awoke many hours, perhaps days, later in his own bed, a canopy of silks shielding him from a nightmare that had felt too real. His head pounded as he sipped the kanwal kakkari, drinking it down like the medicine it was meant to be, trying to block out the flashes of memory that burned bright in his head. The puppets with their gaping jaws, the blackness that lived inside their eyes and throats. The way they'd reached for him as they taunted. He could still hear their words echoing in his ears:

Ek tha raja, ek thi rani, dohno margeh, shuru kahaani.

The king must die, a queen will, too. A prophecy. The prophecy.

The one that would mean the beginning of the end.

Just another hallucination, the boy told himself, ignoring the gash that marked his forehead. Now it was time to be steady and sure. Soon the badshah would return from his latest adventure, bringing new treasures to assess and catalog, new stories to capture forever in ink and blood. Aaryan might not be destined to rule as a warrior king, but being the scholar prince was no small burden to bear, and it suited him immeasurably, the badshah always said. What delight would his father bring this time, the boy wondered, as Mai floated just beyond the curtains, stoking a fire, laying out a nashtha of khichdi and nihari, staving off the other servants who would lure the boy toward the bustle of another day at court.

Perhaps today's accounting would include a mermaid's tail from the salty waters of the Kaveri, or fine miniature gold-worked paintings from Jaipur. Maybe there would be banarasi silks from the ghats on the Ganga, or priceless stems of saffron and spices from the storied lake that centered Kashmir. Contented already with the work that lay ahead, the boy dug into the rich, thick, and meaty stew, scooping up the bone broth and lamb with pillowy khameeri roti.

But before he could take another relishing bite, a voice assailed him through the billow of the curtains, startling him out of his skin. His half brother loomed over the bed, talwar unsheathed, ready for battle, as always.

"The Multani caravan threatens to storm again," Akashvir roared, stabbing the bed as Aaryan stretched just out of reach. "Rumors rise that the shah has fallen. Our father may be dead. Do you stand with me, brother? Or against me?"

Aaryan barely blinked. Worries about his father's safety were a constant companion, as stories of the emperor's untimely demise abounded. But the boy knew that half the time, his father stoked the flames of rumor himself. And strategy was hardly his brother's strong suit, whether it be games or battle.

"I am battle ready. And you lay drunk in bed clothes, feasting and failing." Akashvir leered, looming large above him. "Truly a waste. I should have finished you when I had the chance."

"Some would say I have my uses, brother," Aaryan said

with a laugh, sitting up in bed. "At least in shatranj, as you know."

But the crown prince didn't bicker or argue or tease, as he usually would. Instead, his countenance grew grim, serious, as he offered a hand, flinching at the touch of the raised ridges that marred Aaryan's palms, scars from battles barely won. They both knew that Aaryan's only true nemesis was his brother, bound to him by blood. "Whether the shah lives or dies, our empire needs us now," Akashvir said, his voice leaden and heavy. "Multanazad looms ever closer to an alliance with Gulabi Bagh. If they join forces and take the foothills, Asmani is done for. We'll be trapped."

Aaryan wanted to tell his brother that he'd always been trapped, a bulbul in a gilded cage.

His brother's sword swooped close this time, his anger unbridled as he lunged forward, stabbing through the silk of the sheets as Aaryan leaped up and out of the bed. "I'll kill you before I let you fail Father," Akashvir said, storming forward again, the sword slicing through the air with a familiar disdain but a vengeance that seemed new, missionary. "You'll do your part or suffer the consequences." A warning shot as the sword cut close, the wound leaving a rose blooming across the boy's pretty face. *The prophecy*, the voices in his head sang again. *The beginning of the end.*

They were to prepare for battle, Akashvir told him, and that mean Aaryan would have to leave his beloved books behind. The thunder in the plains grew ever louder, closer, as the sun began to settle. But the boy lay reeling, Mai's needle and thread still damp with royal blood, the wound that marred his cheek still fresh as the icy fingers of Asmani air curled around it. He could still taste the salt of Mai's tears as he sipped the brew, hoping for the seductive lull of the neel kamal nasha. He wished he had succumbed to the pain this time, asked her to let him bleed out so he could claim moksh and abandon his excruciating reality. But as much as he wanted to, he wouldn't give up. Not with the future of an entire empire at stake.

He wove in and out of that familiar dream stupor, following the voices as again he heard them beckoning, taunting, dancing. They climbed up and down the carved wooden shelves like monkeys on the hunt, their eyes flickering dark, their laughter echoing in his head the way his brother's sword had, the clanging loud and endless. They sang the same endless rhyme, the one he could not put reason to, the prophecy he didn't want to claim as his own.

A prophecy, the prophecy, the puppets had reminded him. *Ek tha raja, ek thi rani, dohno margeh, shuru kahaani.*

Dragging himself from his bed, the prince went looking for his tormentors, sure they held the answers. Again, he lurched forward, feeling his way in the darkness as the voices grew closer, louder. But this time, there was another voice, familiar as the scars that lined his own palms. Mai.

He peered at the puppets, once again alive and possessed, laughing as they did their merry dance. Mai hushed them, motherly and tender, her voice low, her words searing.

"Down is the only way out," he heard her say, the sound disappearing into a rustle of raw silk. "I'll carry you, but you mustn't make a peep. The foothills are full of Multanis, awaiting our cue. But we'll have to find him and undo the curse before you can be free. There's only one way, and everything must be done perfectly—"

At this, Aaryan stepped forward, and Mai stumbled, surprised, as the puppets squealed with delight. *He's come, he's come. It will be done.*

And when he stared into their gleaming black eyes, their wide and wicked grins, he knew it was true. *We see it in the stars*, they claimed. *The Guriya of Gulabi Bagh. A girl like a doll, with roses in her cheeks. The pinnacle of your collection, here in this library of souls. She will bring with her the end and the new beginning, the destroyer of empires and the savior of worlds.*

His hand rested taut, unwilling, on the handle of his ruby-studded katar, a gesture not lost on Mai, who indeed had roses blooming in her cheeks.

"You mustn't misunderstand, Kuwarji, for you, too, have a part to play. But you must listen. The girl, the guriya—"

It had to be her. She'd been there all along, the pinnacle of the treasure his father had gifted him. *The beginning of the end*, the puppets squawked. *The king must die, a queen will, too. But that's merely the start of the story.*

This time, he listened, rapt, as they told the tale. *A long-lost city, the fires raging, the stench of burnt roses, and rivers red with blood*, the kathputli shrieked, wooden limbs flailing as they danced with glee. Just like his father had promised him. He could nearly smell it, then, the sulfur and cinder of burnt roses, almost see her. She who would mark the beginning of the end.

The king must die, a queen will, too.

That's when he knew. It would be up to him to stop it.

As he stumbled forward, unable to control himself, the puppets laughed and began their dance again, their taunts loud and shrill, their dark eyes glistening. *Ek tha raja, ek thi rani, dohno margeh, shuru kahaani.*

His eyes locked on Mai's face and he shuddered, the pain of his wound flashing anew, as he realized the depth of her betrayal.

What if his brother was right and his father was dead? What if it was here, the beginning of the end? And it was all his fault. Like a bulbul in a gilded cage, he'd let his only need lead him astray.

When Mai first arrived, in the same caravan as the puppets, she had been a young girl of about sixteen, barely older than he was now. She was the more beautiful than any of his treasures, with bright, liquid eyes, silk ribbons in her hair, her bandhani silks wind-whipped and desert-worn. Her voice was hushed and sweet, the soothing salt of her tears could heal wounds, and souls, yes. But as he saw her now, he realized there was one thing he'd missed. Perhaps, as the puppets had claimed, he could see those roses in her cheeks.

"Aaryan," the mai said now, using a word she never had before. "My sweet, you mustn't misunderstand. She's on her way, the Guriya of Gulabi Bagh, the girl with roses in her cheeks. And we can fix this if we work together. If you'd only understand. I tried so very hard to save them. To save us all. But they're trapped, as you are, in this gilded cage, their souls forever imprisoned. I must set them free. And I can set you free, too, if you'll let me."

The boy shook his head, unsure of her words, unsure of his heart. He didn't grasp what she was saying, only that he'd been right the whole time. The delusions were real, the puppets possessed, the prophecy playing out in his head. *A girl like a doll, with roses in her cheeks, the pinnacle of your collection, here in this library of souls. She will bring with her the end and the new beginning, the destroyer of empires and the savior of worlds.*

The beginning of the end. Of his father's empire. Of his legacy. He couldn't, wouldn't allow it. No matter what it cost him. Even if it was everything.

"You must understand, Kuwarji." Mai's eyes were wet with tears; he could see her pulse racing in her throat. "He's destroying it all, the very cycle of life and death, trapping us all here in his library of souls. Even you. His prized possession."

He'd heard his father call it that once—*atma jahan*, a place for souls to rest. But she'd twisted it, cutting through tender flesh like Akashvir's talwar, the wound still fresh.

"He's been collecting them forever, long before you were

even a thought in his mind, my little prince. Every object he found, some merely centuries old, others as ancient as time itself." Like the kathputli, who danced, delighted, and deviled, as she told him a new version of the story the boy had always known. "You must know, Kuwarji, listen and understand. It's not natural, what the emperor is doing. He's a collector, but not the way you think. Each object he's claimed contains a living, breathing soul. Captured and captive, imbued against its will into sand and stone, hewn of cloth and wrought of metal, through a magic as ancient as time itself."

She unfolded her small palm, revealing an object within it. She'd swiped the ruby from his desk, a stone no larger than a child's fist, but perhaps more beautiful than any other such object on this earth itself. He could feel the power of its pulse from where he stood and hear its heartbeat thrum alongside his. As it glittered by noor and night, it cast grand shadows, throwing the outlines of storied havelis and deep, still waters across the marbled floors of the library.

"She's coming, Aaryan, the Guriya of Gulabi Bagh, the girl with roses in her cheeks. She doesn't know her role yet. It's up to you to tell her, Kuwarji." Mai took a step forward, tentative, scared. "Most of the objects that storied these shelves became home to one soul, or perhaps twin flames, locked together for an eternity, like my kathputli," Mai explained. "But this stone glitters with the energy of thousands, locked away, imprisoned for a millennium or more now. Come with me, and we can set them free." She knelt, hushed, awaiting his answer.

He wondered then if he might still be dreaming, but Jantar-Mantar, their grins growing ever more bold, mocked him with the same wicked savagery he'd grown to expect, a perverse delight in duping a boy who would never really be king. Because they knew—as he did—that no matter what the game, be it shatranj or swords, seduction or shayari, he'd always shrink under the shadow of his brother Akashvir, forever the victor, the claimer of the crown. He'd always remain the motherless child as his own mother, the queen, chose to wipe the other's tears, mend the other's wounds. And now the one source of love, of comfort, he believed he could claim as his own had too betrayed him.

"Come with me, Kuwarji, and let's find the girl." Mai said, urgent now. "There is no place for you here, after all. Your father has shown you that. Your brother will kill you the first chance he gets. You can be the leader we need, the one who frees all the lost souls."

His eyes followed her gaze up and down the storied shelves of his library, his beloved haven, his gilded cage. Did he have it in him to fly? Doing so would mean betraying his father, his kingdom, his fate.

A prophecy, the prophecy, the puppets whispered somewhere deep inside his head.

The king must die, a queen will, too.

She will bring with her the end and the new beginning, the destroyer of empires and the savior of worlds.

His father's empire. And his own little world. He couldn't, wouldn't, allow it.

As she knelt, the salt of her tears marring the marbled floors of the kitab khana, he made the choice. He could take it. After all, he'd always been a motherless child.

Mai's head rolled with a single, clean slice, one he'd learned from the thousand times Akashvir had taken aim at him, teasing, taunting, threatening. One that would do his big brother proud. One he could use, perhaps, with practice, to claim what was meant to be his.

Blood and salt mingled, marring the sanctity of this temple he'd built, as he knelt by Mai's side to reclaim his stone, its heartbeat thrumming loud and expectant as he touched one cool, pale cheek.

The kathputli stood, disjointed, stricken, their black eyes vacant. And then, just as he could breathe again, as he'd finally silenced the voices, they spoke again.

A prophecy. The prophecy.

Ek tha raja, ek thi rani, dohno margeh, shuru kahaani.

AUTHOR'S NOTE

This short story is a slice of a bigger fantasy that I've been working on for a while, infusing magic into a few historical objects from the Mughal Raj within South Asian history—specifically, the legendary Peacock Throne. The fantasy itself centers on the Guriya of Gulabi Bhag, who is part of the prophecy here, but this piece ends up as sort of an origin story for the villain in that one, Prince Aaryan of Asmani, the spare heir, a scholar and motherless child. In the story, I wanted to explore the idea of empire and both the reluctance and seduction of that level of power. What do you have to sacrifice to embrace it? And are you willing to pay that price?

ART BY NIMALI

UNRAVELED
By Preeti Chhibber

"You don't deserve this, Jaya Josh. A woman? Leading this city? Disgusting." The bird monster's voice is as sharp as his beak. Jaya grins, ignoring the blood pooling and dripping from the corner of her mouth. She's nearly done. The magic pulls together in her belly, and she reaches for it. She beats her fists together, and then moves her hands into the shape of a lotus. A blast of white light launches from her fingers, pushing the bird back. It calls out, "You may beat me back today, witch, but you'll never be free of me—you or your line. I'll have what I'm owed."

Jaya laughs. "Try it. My family will be ready. I have faith in them to hold against you, Sarsh."

It starts with a glance. The quick slice of Arit Josh's eyes meeting hers and then back to the front of the room, where their

teacher is explaining *language* and *intent* and *magic made real*.
Shweta tries to focus. Her magic has always been in her language, in the intent behind her words. But she glances at Arit again. Twin pairs of mirrored blackness holding each other for just the briefest pinpoint of time. It's a short, fleeting thing, but the feeling of his gaze settles warm in her belly. Shweta's cheeks pull at the corners of her mouth, and she looks down at her hands, lest Patil Sahib accuse her of daydreaming again. She listens as her teacher tells them to pour belief into their words, to make the betel leaf dance across their desks. Still, she can't help but sense Arit across the room, their energies searching for each other, eager to twine up into a shock of something new. She doesn't look up again, chanting the words *naach, naach, naach* to make the betel leaf lying on her desk twist and turn and curl in on itself in front of her. She grins and wonders if it's her magic that got his attention, or his attention that bolstered her magic.

It's the beginning of it all—for her. *His* story is long. His *family's* story is long. She knows that. It took war, battles, and arduous campaigning for the Josh parivaar to become what it was. It was built through jealousies and monstrous fights. Arit and his family are what everyone in their city wants to be. He's handsome, rich, well-liked. Powerful in stature and magic. The kind and dutiful son of a prosperous family. The backbone of their home. Everything Shweta isn't, with her lack of history, her missing relatives. Her solitude. Sometimes, she can't stop the anger that blossoms out of her

162

circumstance. But after that day in the classroom, she thinks of his eyes and her fury calms a little.

A few weeks later, she's walking through the school when he finds her on her way to the library.

"Shweta." Arit says her name like a blessing as she passes by him in the wide halls. Classes are in session and the space is empty around them. She stalls, but doesn't answer. He whispers to himself and twists his hands into shapes. Arit uses his hands to push his magic out, reflecting the way Shweta uses her voice to manifest her spells. She gasps at a sudden heat, the energy of his spell running galvanic along her arms. The space in front of her is alight in the shape of flowers made of flame. A symmetrical design of lotus and jasmine flowing out from a small circle of fire in the center. A softness unexpected in the harsh geometry of their school.

It's beautiful.

"Shweta," Arit says again, standing behind the fading design, waiting with a hand outstretched to her. She takes a halting step toward him and his hand wraps around hers, pulling her closer. His palm is soft, encircling her hand in a loose grip. "I can see you thinking too much." She can't tell him he's wrong, so she doesn't. She lets herself be pulled.

He kisses her and it's not what she expected. Their teeth click uncomfortably; his lips are too dry. She pulls away laughing.

"I guess not everything comes easy to Arit Josh," she says, teasing.

"I just need some practice," he answers, with a wolfish grin. Then he leans back in, and it's better the second time. This kiss is soft and inviting. There aren't sparks—those burn out so quickly, like they were never there at all—but instead a steady building of warmth. His arms go around her and she lifts her hands to his face. His cheek is smooth under her fingers, and he presses his forehead against hers. This feels like something that could be hers. She edges forward and touches her lips to his again.

That persistent anger in her chest never fully dissipates, but with Arit . . . it's softer. Quieter. A whisper.

She meets his family; their lives integrate. She's surprised, but no one in his home seems to care that she doesn't have a history. His mother calls her *beti* and his father always insists she stay for dinner. His brothers and sisters yell *didi* when they're trying to find her. They study together in his home and his chacha and masi give her tips to grow her magic and Shweta feels . . . not loved. No, not yet. But a sense of belonging-once-removed.

They decide to take a trip into the forest together. Shweta, because she wants Arit to see one of the few places she's connected to. She suspects that Arit wants to go so they can spend time alone. It's one of her favorite places. As the elders tell it, she was found at the edge of the trees, abandoned and crying. It's all she knows of how she started. She wonders if Arit can braid that small piece of her story into his life. She hopes so.

The forest around Shweta is ripe with power. The air is heavy with moisture, and the trees themselves are all but sweating. She's lying on the soft grass staring up at a jagged slice of sky, framed on all sides by the silhouettes of huge teak leaves. She always feels strong when she's closer to the ground. Stronger in the forest where she was found. Sometimes, she thinks she hears it calling to her. Lazily, she lifts a hand up and points at the bright blue, moving her hands in an easy loop. She narrows her eyes and briefly tracks her actions. She likes working on her magic—it provides a steadiness to her life, this thing that she can control.

"*Hawa*," she breathes out. For a moment, the word just hangs there in the thick air and nothing happens. Then, as intended, the wind pulls a tiny parcel of dirt up from the earth around her and she draws an infinity symbol with the trail. It's breaking and stuttering. Something in her blood burns. She needs to get better at this.

"*Shweta!*" Arit's voice calls to her from somewhere behind the trees. Shweta's grin grows even bigger. She warms at the sound.

"Here!" she yells back. She hears rustling and heavy footsteps falling, eventually feeling the rhythm of them all down her spine and into the heels of her feet resting against the ground. Above her, the dirt stalls and then showers back down around her. A dark, sun-kissed face pops into her vision and she finds Arit looking down at her, round cheeks bracketing a toothy smile. The sharp line of his jaw cuts into the blue behind him.

"Hello," he says sweetly, running a finger along her face before falling onto the ground gracefully beside her, leaning back so they're side by side, his head cocked toward hers. She rolls onto her side and rests a hand on his jaw before kissing him. His lips are warm and welcoming. He sighs into her mouth. When she pulls back, her cheeks feel hot and his gaze is unfocused.

"Hi," she says, and he grins.

"Your spells are getting stronger. I saw that spiral of earth from a way back. It was big!"

"You think so?" she asks, meaning it. He nods, and there's nothing in it that tells her he's lying.

"I told you the intent comes from within," he adds.

She wants to ask him what he thinks she could do out here, but before she can, he reaches into his pocket and pulls out something small, wrapped in bright red paper. He holds it out to her.

"My mom sends her regards," he says, joyful. Shweta puts her questions about magic aside.

"Your mom is the best." She takes the gift from him and unwraps it eagerly, knowing she'll find a small tin of Suhana's perfect besan laddoo—four round sweets nestled together, deep brown like the earth around them.

"Honestly, she didn't even say anything weird when I was leaving." Arit laughs. "I was really expecting some kind of lecture—" His pitch rises in an approximation of his mother's voice. "'Make sure you send a message before bed and when you wake up, Arit. Are you sure you don't want to take your brother, Arit? Make sure there are *two* tents, Arit!'"

Shweta cackles at the impression, but then goes quiet, considering.

"*Are* there two tents?" she asks. A mischievous smile shifts Arit's face before he shrugs and leans his head back onto the ground.

"*You'll* see."

"*Hawa*," Shweta says again, imagining the wind moving in a smooth arc. Bubbles of dirt come up and rain down over Arit, who throws his hands up in an attempt to block them.

"Yes! Yes," he says, but it's hard to understand in between his peals of laughter. She knows he'd never actually disobey his mother. Arit's hand reaches out, searching, and Shweta can see that his eyes are closed now. She drops her hand into his and again the air is clear of earth. Arit pulls her to him so her head is pillowed on his shoulder and his arm is wrapped tight around her. "We'll sleep however you want. I just wanted to be out here with you."

Later, together, they build their campsite.

There's something in the air that's got the hair standing up on her arms and sending pinpricks of shivers up and down her spine. She turns to look at Arit, crouched in the dirt, quietly speaking the words and breaking movements to build the tent. His shoulders are tight, and she can tell he feels it, too. Something is . . . off.

"We should hur—" But Shweta doesn't get a chance to finish. A bright flash of light overtakes her vision, and there's a cacophony of sound around her. Shweta doesn't wait. *"JAL!"* she cries out, but the sound, the words, her voice is lost in the violent movement all around her. Shweta plants her feet and bends her knees, anchoring herself to the ground. The dirt is flying up around them, and the tent is whipping in the wind. It loosens and flies away. She can barely see it in the disturbance, just a flit of fabric across her vision. Whatever is happening feels like nothing she knows, nothing earthly. There's a sharp needling of magic up and down her arms. It's aggressive. Arit is still behind her, she can feel the energy of him, coiled and ready.

The light dims suddenly, and Shweta blinks in rapid beats, willing her vision to clear. The forest comes back slowly, by degrees. She sees the trees, and then their things littered about them. The blue sky and the red of the dirt. And . . . in front of her . . . Her jaw drops. A massive, white-feathered bird stands on talons in their campsite. Its predatory gaze is sharp and terrifying. Shweta's heart hammers in her chest, a quick and anxious beat. Any words of magic sitting on her tongue shrivel and die in her mouth. Her brain goes blank. But the bird isn't looking at her. It's only Arit that it seems to see.

"Give your family my regards," the bird says to him. As if Shweta is not worth speaking to directly.

Furious, Shweta feels the earth under her feet. She opens her mouth and starts to speak. "*Ro—*"

The bird cuts her off, finally turning to her.

"No, I don't think so," it says. She doesn't like the calculating way it's looking at her now. She takes a step back, but with quick movement, the bird's sharp clawed feet come around her waist. Shweta struggles fruitlessly against the iron grip, her skin rubbing painfully against the roughness of its talons. She lashes out with the magic she can focus on, the words she can control—*hawa, jal, rukh*—but nothing affects this monster. It's looking at Arit again, and she's just a thing in its grasp. She catches Arit's eye and sees terror on his face for the briefest second before he yells out a spell. There's a slice of fire through the air, but the bird just raises a massive wing and blocks it. It laughs once.

"Come and steal your prize back if you can, little Josh."

Then she's being lifted into the air as someone lets out a scream. Shweta isn't sure if it's her or Arit.

The air is freezing, and Shweta can't get a handle on which direction they're heading. The wind bites at her face, her arms, her feet; she feels a sharp stab of pain and wetness under her right rib, where a talon must have nicked her skin. If she could see, she's sure she would see red blood spreading along the light color of her cotton salwar.

"Let me go!" Shweta screams more than once. Finally, the bird falls into an abrupt descent before opening its feet and dropping her. Her elbow takes the brunt of her fall. It's jarring, and the pain radiates up through her arm and into her shoulder. She hisses once, but bites her tongue, unwilling to appear weak. She has to survive this.

"You're lucky I didn't drop you from the heavens, little thing," the bird says, but it's looking back the way they came. Shweta gets to her feet, holding a hand against the cut on her side. She's shocked to see it wasn't the ground she fell on, but a floor of deep red marble. It's cold under her soles. She's in a large room with columns running in parallel along the edges, and a massive, ornate golden throne behind where the monster landed. At the other end, she can see the outline of a doorway. Above her the ceiling is dark, but the sky cuts through a sizable opening, allowing the bird's entrance. The monster itself is still looking away, and Shweta takes the time to think. She needs information.

"Who are you?" she asks. The bird turns back to her and cocks its head to the right. It's unnerving to see a shrewd gaze from the animal. She'd heard tales of beasts like this, but no one had seen one in so long that that's all they were . . . *tales*. As she stares into its eyes, something starts to shift. The bird begins to morph and shrink, its feathers pulling into its skin as it becomes a man. Handsome and fair-skinned, with dark eyes and hair. His shoulders are broad, and his chest is strong. There's a thick black belt of feathers at his hips. Somehow, he's more frightening in human form. Shweta retreats a step.

"You won't know my name," he says in lieu of an answer. "It's not yours to know." Then he's next to her, gripping her arm so tightly it hurts. He yanks her down a staircase and into a sparsely furnished room. She pulls away from him violently. The walls around her are stone, with no windows or natural light to speak of. Candles burn in a few sconces on one side. The uneven lighting gives the room an off-kilter feeling. Shweta looks to the bird-turned-man; he's facing the dark side of the square room.

"Why?" she asks. He studies her again, and in a strange reversal of his earlier shrewd look, Shweta can see the animal in his eyes—like he can't quite grasp why someone would want to know anything. He shakes his head.

"You'll stay here," he says, gesturing around them. There's a bed and a small table with a jug of water on it. "He'll come to save you. First, he'll watch you die, lose all his hope, and then I'll kill him. The favored son will pay for the sins of his parivaar." Shweta has no idea what he's talking about. There's a history here she isn't privy to. One that *isn't* hers.

"I'm not a part of this . . ." She hesitates. "I'm just—"

"This isn't about you. But you *were* with him. I watched you both. You're something to him." Shweta's anger rises again.

"I'm not a *thing*," she spits out. But he just shrugs.

"You're a tool for me. A taunt for him." He turns to leave. Shweta's heart drops. This isn't all she is. It can't be.

"Wait!" Shweta calls. He stops and looks back at her, face impassive. Shweta has the painful realization that nothing she says will matter. She doesn't matter. This isn't her story. But she tries anyway. She'd taken in the low lighting around them and the careful way he'd kept his face to the shadow. Shweta pulls at a spell she believes will work. She has to believe, or it won't. "*Heer.*"

There's a flash of lightning and the man staggers back, hands in front of his face. He shouts in pain and Shweta takes off past him. Her side is on fire and her elbow throbs, but she can't let that slow her down. Behind her, there's no sound and somewhere in her brain she knows it's strange. Is he not in pursuit? Is he shifting again? She rushes back up the stairs and into the throne room, heading straight for the door on the opposite end.

And then she stops. On the other side of the door is a sheer drop down the side of a cliff. She's so high up, all she can see below is mist. She thinks of the silence behind her and the lack of hurried footsteps. He knows she has nowhere to go.

"*Udana,*" she whispers. The word travels up and down her skin, and there's a lightness to her, an airiness in her blood. Her body lifts and she's hovering, just centimeters over the marble flooring. But it's a shaky thing, and Shweta isn't sure she can sustain it long enough to make it to the ground. She can feel blood again at her side, the effort opening up any clotting.

She'll have to find another way. Dropping back to the ground, she eyes the open air in front of her with a painfully impotent anger.

It's night and the room is cold. The man didn't bother to provide any kind of blankets, so Shweta huddles in her clothes and wraps her arms around herself. Without anything to track the passing time, she can't be sure how long it's been—but several hours at least. Up here, isolated and frigid, her magic feels like a useless, sputtering thing inside of her body. She thinks back to her professor's lecture on intent. Her intention is lacking. Her confidence is gone. She'd been taken as a thing, as a way to hurt someone else, as a ploy.

"*Jal,*" she says, and there's a small spark at the end of her fingers, but it dies so quickly she's not sure she felt it at all. Twice already she'd attempted escape, but both times the man had found her, gripped her by the hair, and thrown her back into her room. There was no chance to find an alternate route down the mountain. Tears gather and start trailing down her cheeks, and Shweta lets out a furious groan. She scrubs at her face.

"Stop crying," she admonishes herself. "Stop." But they still come, the tears, and Shweta curls her hands into tight fists, digging her nails into her palms. She tries an old trick, taught to her before she could remember. A deep breath of air sucked deep into her lungs, holding it, and counting to five in her head. *One . . . two . . . three . . . four—*

Before she can get to five, there's the loud sound of wood hitting stone as her door flies open and the man glides into her room.

She's noticed his movement is always smooth—like he's floating or flying, even without wings. It's disconcerting. People don't move like that. He reaches for Shweta's throat and squeezes once, very tightly, before letting go. A promise.

"Where is he?" he bites out, and Shweta can see that his teeth are pointed. This is the closest she's been to him.

"I don't know," she gasps. "He won't come. They won't let him." She thinks this is true. Arit isn't expendable, not to their city. Not to his family. They won't—they *shouldn't* let him come when he goes back for help. But she hopes *someone* will come. "This wasn't a good plan," she adds spitefully. "This was shortsighted. Absurd. You're absurd."

The man stares at her, unblinking. *Unseeing*, she thinks. Like she's not there at all. And the fury in her heart grows a little more. He leaves without speaking. *"Jal,"* Shweta says when he's gone, and this time the edge of the mattress catches in a small flame before sputtering out into nothing. It's a start.

It's another two days before she sees him again. He keeps her fed and watered. In the mornings and evenings, small bowls of dal tadka and chawal appear through a slit at the bottom of her door. She can't tell who brings them. There are no sounds of footsteps or voices to accompany the trays. No one comes to take the dirty dishes; two days' worth are stacked in the corner of her prison. Two days for her to focus her anger into something usable. Into something she can build on. Two days, and then he comes in with a large, metal knife. His brows are low over his eyes.

"A punishment for his absence," he says, voice cold. "When he gets here, you'll be broken." Shweta's breath gets caught in her throat for a split second before she can focus. She's been waiting for him to come back. This is what she's been building up to. She can't lose her chance. She doesn't *think* he'll kill her. He needs to use her, still. He takes a step toward her, then another. Shweta tenses. The knife gleams. "This is your role, little thing." He says it matter-of-factly. Shweta's blood burns.

"Hato!" she yells, flinging out an arm. The man goes flying backward, twirling through the air like one of the fancy spinning toys of her childhood. He rebounds hard against the stone wall. She's already up and running toward him—she knows she can't win this fight if he gets a blow in. That *would* kill her. There's no doubt in her mind. He moves to stand, curling up unnaturally, and she can see black blood cutting its way down his forehead in thick lines. Grimacing, he darts his tongue out and licks the blood off his lips. He opens his mouth to speak, but Shweta doesn't let him. She shoves a hand against his chest and pushes with all her might.

"JAL!" The word bursts out of her mouth, loud and angry and *kinetic*. Fire explodes from his birded belt and the man lets out a screech, and something avian in it grates at Shweta's ears. He starts to shift, his eyes going beady and black first. She tries to pull her hand away from his chest, from the fire inching its way up his torso, but he's got his fingers wrapped

around her wrist, and she can feel the points of his nails digging into her there, drawing blood.

"I might survive this," he says. "But you won't. And they'll say you died because of me, because of a feud you had no part in."

This is how it ends, she thinks. There's a frantic energy enveloping her, and she pulls as hard as she can. Her mind is blank, and she can hear herself screaming sounds, anything, to get out of this. The heat is everywhere now, and she can smell the sick scent of a burning body, but still he stares at her and holds on. *"Jaane do, jaane do, jaane do,"* she chants, but there's little power in it. Still, the grip around her wrist weakens ever so slightly. It starts to give. She hopes he sees the triumph in her face. But his eyes are black, and his face expressionless, until—

"No!" a voice cries out behind her, and just before Shweta is yanked away from the burning man, she sees the corners of his lips go up in a smile. And then the world disappears, and her last thought is that she'd wanted to see his end.

Shweta wakes to the feel of a pair of strong arms wrapped around her middle. She's sitting on the red marble floor, and there's a heavy body behind her, tethering her to the ground. They're in the throne room; it's empty and quiet around them. But she can still smell charred flesh in the air. Her stomach turns.

"Shweta? Are you okay?! Shweta—what happened?"

Arit—it's Arit behind her. She twists suddenly and falls into him, hugging him as tightly as she can. His fingers dig into her ribs, holding her to him. He came—she didn't think he would, but he was here, in her arms.

"I'm here, I'm okay. I'm okay. I'm here." It's like a mantra that she whispers against his throat, over and over. "I'm okay. I'm here. I'm here. I'm okay."

Arit moves his hands to her shoulders and pushes against her lightly, so he can look at her face. She starts. There's something in his eyes now that wasn't there when she was taken. Before she can ask about it, he questions her again. "What happened?"

She tells him everything—that she was just bait, that the monster was angry with *Arit's* family. How he had kept her and threatened her and how she'd finally fought back. When she's finished, that hard look is still in Arit's eye. He doesn't say anything, and then he stands. He reaches for her, but when she offers her hand, he wraps his fingers around her wrist instead. She tries not to think of the monster. He looks at something behind her and she turns to find one of his family's flying machines. Arit still hasn't said anything, and his quiet is starting to unsettle her. She climbs into the double seat in the front, sliding to the side so he can fit in beside her.

"How come you came alone?" she asks finally.

"My dad knew about this," he says, waving vaguely at the throne. It's not an answer. There are secrets in that sentence. She thinks of her place in Arit's life—in his story. The monster had called her a thing. A tool. A taunt. "They didn't want me to come." *For you* goes unsaid. "But I convinced them. They had to allow it. They *had* to." As he says the last bit, he drives his fist into his seat. Instinctively, she puts a hand on his knee and is surprised when he flinches. She snatches her hand back.

They make it to the edge of the city and Arit puts the machine down with whispered words and two hands flat, pressed against his thighs. They disembark, and she starts to move quickly toward one of the gates to the interior streets. Arit stops her.

"Wait," he says. "Hold on. Come back. I have to—"

Shweta turns to him and cocks an eyebrow. He's silhouetted by the forest behind him, a thin line against wild openness. *Now what?* she wonders. *What else could he—*

"I think I should go in first. Alone. Wait here, and I'll come get you when it's safe."

"Safe?" She bites out the question. Her skin itches.

"Yes." He's unapologetic in it. "There were . . . questions. It's been three days."

"Three days," she repeats, confused. "Yes. He took me away from you for *three days*. I want to go home."

"*Three days* in the presence of Sarsh."

A question flits across Shweta's face before realization settles.

"The man who is a bird, that's his name," she says, and

Arit nods. He's so far from her now, she can't read him. She steps forward, as if closing the distance will help.

"He has a history with my family," Arit says. "My father, his parents, *their* parents—they've long told what kind of man he is. Was." Shweta thinks of the charred smell behind them and the smile and wonders if "was" is right.

"I don't understand."

Arit closes his eyes and groans. He digs his fingers into his hair and pulls.

"How did you survive, Shweta?" he asks, finally looking at her again. "You were never so strong. Everyone will wonder."

Then Shweta gets it. There's a surge of anger. She moves forward, into Arit's space. Twining her arms around Arit's neck. Leaning forward, she presses their mouths together and then rests her forehead against his.

"Do you think it was this?" she asks, voice cloying. Arit starts and pulls away with a jerk. She tightens her hands against the back of his neck. The bird monster's—Sarsh's—voice echoes in her head. *A taunt, a tool, a thing.*

"No—I-I . . . ," he stutters. "There are *questions*," he says, "and you aren't answering them."

"I shouldn't have to!" she cries. "How did I survive? Do you know me at all? Did you ever know me?" Arit flinches. *Good,* she thinks.

"You don't see it. They don't know . . . how could they understand . . . you don't have any—" He cuts himself off and starts again. Shweta is afraid to think what he might have said. His eyes shine, and his voice is weary. "Just tell me the truth. Then we can be together. You'll fit right back in. Everyone will trust you again."

"*Again?*" she spits out. "You're so focused on how I need to earn something I didn't do anything to lose. What have I done to deserve this except love you? Loved your family? Been *didi* and *beti* and *mere jaan*." But she doesn't wait for Arit to answer before she continues. "So quickly they turn." She laughs, and there's no humor in it, no joy. She yanks her arms away now and presses a palm against his chest. She looks down at her hand in puzzlement. "I can feel it beating, and yet . . ."

"Shweta . . . ," Arit tries. "*I* trust you—"

"No," she says. "You trust the thing you think I am. The maybe-bride, the damsel, the future bahu." She runs her hand down his arm and lifts his hand, her fingers dancing across his palm. "Hold my hand. Walk back into the city with me right now. Show them all that we're united. Together." His hand twitches in hers, as if he's considering it. She holds her breath for a beat, and then, quietly, "*Kuhaasa.*"

The mist gathers behind Arit, on the edge of the forest. She can feel the wet in the air, the dampness encroaching on her skin. Then he pulls away. Shweta takes a deep breath in and starts to count. *One . . . two . . . three . . . four . . . five.* She takes him in, his beautiful dark brown skin, his bright eyes. He's looking at her like he doesn't know what to do, but that isn't her problem. She's not here to be *a taunt, a tool, a thing.* The weight of wanting to braid into his life lifts off her, and she settles into her unknown story. As if her thought itself manifested it, a peculiar magical current fills the air and crackles across Shweta's body. It wraps around her and the trees, and when it pulls at her, she listens.

Shweta steps around Arit.

"Shweta?" he asks, puzzled. She ignores him and walks toward the trees, following the buzzing of the magic. "Where are you going?"

The ground calls her forward, and she can see the wind whipping sand into a trail to follow. She doesn't answer Arit.

"Shweta?" he calls. His voice is quieter, farther away. Shweta cannot be a small piece of his life. She can't be an easily excised footnote. She'll make her own. "*Shweta! Shwe—*"

"*Chup,*" she says and the voice cuts out.

Shweta steps into the forest.

AUTHOR'S NOTE

I'm obsessed with the women of Hinduism. Draupadi, Yashoda, Sita . . . the list goes on full of strong women making difficult choices. It was Sita's story I returned to here. She goes through intense hardship with her husband Rama, and it's his story. But there's a version that ends with him questioning her purity and instead of staying with him, she chooses to go back into the earth. She takes the power she has and uses it to show what she's worth.

ART BY NEHA SHETTY

SHE WHO ANSWERS
By Shreya Ila Anasuya

In the darkest deep of the mangroves, Bonbibi's skin gleams green. The rich forest green of an overflowing canopy. Neon green like sunlight shot through summer fruit. Green like a newborn tendril, green like an ancient tree. But here, in the city, it is a burnished brown, melting her into her surroundings. She eyes the river, seeing what the people around her, hurrying to work, cannot—dolphins under the surface of the brackish currents. She pauses, watching a ferry pass noisily through the water to the other side, and catches the eye of a little girl sitting on her father's lap on a bench nearby, staring at her. Bonbibi considers what the girl sees—herself, in this mortal guise of a girl no older than sixteen, thick hair plaited loosely down her back, wearing salwar kameez the color of bougainvillea. She smiles at the girl, who smiles back shyly. Bonbibi walks on, the city swirling around her.

Even in the city, the forest thrums within her, and she can hear its great old banyans and flowering gulmohar trees turning their buzzing minds toward her presence. If Sajangali—her brother—were here, he'd enjoy the city's arboraceous interludes, the quiet, lush spaces that erupted from every possible crack and crevice, sometimes stretching over abandoned warehouses, sometimes knotting over old buildings. He would stop to explore them, to ask them questions. He and Bonbibi are twins, part of a larger whole, mirrors to each other, opposites, the sun and moon of the mangroves. Between them, they had a pact: one of them must always remain in the land of the eighteen tides, their domain and their home.

They must deal periodically with Dokkhin Rai, the Lord of the South, known to the people of the mangroves by his favorite disguise—a tiger, striped orange fur, deep roar, padded feet. He isn't actually a tiger, of course; just a man who inherited too much land and the gift of shape-shifting.

Rai had a propensity for stealing away children, taking their youth and vitality from them until they had none left. Not a week passed without a child disappearing, a home erupting in wails. Until Bonbibi intervened. Until the people opened their hearts and let her in, knowing she would keep them and their children safe.

In the mangroves, her people tie colorful fabric on tree bark before they enter the heart of the forest. The thread on the trees is an offering to her, to protect them when Dokkhin

Rai is on the hunt, calling on the dark forces that inhabit the Sunderbans to aid him in his avaricious desires. The body of the mangroves is her body, and each time they tie a dua on a branch, it is her wrist they are adorning. She collects prayers and petitions by the hundreds each day, not just from people, but from each insect and bird, from each leaf and stone. Entreaties trickle in, too, by the dozen, from the city. From ever-expanding Kolkata. Some of her devotees work here, and although they no longer live in the land of the eighteen tides, they still whisper an invocation before they dive into the life of the city, which opens its maw and swallows them, their time, their work, their magic, like a spider does a fly.

It has been a while since she has roamed the streets of the city, answering a desperate plea. But in the past few weeks, a call has become insistent, tugging at her, whispering her name urgently. She grew restless in the forest, disturbed that someone needed her protection here, for her to ferry them to safety. Finally, she has arrived at the source—close to the Keoratala crematorium—drawn by the invisible thread the prayer forms between her and the voice that calls her. The voice of a boy. But before she goes to see him, she must see an old friend.

She stops before the cremation ground, where smoke rises in the air, and spots an old woman who turns implacable, magnificent eyes toward her. Dhumavati. The goddess of widows, of crows and jackals; she who takes ashy smoke and creates from it the breath of life.

Bonbibi inclines her head, waiting for permission to proceed. Dhumavati smiles, her silvery hair whipping in the wind. Among the forlorn crowds of people pouring into the grounds, only Bonbibi directly approaches her.

"Hello, Didi. Thank you for receiving me."

"Of course. Would you like some refreshment?" Dhumavati was gracious, but slightly distracted, looking absently at a crow that had settled near her, a glint in its eye.

"No, Didi. I cannot stay long, there is a boy here who has been calling for my help. But I came here to ask you for something. If you will grant it."

Dhumavati nods and raises an eyebrow. Another crow joins the first.

"If I need assistance while I get the boy out of whatever predicament he is in, may I call upon you?" Bonbibi asks plainly.

Dhumavati looks amused. "What need have you of an old woman? Don't you control and command every particle of dust in your delta?"

"I protect and cherish it, yes. But here, as you know, my devotees are fewer. I do not know what is afoot. I hope you will come, if need be."

"A long time ago, I realized that you have to let some of your worshippers go. Let them find new deities in new lands, new ways to worship . . ."

"I have never stopped anyone," Bonbibi says, a little curt.

"Don't be so afraid to let go . . . this anxiety of holding on to your children will weaken you, in time."

Bonbibi does not answer. She hadn't expected Dhumavati to be contrary—but she has come to the city to do what she must, whether her friend agrees to help or not. Finally, she says, "I hope you will come if I call. It was nice to see you."

Bonbibi arranges cones of incense before her, lights them, and, with one backward glance at Dhumavati, leaves the crematorium, the wisps of smoke following her—her mind squarely on the prayer that tugs at her.

"Bonbibi, mother of the forest, body of the forest, I invoke you. I love you. I open my heart to you. Keep me safe. Bonbibi, mother of the forest, body of the forest, I invoke you. I love you. I open my heart to you. Keep me safe. Bonbibi, mother, forest, I love you, please keep me safe." Dukhe leans against the heavy door, whispering the dua his mother taught him when he was little.

The knot in his stomach is painful and his lips are dry, but he keeps his mouth working in his fervent prayer, the song hissing out with each breath, the invocation, his mother's nudge to remember Bonbibi whenever he found himself adrift on the boat of his life. "No matter how wild the waters, Bonbibi will ferry you home, son," she'd told him time and time again. "Remember her with an open heart and call on her to help you. Now, let me hear you say it."

Clammy and terrified, in this strange, darkened room, he thinks about his mother, the light in her eyes, her voice raised in laughter. "Bonbibi will always protect you." His mother's words echo in his ears. "If you are ever in trouble, and I am not with you, call on Bonbibi." So he swallows his fear, and keeps whispering.

What he doesn't know yet is that Bonbibi is listening. She

has arrived at a house in Kalighat. She enters unseen, tip-toes to his door and stops on the other side. The thread that connects the boy and the goddess thickens with his whispered pleas, and she pulls at it to understand why he needs her so desperately. She weaves her magic and asks the thread to reveal its secrets. When it does, she listens.

Dukhe has been entrusted to his uncle, Dhona, because his mother, Jharna, works in a house in the city, taking care of someone else's children, washing their floors and clothes. The family she works for has given her an uncomfortable mattress in a dingy room at the back of the house and utensils they never touch, kept away from their own. The family does not permit her young son to live in their house. Jharna keeps the job because she needs the money to send Dukhe to school, she needs it so that Dukhe doesn't have to work.

What Jharna doesn't know is that Dukhe works anyway, in the mornings before school and in the evenings after. Putting stickers on the honey his uncle sells, amber bottles decorated with identical roaring tigers. Carrying huge boxes full of beeswax candles to load on trucks for suppliers. Helping his aunt take care of his young cousins. Doing his homework only after his evening chores are done. Putting finishing touches on his sketch of Bonbibi that he has been making for months, in the few moments he gets to himself before he gets up the next day and has to do it all over again. His uncle has no idea he can draw, or whether he finishes his homework, or what he likes to eat. The particulars of Dukhe's inner world are irrelevant to Dhona. As long as the honey is sold, as long as the candles are packed, as long as the children are asleep.

The thread is taut; Dukhe cries now, silently, his whispers broken when he has to stop for a breath. *Enough*, thinks Bonbibi, and raises her palm toward him gently. She will not appear before him yet, not until she fully understands what is happening. But she knows enough now to know he is lonely and afraid. She does what she can to ease his pain. To Dukhe it feels like a cloud bursting, rain coming down. The tight fist around his heart loosens. A surge of hope comes over him, though he can't tell why. He falls into an exhausted sleep.

Bonbibi continues to search the thread for more information. Where is the boy's mother now? She finds her last visit: the tight smiles on the adults' faces, Dukhe sitting silently with them, while Dukhe's little cousins roughhouse and tumble around them.

"How are you, boudi?" Jharna asked Dukhe's aunt Lalita, her sister-in-law.

"How will I be? Your brother is tense all the time, worrying about the business," Lalita answered, her bangles jingling as she adjusted her saree. "And the children are so much work. And with an extra mouth to feed . . ."

Jharna nodded but did not smile. Dukhe noticed the shadows under her eyes. She held out sweet, crisp batashas for the younger children, who eagerly took them. "I hope Dukhe has not been too much trouble?" she asked, when she could trust herself to speak again.

Dhona grunted while looking down at the newspaper. Lalita said nothing, letting the silence thicken and become uncomfortable. Dukhe shifted, growing irritated, starting to understand what his mother endured on these visits.

"Dukhe, how is your schoolwork going?"

"It is fine, Maa." It was all he could bring himself to say. Anything more would do no good. Dhona and Lalita sat, taut, looking between mother and son, waiting for the inevitable offer of money from Jharna.

"Dada, here, please keep this." Jharna pressed some folded notes onto her brother's palm.

"Arre, no, no." Dhona always made a show of hesitating for a second or two, but then, sure enough, his hands would reach out for the money.

In the few moments Dukhe and his mother had gotten to themselves in the small room where he stayed, Jharna had hugged him and kissed him on the forehead. "Remember, it will not always be like this," she had whispered. "Remember to pray to Bonbibi if ever you are in trouble. I'll see you soon."

After she left, he immediately picked up the teacups and saucers and hurried to wash them, bracing his whole body against the jibes that might or might not come, depending on how much money his mother was able to leave. Then he went quietly to his room to work on his drawing some more, to feel the crayon blues and greens coming together under his careful eyes, flowing like a river. Before he went to sleep, he said a prayer, knowing that across the city from him, Jharna would do the same. "Bonbibi, mother of the forest, body of the forest, I invoke you. I love you. I open my heart to you. Keep me safe."

Dhona's house is on a street near the temple, choked with little shops all the way up to the front entrance, where priests corner everyone wishing to go in to pay their respects. They control the relationship between the people and their goddess, extract the money for the rites and rituals they claim only they can perform because they deem that they are better and purer than everyone else. One day Bonbibi would dearly like to tell them what the goddess thinks of greed and contempt in the name of devotion.

The Keoratola crematorium is close by. Dukhe has been there once before, too early in his life. When Jharna and Dhona's father passed away, they brought his body here. The place of sadness. Dukhe passes it on his way to school or to the shops, and he always notices the people streaming out or going in, the tightness in their shoulders, how brave they have to be. He knows that set of the jaw. He knows that pain; he has seen it on his mother's face, even his uncle's.

But it is not a regular week for Dukhe, and this place is not his home. Bonbibi sees that after Jharna's visit two weeks ago, a man came to see his uncle Dhona. There was a ferocious brilliance in the man's face, his wide stride, the rough way he patted Dukhe's head when Dukhe brought him a cup of tea and snacks. Dukhe felt an uncomfortable prickling in his neck when the man looked him up and down, his eyes lingering on Dukhe's face before flicking away, back to his uncle. He was entirely self-possessed. A man who had, for his whole life, known a world built around his convenience.

A man who was used to getting what he wanted. A man who always wanted more.

Bonbibi recognizes the man with a wave of irritation.

Dokkhin Rai.

Still walking around like the world owes him something.

Dukhe had quickly left the room when his uncle dismissed him with a grunt and a wave of his hand. While his uncle ingratiated himself to the stranger, smiling too widely, inquiring loudly after his well-being and that of his family and his business, he took for granted that Dukhe was someone who'd obey him.

Usually, Dukhe would have gone dutifully straight back to his room or to see if his aunt needed anything. But this time, after making sure he wasn't seen, he stood, ear to the door, curiosity driving a desire to hear what his uncle was discussing with this strange man. He felt the other who grew inside him twisting in impatience, the Dukhe who was neither made of the city nor a series of reactions to his uncle's behavior, the boy who would be the master of his own life as an adult, the complicated man he would become, the stranger he would shed the sweet boy for. The growing took his breath away. Its power was the thing that enabled him to observe quietly, missing nothing.

This was, Dukhe thought, his secret strength. None of his teachers, nor his uncle and aunt, ever realized this, but when he was seemingly just doing chores, housework, or his lessons, he listened and heard more than they knew. Lately, he had been discovering how to make of this a skill. From eavesdropping on his teachers, he'd found out that they'd been instructed to keep his schoolwork light. And there was a reason his uncle wanted him to spend so much time working on the products he sold, on the honey and beeswax that came from the Sunderbans. He'd overheard a private conversation between his aunt and her sister: "My husband has lost his mind. When the boy packs the shipments, apparently they sell five times faster than usual." The two women had laughed, and Dukhe had moved away, his ears buzzing.

As Dukhe stood at the door, straining to hear Dhona and the stranger, he almost cried out when he felt it. The terrible heat on his forehead, accompanied by a rush of sound in his ears like a wind howling. His secret eye, opening on his forehead, letting him see beyond the door. Dukhe almost yelped in shock. It was the grown man inside him that held him quiet, steady. He watched the terrible transaction that was taking place; his uncle, dropping to his knees before the man with the ferocious smile, who had turned himself into a beast, a tiger glowing with the weight of his own transformation.

Behind the wooden door, Dukhe stood, his three eyes widened in fear and surprise at his new strength. His mother had the power of sight, and he had witnessed it ever since he was a small boy, but neither of them had ever seen any traces of it in Dukhe. Her mother had had it, too, but Dhona did not, and Jharna had always told him she assumed it passed from mother to daughter. Dukhe had no siblings, so Jharna had always said the power probably stopped with her. This had made him feel small and sad. But it turned out he had been molded and glazed by life, year after year, until he was ready. His heart flooded with bittersweet relief; what a difference it would have made, to know that he had this power inside him all along. What a time to welcome it, while he witnessed this unpleasant, frightening beast bully his uncle, instead of being with his mother, celebrating with her the gift that was theirs to share. As he kept quietly watching, though, the churning of his feelings curdled into dread.

A deal had been made behind that door. One that Jharna knew nothing about, one that Dukhe would have known nothing about had he not come suddenly and violently into his abilities. Dhona had been dealing in honey and wax without paying the illegal tax that Dokkhin Rai extracted from everyone in the business. Dokkhin Rai's ancestors had commandeered the resources of the Sunderbans, and no one who harvested the fruits of the delta was allowed to do so without paying the family.

Dhona had toed the line for a good long while, but lately he had gotten confident, with the expansion of his business. He had grown certain that the city, which seemed so far away from the delta, protected his interests. He had grown complacent in the knowledge that Dukhe's magic touch would continue to make him money. Until Dokkhin Rai had shown up and invoked the old code, the code of name and lineage and caste. The code that demanded obeisance. The code that promised vengeance if flouted. It was this code that had led to whispers back in the Sunderbans about the new heights of success that Dhona had reached. It was this code, one of entitlement and violence, that made Dokkhin Rai rush to the city to put Dhona back in the place Rai deemed fit for him.

It was too late for apologies or back payment on taxes owed, even with interest. Dhona needed to give up something precious, something beloved, something that he could not afford to give up. Something that would make him remember, forever more, the consequences of stepping out of line. Rai's eyes rested on a framed picture of Dhona's family—his wife, their three children, and, with them, Jharna and the boy. The boy.

Dhona had tried hard to negotiate. But pushed into a corner, Dhona would not give up his own beloved family, as much as he could bear to give up his sister's son. He would have to explain it to Jharna somehow. It would be a horrendous undertaking, having to come up with an explanation that would calm her. But his wife and children would be safe.

Dukhe had backed away, the stranger inside him bristling in terror and rage. He'd kicked and flailed when Rai's men came that night to tie him up and gag him and take him a few streets down, under the cover of darkness. Dokkhin Rai had set up a bungalow in Kalighat for his time in the city. There he stayed with his mother, Narayani.

The men threw Dukhe into a cold, damp room. He shook, shouting and banging on the door of the tiny room he was imprisoned in, desperate for his freedom, sensing that when the door opened again, he would be met with something monstrous.

But Bonbibi saw that days had passed, and the door had yet to open. At night, Dokkhin Rai, hungry, restless, paced the streets of the city, walking up and down Kalighat like true tigers had, once upon a time. From the shadows, the city's goddesses, spirits, and even its ghosts and monsters secretly watched, but did not act. They waited, because Dukhe's frantic chants came through, loudly and clearly, for the green goddess of the tidelands. Bonbibi.

In a few days, it would be time for Jharna to return to Kalighat, to see her boy and ask him how his studies were going. That had been the plan all along—keep her head down and work steadily and get him through school and into university, into a steady job, into whatever other life these roads offered. They had worked as a team, looking beyond the grimness of now into the indistinct but vibrant glimmer of the future. One day he would see the vision of her in comfort, in rest, laughing with friends, tending her own garden, nobody demanding anything of her. That day might be far away, but it was coming, her eye was on it, and it was powerful.

As the days passed, Dhona felt his trepidation growing. His wife looked at him in a way he didn't recognize as familiar, and didn't like very much. His children were subdued. At the thought of Jharna, Dhona's skin felt like it was burning. He knew he had gone too far. Children never returned from Rai's lair. It was not known exactly what he did to them, only that their families did not even find bones to bury—just an absence that would stretch on forever, an everlasting grief. Dhona went to the Kalighat temple, where he gave the goddess gifts of hibiscus, fruits, and incense, praying for a forgiveness that would not come.

On seeing Dukhe's story, Bonbibi was consumed by anger. Dokkhin Rai had been brazen before, but in front of Bonbibi and her twin, he and his family had made an elaborate show of behaving. His mother, Narayani, had called her soi. *Friend.* On her son's head, she had promised that she would not permit him to harm people. On her son's head, she had vowed to find a way for everyone to coexist.

But here he was, using Kolkata to cover up his greed. Breaking promises he should have kept. Bonbibi knew what she must do now; she could free Dukhe if she wanted, apply the salve of her benediction on his wounds, promise him he was safe. But until she confronted Rai, until she put him right, until she showed him the consequences of his own arrogance, she could not make that promise.

She saw that the boy was scared for his mother's safety, not just his own. Dukhe knew what would happen if Jharna found out that he had been pulled out of school and imprisoned by Dokkhin Rai. She would rush to him and be met with Rai's malice. And Dokkhin Rai, his tongue licking the night air, ravenous, pacing the street, knew this, too. He was hoping for a fight, for rebellion, for an excuse to turn into a tiger, or a snake, or a demon, and feast upon flesh. Dukhe could sense Rai's hunger. Dukhe's blood had run cold at the thought, and his nonstop prayers were the only thing holding his mind together. When the moment of reckoning came, he'd throw himself between Rai and his mother. It would be the end of everything—a life together, all their dreams, visions, and prayers.

So Dukhe prayed to Bonbibi, willing her to come, hoping to feel her nearby, hoping to feel again the same assurance that had animated his mother, that had illuminated both their dreams like a flame. "Mother . . . forest . . . I love you, I open my heart to you, keep me safe." As he prayed, his body went taut, every particle of him never forgetting that Jharna was due at his uncle's house any moment now, knowing she would run to save him, and run straight into the mouth of the tiger.

"Dukhe! Dukhe!" Jharna screamed, terrible in her rage. She hurtled down the streets of Kalighat, not caring who saw, not caring who heard, drawn to Rai's ostentatious building. She was incandescent with anger, screaming her son's name, her eyes red, her third eye wide open.

Inside, Bonbibi heard the creak of footsteps on the wooden floor. Rai had finally come for Dukhe. He burst into the room and held the boy by the collar, grinning hideously, spoiling for a fight. Narayani was fidgeting in a corner, appealing to her son.

"What have you done, what have you done? Why are you inviting fresh trouble upon your head?" she was muttering, her words falling on Rai's uncaring ears.

Absolutely not, blazed Bonbibi's thoughts. It was Dukhe who saw the goddess first, still in her city outfit of bright fuchsia, but now making no effort to hide her skin in all its fullness—the dark greens and blues and browns of the tidelands.

Dukhe was filled with awe and terror, realizing that Jharna had been right, that his fervent calls had been answered, but that even so, he was still afraid.

"*Soi,*" Narayani whispered, but Bonbibi shook her head.

"So you have decided to set up in Kolkata," Bonbibi said.

Rai jerked around, his wild eyes on her. "Bonbibi! I—"

"Bonbibi!" Dukhe screamed, squirming and kicking.

"Unhand the boy," Bonbibi said.

"I . . . no . . . No. I won't." Rai got over his surprise very quickly. "I will not give him up. I won him, fair and square. His uncle gave him to me."

"He is not his uncle's to give. He is not your property. Or anyone else's. Unhand him before I make you."

Rai burst into fervid laughter. "You are a forest ghoul. You have no power in the city. There are many deities here, as many as there are people, and none of them waste a second's breath on you."

Bonbibi's lip curled in disgust, and Narayani saw what her son was too foolish to see—no good would come of insulting the goddess of the forest.

Bonbibi lunged toward him, but his mother stepped between them.

With her fullest might, Narayani summoned the spirits of her family, hordes of them, to come to her aid. But Bonbibi held up her brown palm and blocked them easily. Narayani began to whisper under her breath the magic that would make her summons stronger. A wraith appeared, growing larger as it emerged from her palm and burst toward Bonbibi, fangs bared. Bonbibi shook her head, impatient, and swiped at it, hitting it cleanly in its terrible throat, and with a screech, it disappeared.

Sweat pouring over her face and neck, Narayani screamed the secret chant to summon ghosts, no longer caring who heard. In her voice the words were a strange song, rumbling from the back of her throat; at her guttural call, a spectral girl arrived, small and neat, an erstwhile goddess associated with Narayani's clan, long forgotten by most except the eldest members of the extended family. Grateful tears singed Narayani's face at the sight of her, and Bonbibi's eyes narrowed with rage. In summoning the dead goddess against Bonbibi, Narayani had severed any semblance of honoring the pact they had once made.

The little girl goddess stared at Bonbibi, slowly raising an undulating smoky arm in a gesture that would have, in her heyday, killed anyone who saw it. Bonbibi's nose bled, sending Dukhe into a cold sweat. Bonbibi transformed from a girl of sixteen into her full form, tall, the uprising power of the forest surging anew through her body. The ghost goddess backed away, weeping, though no tears emerged, and hid her mournful face before she disappeared.

Ferocious with anger, Bonbibi turned to Narayani, stepping toward her as Narayani winced. "Are you done?" Bonbibi asked.

A roar. Rai had been itching for this, and Bonbibi had given him enough reason for it, or so he imagined. He transformed into a tiger. A man pretending to be a tiger does not understand the tiger's heart. A man like Dokkhin Rai only understands tigers superficially, excels in copying a tiger's proportions, maybe even amplifies a tiger's strength, but does not essentially understand that a tiger is simply a tiger. Its strength is never malice. His vanity could never become the animal grace of one of Bengal's actual tigers.

He lunged for Bonbibi, pinning his jaws around her neck.

"Dukhe!" shrieked Jharna from the doorway, walking into the fight. She rushed to her son, to help him up, hold him against her, run her hands through his hair.

To Bonbibi's surprise, Rai's jaws hurt her. He was right— her power was concentrated in the land of the eighteen tides. Bonbibi hid her pain from Rai's bite but wondered how long she could last. Rai felt her flinching, which only emboldened him, because he clamped down harder.

Smoke filled the room, rising in thick gusts that looked like fog on a mountain's head. Something intense, inexorable, pulling those deadly jaws away from Bonbibi's neck. Dhumavati, the goddess of widows, flanked by crows and jackals, had come to her aid. Bonbibi's strength rushed back to her, as her green heart filled with the nonstop whisperings of a woman and her boy. *Bonbibi, mother of the forest, body of the*

201

forest, I invoke you. I love you. I open my heart to you. Keep me safe. Bonbibi, mother of the forest, body of the forest, I invoke you. I love you. I open my heart to you. Keep me safe, Bonbibi, mother, forest, I love you, please keep me safe. Their whisperings thickened the invisible thread between Bonbibi and the worshippers; the prayers gave of themselves and transmuted, in Bonbibi's body, to unearthly power.

Bonbibi pinned Rai to the wall, his face staring back at her until his body slackened in defeat.

"I will deal with you later. See you in the tidelands," Bonbibi said to Rai, as he crumpled into a heap in a corner and Narayani moved to comfort him. She knew what would happen. He would seek the counsel of the wise Gazi Pir, who would plead with Bonbibi and Sajangali to pardon him. She knew Narayani would pray to her for forgiveness. This time, Bonbibi would ensure Rai knew what it meant to promise her he would not harm her people.

Dukhe was in Jharna's arms, heavy with consolation, tears finally taking over the boy, still so far away from fully merging with the powerful stranger inside him. Dukhe looked up at Bonbibi with a mixture of reverence and complete relief, his freedom restored. She turned tender eyes toward mother and boy, meeting Jharna's grateful, loving gaze as she held her sobbing son.

And in the corner, beyond the door, the unconquerable eyes of Dhumavati, goddess of widows, of life and breath and smoke, turning the world inside out, watched as Bonbibi walked toward Jharna with a smile playing on her lips. The crow on her shoulder flapped, and Bonbibi burst into a peal of laughter that every creature in her realm felt bubbling in their bodies.

Bonbibi cupped Dukhe's small face in her green palm. "I will always protect you, my darlings," she murmured. Dukhe and Jharna felt Bonbibi's enormous love bloom in their hearts. "Thank you, Mother," Jharna answered. "Thank you," she said, her eyes glistening, looking forward to the days stretching out beyond them, streaked with color and light, even their shadows cradled and consecrated by this moment.

AUTHOR'S NOTE

Bonbibi is a beloved deity in the Sunderbans delta in Bengal, adored by the people who live there, regardless of who they are. This is a retelling of a story that is told about Bonbibi and Dukhe. One of the most beautiful things about India—and the whole world—is our plurality and diversity, and the worship of Bonbibi is a reminder of exactly this. I hope this story helps you taste her magic, and stokes your curiosity about stories and folklore you may not have heard of before.

ART BY TARA ANAND

THE HAWK'S REASON
By Naz Kutub

Made of mud, of spilled blood, when you shall nearly fall
Prepare to heed, ready your steed, choose to answer the call
The sky unkind, with vision blind, still you must muster through
A spirit bare, let talons tear, for the hawk will save you . . .

For the hawk will save you
—Prophecy of Qhairan Al-Shekhar

The rain came, as it was foretold. Signaling the final day of war.

It muddied the battlefield. Slowed movement. Decreased visibility.

And washed all armor clean, robbing it of red stains—evidence of wins that conjured pride on every face. Victories against the Mongol invaders from the north who had arrived a fortnight ago. Mongols hungry for conquest. A hunger that wouldn't be sated until the foreign kingdom was staked under their bloodied banner and its people enslaved.

Our allies from the south answered our call a week later. Yet, my father's kingdom—a tiny piece of the Maratha Empire—might still be ripped apart like a feeble linen cloth rent by sharp talons.

I stood up high on the southern tower, a prince looking down at his people, reeking of royal uselessness. Because the king had commanded his only son to stay up here and watch.

The latest scout reports estimated that our enemies were an hour from breaching the walls of our palace. Stout and seemingly impregnable walls of granite that had withstood floods, earthquakes, and hurricanes. Soon to fall after being attacked with impunity by ten thousand invaders.

There, on the muddied field below, were throngs of my men in drenched leather, swinging talwar and spears and slinging arrows at the invaders as they charged with determination. Where one Mongol fell, two more would take their place.

The rain came. And still one more piece to the prophecy remained:

The hawk will save you.

But no winged bird dotted the skyline. And there was no sign of the downpour yielding, not with the sun turning its back on us, draped behind that cape of everlasting gray.

I had to do something, or we would lose everything.

There was just one obstacle for me to overcome.

My slippered feet shuffled down the hundred steps of the tower, each one sunken and weathered from the treads of tens of thousands of men before me. Through to the gardens in the courtyard, where the rain drenched me and my clothes, and into the main chamber of my father's palace.

There he sat, on his throne, beads of sweat rippling down his forehead, gripping his royal talwar. Next to him stood Qhairin, his mysterious adviser, wearing a magnificent dress spun from platinum thread and bedecked in gold chains that glittered with rubies.

I had to look twice to understand who was in charge.

"You lie. You've always lied. No hawk will save us," I snapped.

But Qhairin's smooth, ageless face bore no sign of betrayal. "I have not lied a day in my life. Everything I've foretold will come to be."

I marched up to the king. "Baba, we should have given up on her long ago. We could have won this easily, if you had just given me permission to join our fighting soldiers. But you refused to listen to me, and instead you remain a coward." I reached for the talwar at his hip, swatting his trembling hand aside. The blade slid out with a hiss.

The weapon was useless before, a mere ornament that was only polished but never wielded. But in my hand, it was heavy—the weight of an entire kingdom could be. Especially when it was about to be put to use.

"I would have broken the rules of our land and sent you if she had instructed me to," was all the king could say. "She is here to save us. We have to listen to her."

Qhairin simply stood there, her eyes fixed on me, as if she'd expected this moment of defiance. Even the guards that lined the hall remained silent, unmoving.

But it was time for me to show my worth, and I walked away as the daggers of my father's stare pierced my back.

Because either I died a warrior, or a prisoner.

I snuck out of the hidden tunnel from the north mountain with Anaar, my trusty steed, so called because of his unnaturally red hide.

My boots sped us up to a canter down the treacherous stone steps, slick with sliding mud, and we joined the battlefield without losing a single ray of light.

There in front of me were thousands of fleet-footed men swinging blades, shields raised. Thousands of faces smeared with anger. All showered by a relentless rain that blurred their motions, dulling the accuracy of their years of training.

It seemed nature was on our side in trying to stop them.

I had been trained by renowned warriors in our country from the moment I could stand, but it was meant to be for show. The prince was never supposed to join the ranks of his army.

But I had not forgotten a second of all the lessons I'd learned.

My aim was true and my instincts were sharp. Arrows and spears flew by my ears, and I leaned this way and that way and all around in the saddle, my feet locked in the stirrups. My talwar felled enemy after enemy, the shine of metal along its entire length now coated with red.

I was here on this battlefield because my king chose to believe in sorcery. That a miraculous winged creature would save our entire kingdom. But I knew it was only the toil of human hands that could bring about victory. And I had to volunteer mine.

Dozens and dozens of dead later, my thighs burned, my hands a fraction slower in response. But still I kept going. This was not the time to give up.

When the battlefield had lost its light thanks to impending nightfall, it became clear my soldiers were being driven back. The Mongols continued to press forward, gaining a steady advantage against us with their seemingly unending numbers.

And that was when it happened.

Out of the corner of my eye, something materialized out of nowhere, flying into view.

The Hawk.

Curiously, it wasn't a bird soaring high in the sky, but an etched sigil on a man's breastplate that blurred in my vision.

And he was one of us.

The peshwa.

Behind him was a column of soldiers in green metal, who then interspersed with the brown leathers of our men and the black furs of the Mongols.

Yet something else sought my attention.

A flash of a spear hurled by a smirking enemy, closing its distance to me.

I raised my talwar to my chest to deflect. But I was still too dazzled by the glimpse of the Hawk to stop the glint of metal-tipped wood aiming for my heart, which suddenly felt exposed, even under the sturdy breastplate I wore.

As death descended, a hand caught the flying weapon a mere hair's breadth before it could drain me of my last breaths.

The Hawk slammed the spear down over his knee with such strength that it broke in half, then swung his sword at everyone around to protect me.

He grabbed my wrist and dragged me to safety behind a palisade, and his eyes glowed with a danger that warned me there was no correct answer to the interrogation that followed. "What are you doing out here? You are the prince of your kingdom. We have come to lend aid."

Was this the Hawk that was to save us, as foretold by Qhairin?

Words fermented in my mouth, his bright brown eyes searing my soul. He shielded me as one Mongol after another fell under every swing of his urumi, a blade that—under years of training—would bend to its master's every whim. No one was spared as the peshwa beat us a path to retreat.

Making our return, we endured the screams of limbless men, some with a drench of white foam at the mouth that disappeared with the rain. The distant beating of drums still flooded my ears.

The muted glow of the sun moved a palm's width closer to the horizon as we finally made our way to the fortified main entrance of the palace.

But I wasn't ready to give up. I had to keep going. I could not let my men die.

So I steeled my courage and marched up next to the peshwa, and together we took aim at the Mongols who still stood their ground.

The Hawk would surely save us.

And by the time the light finally failed, even as the rain continued, not a single Mongol remained standing. Tired bodies in green and brown stood leaning against each other for support, as they raised weak but celebratory fists at the escaping invaders.

The peshwa grabbed my arm. "Are you hurt?"

How could I explain the ache in my chest? The one caused by the sudden realization that I owed this man my life? I grabbed his upper right arm, where a forefinger's length of skin had split open, revealing a slow river of red that refused to crust over. "Let me tend to your wound, Peshwa."

He looked down at me with a gaze unwavering, as his large brown lips took a sip from the rain slicking down his face. There was a moment of hesitation before he said, "Call me Bajirao."

I signaled to the men at the top of the towers to let us in.

"And I'm Mastan."

Our steps echoed through the bustling hallways, which were now lined with soldiers, barely alive, pumping shallow breaths out of winded lungs.

My poor people. Countless gone, lost to a bloodied battlefield. Led into a war by a prophecy. A war we could've avoided, if my father—whose ears were easily charmed by oily tongues—had just stopped listening to Qhairin. A woman who convinced the king that her foretelling was the only working tool for our kingdom.

Though I would be wrong to say I didn't have mud on my face when it came to her prediction of the hawk. Embodied in the sudden appearance of this man.

The man who had saved us all.

We made our way into my chamber, and I swung the door shut. No one disturbed me unless I asked to be. And especially now. I did not want to have to explain my actions to my king—not yet, not while Bajirao was this close to me—for fear my feelings would betray me. "I have to tend to you."

An eyebrow quirked up behind that helmet, and it very nearly stopped my heart. "And so you shall."

My bedroom was sparse—ample space for a quiet mind. It was just a bed—a mattress packed firm with cotton, resting on a teak frame—which would fit two, if I were to ever find a partner. And nothing else but a window, from which to stare at the sprawling palace grounds.

Just like my father sought miracles, I labored for my wins. Where my father sought excess, I worked at austerity.

I led the way to the adjacent wash chamber on legs that

were as unsteady as kash that swayed in the wind. Central to the chamber was a tub carved out of marble—opulence I'd never asked for, but that the king had insisted on.

The peshwa followed behind with ragged breath, and rested his weary body on the bench made of stout sal.

I grabbed the washbasin and cloth and made my way to him, setting both by his feet before reaching out, grasping his helmet—which, I realized, resembled a hawk's face, with its down-tipped beak—and lifting it off.

The Hawk from the prophecy.

A boy no older than I was.

I suppressed the shudder making its way to my shoulder blades. Something about him commanded every ounce of my attention. His body poised to spring at the slightest provocation, each corded rope of muscle flexing and unflexing.

Yet I knew he'd never hurt me.

His topknot, which had been swirled into a bun, fell from the top of an otherwise clean-shaven head.

The damp strands whispered against my arm, sending jolts of a foreign emotion through me.

Then he removed an especially beautiful dagger with a ruby in its hilt and set it carefully aside on the bench.

I rested the helmet by his feet, lowered myself to my knees, and lifted his chin with my forefinger so I could stare into his eyes. They were wide open, focused on nothing, even though he was looking directly at me.

"You saved us," I said.

Those deep brown pools finally focused. "Mastan, I left

Pune at the emperor's request. To provide aid to the kingdom of Bundelkhand. And for that, I am glad."

I didn't have the strength to read into his words, because I only had the courage to make a promise. "I, Mastan, swear that I will always be indebted to you, Bajirao. A Muslim prince to a Hindu warrior. Something unheard of in our history books. Now, will you stay awhile?"

He grabbed my hand and pulled it toward his chest gently, laying my palm over his heart. "Only if I have a reason to."

The racing rhythm of my pulse seemed to match his.

With my free hand, I dipped the washcloth in the basin and wiped the dirt off his body, rubbing away the day's fatigue with it, along with the blood from his open wound. Then I released my palm from his chest—afraid of burning to death from the heat he was giving me—and reached over his shoulder, my fingertips working his upper back, stretching away knots that shouldn't have formed in muscles so young.

And he let out guttural sounds at their release.

Oh, I could do this forever.

I couldn't stop staring at that face, one seemingly carved out of stone, as he leaned into me and clung on for dear life, digging into the flesh on my bare shoulder. How could any man make me feel like this, rip every breath out of my lungs? Make turning away from him inflict actual physical pain deep in the pit of my stomach, leaving me a raggedy mess?

It felt as if I were taking all his pain—along with his worries—and piling them onto my soul.

When I was done, he took the basin and cloth and did the same for me. But his fingers wavered at times, his breaths unsteady. Conflict seemed to stir in him every time our skin touched, almost as if he wanted to draw away, yet his fingers would always right themselves, plant themselves somewhere on me.

Once our bodies were dry and wrapped in fresh silks, and his wound bandaged, we stepped into the bedchamber.

A quick exchange of a glance, and he blushed.

"I would be glad to share a bed with the man who risked it all for me." Words I couldn't wait to repeat again and again. To him. For the rest of my life.

A smile lit up his face for the first time since our meeting.

And I found myself lost in it.

In my simple mind, with the prophecy fulfilled, the tale of Mastan and Bajirao could begin.

We spent the following days together, laughing and chasing after each other in the royal gardens like we were unaware of the dangerous world beyond our walls. Because for just this moment, we rejected the future that was being carved out for a pair of eighteen-year-olds—one meant to be king of an entire kingdom, the other the warrior-general of an entire empire.

For this moment, we were just boys enamored of our first loves.

But the nights were the moments I looked forward to the most. When our bodies would melt together and our lips locked, afraid of letting go. Hands explored slick skin, warmed by the summer winds. My eyes would rove over every inch of the peshwa's face, memorizing lines that appeared with every smile.

We belonged to each other. And we were unwilling to ever part.

The sun had set seven times by the time our kingdom had accounted for its damages and losses—a scale that would set our growth and progress back by decades. It was also when our kingdom received word from the emperor that the peshwa was to make haste for Delhi, where rumors swirled of an impending war against the empire, one that needed his expert leadership.

My father—who'd actually forgiven me for my willful transgression, seeing how our kingdom was saved—hadn't been overjoyed at a foreigner staying on the grounds of his palace and sharing my chamber, with its solitary bed. But given the peshwa's exemplary skill at saving our people, there was nothing for the king to say. Not even with Qhairin by his side, still whispering into his ear.

An emptiness grew inside me as Bajirao donned his gear, washed clean of blood from the battlefield. It had weighed down our steps, which dragged like molasses, our fingers brushing against each other's every moment they could.

There was only one thing I wanted before he left.

As he put on his helmet, I rushed to him and laid a hand on his chest. "Bajirao, take me as yours."

He could only look at me, eyes glistening as he held back emotions that couldn't be put on public display. "The Maratha Empire will never let that happen. They will never understand what we are. No one will let us be."

My laugh was bitter, cold. "Because you're Hindu and I'm Muslim? This country and its backward thinking. We could be more powerful than we were if we stopped acting like cobras hissing at each other in our own basket. We could make the entire world fear our every strike."

"That"—he dropped his helmet to one side and grabbed my cheek with the other—"and this."

His soft lips landed on mine. And my world would never be the same again.

This was what I'd been waiting for my whole life. That longing, that emptiness, that need. They were all because of him. I had finally found my reason. And I couldn't imagine it any other way. Not with anyone else.

I was Bajirao's. I would fight anyone who declared it otherwise. Even if no one would let us be.

Whether it be a king, queen, or prophecy.

And as he pulled away, sliding under the anonymity of the hawk breastplate and helmet and taking his leave from me, I knew only one thing.

I would chase after him, or I could only deem my life worthless.

Before he could even take a step away, I grabbed the first thing I saw—his dagger with the ruby laid into the hilt. He didn't stop me. He only smiled as he disappeared through the front gate.

The dagger belonged to me now. And soon, so would he.

My father warned against my departure, that setting foot outside our kingdom to follow a stranger would mean abandoning the people I had grown up with. But I couldn't find a way to tell him that my home wasn't here.

It was wherever Bajirao was.

A week after he left, I made my way to the secret tunnel in the still of night, with Anaar by my side as my sole companion.

Only one person appeared. The last person I expected.

Qhairin.

She stood alone in a blue shift, glimmering twice as brightly as she ever did, gems weighing down her neck and forehead. Obviously, my father had compensated her well for her remarkable work.

"Bedecked in more jewels, I see. What wise words do you have for me now?" I snapped.

Her face betrayed an emotion that was indecipherable. She almost looked sad. "What glitters is temporary. But what remains is duty. And my duty is not to king or kingdom. But to the prophecy."

"Why do you speak in riddles still?" I asked.

She refused to look my way, chewing on a lie or a truth. Her gaze was still fixed dead ahead on empty air when she finally uttered, "The hawk will save you."

I could only laugh. "Bajirao has already saved our kingdom. Tell me something new." I had had enough, and I pressed my steed on. But as I stepped into the tunnel, I could hear her last words as they faded with a faint echo.

"Not the kingdom . . ."

The ride from Bundelkhand to Pune took a fortnight, and the sun was just setting when I finally dismounted my horse in the city.

The streets were loud with throngs of people, a smile painted on every face, garlands of frangipani and jasmine decorating every other neck. Every window was lit, filled with bodies garbed in vivid colors, moving to the rhythm of a distant beat reverberating against the buildings' walls.

They seemed to be celebrating the return of the peshwa, even though it had been weeks since his homecoming. Fresh flowers perfumed the air and drugged every inch of my being.

The joy at seeing his people made my heart soar as it danced up in the sky with the crescent moon that was just peeking over the horizon.

Oh, to see his beautiful face again, to brush against the rough stubble with my hands. I swore I'd bring a razor to it one morning, but only after smoothing his skin with coconut oil. The thought of it brought a kick to my step.

I wanted to inhale all of him and fill all of me with all of him. Again and again.

It wasn't difficult to find his domicile, since all roads led to the heart of it.

I stood at his doorstep, staring at the wide-open maw of the compound, bone weary but spirit renewed. The home was regal, full of splendor, as befitted someone so decorated. Two stories, with a large courtyard, garbed by fragrant, multicolored garlands that had been hung everywhere to decorate the dull brown stone.

I stepped over the threshold and asked the first person I saw—a guard dressed from top to toe in white—for Bajirao. He left me waiting in the center of the courtyard.

An hour later, an austere older woman dressed also in white greeted me. Her eyebrows were knitted with years of worry, or resistance. "Who comes looking for the peshwa?"

I placed a hand on my heart and said, "I am Prince Mastan of Bundelkhand, and I come looking for my . . . friend."

She glowered, as if someone had struck her hard across her face, but stood her ground. "My son has already given your kingdom more than enough assistance. What more can you want?"

"I wanted to return this to him," I said, as I pulled out the dagger, its jewel gleaming even with the dim light from the torches around us.

His mother's eyes narrowed. "He told me it was lost in battle."

Why would he lie to her? "Yes, and one of my men found it. I thought it prudent for me to return such a precious thing. For his own protection."

I held it out for her to take. A small piece of my heart was a fair price to pay, if only to see him again.

She refused to touch it. "I do not know when Bajirao will

return." She beckoned a servant, who bowed to her. "Take this man to our guesthouse at the edge of the city. He's not to be let in this household ever again."

I waited patiently in my temporary abode—a run-down abandoned shack that had a roof in severe need of repair—for an entire week, with only Anaar to keep me company.

And when there was still no news of Bajirao's return, I stormed my way back to his home, expecting to be rejected instantly.

But alas, I learned from a sympathetic servant on the outer grounds that Bajirao had remained in Delhi after a recent battle, and that he'd sustained serious injuries.

A cold fear took root in my heart. My warrior was wounded, and I was nowhere near him to provide comfort.

Apparently, rumors had flown among the household—those who'd overheard his mother in conversation with religious leaders—that the famed peshwa had seemed distracted for the first time in his life.

I didn't dare believe I could be the cause of any harm that had befallen him. Was I the reason for his current plight?

Was I the one who may have sentenced him to a premature—

No. My stomach would empty itself if I tried to finish that thought.

An hour later, the dark jaws of the night swallowed me as I rode out of Pune.

I was near delirious by the time I arrived in Delhi. Lacking food and water, Anaar and I scraped by on the small pouch of coins I had left. Which wasn't much, compared to the bundles of gold I had left home with.

I was a prince turned pauper. And no one paid the latter any mind. It took me from sunrise till sunset to find out Bajirao was housed at the military command center, and all hope left my soul at witnessing how heavily fortified it was at every entrance and exit.

Was such security meant to keep him in, or me out?

But the one most important person saw fit to acknowledge my presence, as she made her way out in pristine white. Always pristine white.

Bajirao's mother.

This was a graver circumstance than I'd thought, if they'd summoned her to be by his side right after battle. But that meant he was still alive. "Please let me see him. Let me see the peshwa," I begged as my knees slammed against stone.

Wordlessly, she tapped her toes to the dry ground, demanding that I pay the proper respect.

Which I couldn't, for my religion, my father, and the prophet himself had forbidden me from bowing my head to another human.

But I did look up without defiance in my face. Because I couldn't afford any of it. "I just need to know he's safe."

His mother finally spoke. "You came here despite being warned. That was your sin. You don't deserve anything." She

222

signaled to a pair of soldiers, who marched over to us.

Words failed me. Weapons would have guaranteed instantaneous death. Any one of those soldiers could have felled me with a sharp talwar, for I wasn't of Bajirao's constitution and countenance.

The pair of soldiers flanked me, dipped down to my lowly level, and gruffly dragged me by the elbows.

Away. Far away from the man I loved.

All I could summon was a weak flailing, like the tail of a headless earthworm just before death. The courage I had that had drawn me here, to the one I loved, seeped out the soles of my feet and into the dry ground.

But he had saved me once. Why couldn't I do the same for him?

That was when it came. Out of the caverns of my tired lungs. The guttural moan that crawled up my throat, unleashing a roar that might've decimated eardrums. "Where is my Bajirao?"

There was a hiss—presumably from his mother—and the dragging continued.

I finally gave in to the weariness and let the two men carry me, as I shut my eyes for a bit of rest. Hoping for strength to fight tomorrow.

I woke in a dungeon of stone blockaded by the stoutest wooden door. A ball of bright moonlight nudged its way in from an oculus in the wall, a hole I couldn't squeeze my head through. Whether it was by design or the handiwork of a prisoner who'd been trapped in there for their entire life, I couldn't tell, but judging by the reek alone, it was probably the latter.

Was I to wait here, in the only prison in the fair city of Delhi, until Bajirao was fully mended and healed? Would he even know I had made my way to him?

Rocked by the waning moonlight, I let nightmares of never being near enough to Bajirao consume me.

A fortnight later, after half a dozen ripped fingernails, blood-ied fists, and a throat gone ragged, the most mesmerizing sight appeared before me.

It took all my energy to flutter my eyelids open. "Qhairin. Obviously my mental faculties have escaped me. To have you present, in this dungeon, in my darkest moment."

She was draped in the finest yellow silk, even if the jewels dripping down the sides of her face seemed extraneous. "You are dying."

"And here I was expecting to shed enough weight to squeeze myself through that hole. Tell me, what's on the other side? Will I make it, or will I plunge down a hundred stories? For that would be a similar fate to languishing in here all alone."

Qhairin stood by my side, then lowered herself to the filthy floor, kneeling in her finery. "He is dying, too."

That was when fear truly gripped my heart. Nothing and no one should've been able to fell the mighty Bajirao, but the man was no match for a rusty sword, it seemed. "Tell me what I can do for the boy I love."

"You're not going to save him." She said the words with absolute finality. There was to be no argument against it. "For he will save you."

It took all the strength from my final reserves—I had been served only water from the moment I was thrown in here—to bring myself up to a seated position. For, as her words faded, the sound of wings arrived.

She looked out the window.

I followed her gaze. And there it was.

The hawk.

And I finally understood. "Tell me one more time."

The magnificent bird squeezed its way through the oculus and landed within an arm's reach of me, its intelligent eyes all-knowing, full of empathy at my plight.

Qhairin looked at it and said, "The hawk will save you."

The hawk would save . . . *me*?

Ah.

As I sat back, my eyes closing for the last time, moisture pooling from my entire body to drain itself as a single tear from the corner of my eye, I could hear it take flight. The heavy rush of wings beating the air and against my face, followed by a swoop and sharp talons ripping into my chest, aimed for my heart

This was no dream. It was no vision.

I welcomed the pain of this escape.

At long last, Bajirao had come for me.

For I was his reason.

ART BY CYNTHIA PAUL

POETRY OF EARTH
By Swati Teerdhala

The stench of musty, rotting earth assaulted Uma the moment her feet touched the ground. Uma's mother had warned her that the mortal world was nothing like their own, that it was a wild, uncertain, dangerous land.

An unnatural building rose up in front of her, a mountain of gray stone and rusting metal. Immediately, Uma thought of storm clouds, dark and foreboding, like the ones Lord Indra would send after wayward celestials who had dared incur his displeasure, each one laden with curses. The building itself was encased in stone, its windows drab gray slats that looked as if they had been stamped across the front. The front door was an ashy black, as if it had been weathered and beaten down by its inhabitants.

Uma dared to look at the words imprinted over the building that would be her new mortal residence, her nerves alive.

Joseph Allen High School.

This was her punishment for disagreeing with Lord Indra. Not a storm cloud, but a mortal school.

In some ways, Uma might have preferred the storm cloud.

She was a young apsara, not even two decades old, so Lord Indra's punishment for her rash words against humanity was to be quite literal, apparently. One year among the humans she so distrusted and dismissed, whose fickle hearts she had heard of from her mom's stories of Earth.

Mortal high school was not likely to change her mind.

Someone jostled her from behind and she lurched forward, throwing her hands out to brace herself with a gust of wind as she would have done at home. But she had forgotten that she had been stripped of her magic when she was tossed down to Earth. Instead, her arms flailed. Her feet slipped on the unfamiliar stone.

A strong pair of arms caught her before she fell.

"Whoa there, you okay?"

Uma was deposited on her feet. She straightened as quickly as she could, ready to tell off the mortal who had dared lay hands on her. Even if he had helped her, she was a princess of the Apsara Court. She was royalty.

A hand waved in her face. "How many fingers do you see? Do you have low blood sugar or something? Did you black out? That happens to my sister a lot."

Uma blinked up at the young man. He wasn't fully developed, his limbs still a bit too gangly for his height, his nose just a tad too big for his face. But there was a kindness there. His eyes were a deep brown, fringed with lashes and warm to their core.

"Fingers?" she managed to get out.

The boy held up two fingers and waved them. "How many?"

"Two?"

"Right answer."

Uma stared at this confusing mortal boy. He didn't wither under her gaze, like she had hoped. Instead, he chuckled.

"That could've been a nasty fall, you know. They just laid in new concrete this summer. I told my sister that it was a total concussion trap. You know how many students have to sprint up these steps?"

Uma wondered if the boy ever stopped talking. She tilted her head, watching him. He was still going, talking about "sleep deprivation" and "finals," both terms she did not understand. What she did understand was that this mortal boy was not normal.

"All this to say, I can walk you to class?" he said. "My name is Parag."

Parag.

What an interesting name. Most of the celestial men had grand names. Warrior of Truth and Light or He Who Basks in the Glory of the Sun. Here was a boy whose name was a simple thing, the pollen of a flower. Small, but necessary. Overlooked, but important.

"Sure," she said.

A week passed by, and slowly, Uma began to learn the mortal realm. She learned that the white lines on the streets were there for good reason, so that cars stopped and did not ram into you. She learned that cafeteria food was quite disgusting.

To be frank, the little she had learned about Earth from books and her mom's stories now seemed woefully inadequate. Most apsaras who came to Earth came willingly and had the knowledge to help them survive. Lord Indra must have thought her struggling would be a fitting part of the punishment. Plus, each day was a tedious blur of school, homework, and hours of mind-numbing TV at the celestial boarding house—nothing like the life she led in the celestial realm. She wasn't sure how the next fifty-one weeks would go, but things could only improve, really.

Uma found a small corner of grass and laid across it, turning her face up to the sun. "Lunch," this was called. The other mortal students were cramming themselves into the small metal rectangles in the cafeteria, all the better to gossip and gab about each other. Uma had set one foot inside and turned around. She had endured centuries of court chatter, and when she returned home, it would be a millennium more.

She escaped outside.

Uma had discovered that Earth's rotting smells were flowers. More beautiful because of their short lives, more precious because of their fragrance. At first, they had smelled like decay. Imperfection. But they had a beauty of their own.

"Hello!"

Uma opened her eyes.

Parag smiled down at her, his nylon bag across one shoulder and worn leather books tucked under the other arm. His wavy black hair shone in the sunlight.

"Hello, Parag."

"You remember me."

She didn't tell him that she remembered everything. It was the curse of immortality. But he was right. She did remember him.

Her smile seemed to be enough of a response. "Sit down, Parag."

He nodded and dropped his nylon bag to the dirt, his body following after. The books under his arm tumbled to the ground.

"I see you're reading the Brontë sisters' entire oeuvre. Impressive," she said, watching him as he hastily picked up the books. "Did you know they originally published under pen names? As men?"

She remembered that her mother had advised the sisters that society was not quite ready to accept their brilliance. Apsaras were only seen as beautiful nymphs to humans, but they were also champions of the arts. She had watched her

231

mom take on mortal form and walk among humans, guiding and advising those who held a creative spark in their heart. Most apsaras did their work from the celestial realm, only visiting Earth once or twice. Her mom had been a rare kind, and she had been battered by humanity all the more because of it. She would come home weary more days than not, and yet, she returned to Earth.

"Oh, um, yes. I'm reading them for a personal project. And no, I didn't know that. That's kind of unfair, isn't it?"

"Indeed. Humans are often unfair," Uma said.

"We are," Parag said, nodding wisely. "It's pretty messed up that we—you know, society—made them feel like they had to hide who they were."

She reached for one of the books. "What are your thoughts on these books, Parag?"

Parag squinted down at the heavy book in his hand. *"Jane Eyre* is probably my favorite. While there are some problematic elements to the relationship between Jane and Mr. Rochester, it's overall a pretty empowering story."

Intriguing. Parag the Overlooked had surprised her. For the first time in a week, Uma wasn't bored.

"Tell me more."

And so he did. The rest of lunch flew by.

"Heathcliff is overrated," Parag said, shaking his head. "Everyone is obsessed with him, but he's really just the typical Byronic hero. Copy, paste, over. I'm kinda surprised you like him."

Uma sniffed. "Heathcliff? I do not like Heathcliff. I enjoy *Wuthering Heights* because it is a nuanced portrayal of humanity's worst impulses. Love turned to hate. Hate turned to revenge."

"A scathing rebuke of the morals of the time," Parag added.

"Precisely," Uma said, nodding appreciatively. "And of the social rigidity of the early half of the eighteen hundreds. You know, it was quite horrible back then—"

And then she was off, ranting about the British Empire and the rampant colonialism of the nineteenth century.

"You're like a walking history book," Parag said, once she had settled down. He was smiling, though. "You sound like you actually lived then."

Uma tensed. "I . . . read a lot," she said.

"How do you know so much about literature?" he said, looking over at her, his fingers dangling lazily near her own. "There's no way you got all of that from AP English."

"My mother is the apsa—a professor of classical literature," she said finally. "I've grown up around the arts most of my life. They're like my . . . second home. Writing and literature, in particular."

She didn't mention that her first home was in the celestial realm up in the stars.

"Oh wow, is your mom published? My uncle always says that's the hardest part of being a professor. I mean, you know, after defending your dissertation and all that."

Uma nodded as noncommittally as she could. A slight tilt

of her head. Parag took it as a yes, his eyes lighting up.

"Her books are out of print, unfortunately," she said. Parag deflated a little.

"That's still amazing," Parag said. Suddenly, he looked nervous. "That personal project I mentioned before? I've been working on a novel."

Uma fought the urge to roll her eyes.

"Well, a novella. And I can't figure out the ending. It doesn't have enough drama, one of the teachers said. I'm stuck at the midpoint, and I just—"

His entire body tensed. Like he was waiting. Like he had said too much.

Something about his uncertainty tempered Uma's initial surge of annoyance. Parag was nervous about his admission.

"I can help you," she said, surprising herself. "I can help you write the rest."

Why had she said that? Uma didn't want to be a hands-on apsara like her mother.

Boredom. That must be it. Why else would she volunteer to help him? She had been here a week already, a week spent listening to lectures and learning the basics of subjects she had mastered years ago. It was tedious. Her fingers itched to get back to her pen, even if that did mean working alongside a human.

And then, another thought.

A plan formed in her mind. A way to show penance. A test of mettle for the mortal. And, perhaps, a triumphant return home.

"Seriously?"

Uma nodded, growing fond of the idea. "I enjoy writing endings. On one condition. You can't read what I've written until I'm done with it. You can't look at my notebook. Ever."

She could help this boy, but perhaps he could help her as well. She needn't stay down on Earth for the full year. He might accept her terms, but there was a chance he would also prove what she knew in her heart about humans.

Parag bit his lip, deciding. He glanced down at his notebook, torn at the edges, the coils that bound it together bent out of shape from frequent page turning. And then he nodded.

"Okay, sure, let's do it. I've always wanted to have a buddy," he said. "For my scribblings."

Uma didn't know if this boy had any talent, but something in her rose to his defense.

"Cowriter," she said. "You're a writer. I'm a writer. We'll be writing together."

Parag's cheeks took on a brick-rose hue. "Me? No, I'm not—I'm not a writer. I'm just an amateur. I haven't even got a short story to my name. Only a one-shot fan fiction from when I was thirteen."

Her grip was firm, but gentle. "A writer." She didn't know why she was taking the time to make the mortal feel better, as if his feelings and emotions weren't anything but a passing breeze in the reality of time. Why did she care?

His smile was her answer.

235

It was a radiant sun peeking out from behind gray clouds. Uma realized she had never seen anything so beautiful, despite traveling the seven realms. So different from the practiced expressions of the celestial court. Plus, she knew what it was like to not believe in yourself.

They met for their first writing date the next day, in a coffee shop, where mortals gathered to drink a vile, bitter beverage that creative human types found to be an elixir. Uma sat on one of the plushy couches, fretting that she had made the wrong decision in involving herself with a human, helping one, even. After everything she had said at court?

She had meant to refute Lord Indra's proposal to dedicate more of the court's time to directly helping humans in a calm, rational manner. Instead, rash words had tumbled out of her mouth in front of the whole court. Lord Indra loved his humans, loved their changeable nature and creative spirits. That was exactly what Uma didn't trust.

Speaking out in such a way had been a mistake.

But maybe it wasn't so dire. Lord Indra had banished her for a year, but good works might commute her sentence. Showing that she could work with humans might smooth things over.

And if that didn't convince Lord Indra, then perhaps her true gambit would.

Humanity was greedy. This boy would never be able to resist the desire for knowledge, especially if it was denied to him. He would fail her one condition of staying away from her notebook, and she would prove to Lord Indra and the court that she had been right all along. Surely, once they saw that she had proof that humans couldn't be trusted, she would be forgiven for arguing against them.

Lord Indra, having seen that she was correct, would welcome her back.

And she would return home.

Which was exactly what she wanted. Right?

Parag appeared before her, a tall, steaming mug of coffee in his hand. He took the seat next to her.

"I've been thinking about your feedback," he said, continuing their conversation. "That the character doesn't have a strong enough relationship with the antagonist, but I can't figure out how to fix it. Any ideas?"

He glanced at the notebook she had spread open across her lap, a hint of interest in his eyes.

"I have a few," she said.

"More ideas from your magical notebook?" Parag said. "Hit me."

Uma squinted at him, before realizing this was another one of Parag's colloquialisms. He did not, in fact, want her to hit him.

"All right. First of all, have you considered that a main character could be their own antagonist?"

"Ooh, like being your own worst enemy," Parag said. "That's an interesting thought."

"Humans often are. Their own worst enemy, that is. They

are presented two paths and often choose the one that is the most destructive."

"I suppose that's true. But isn't that what causes growth? Mistakes? Making the wrong choice and then learning from it? *Humans* learn. That's what makes us special, don't you think?"

Uma had never thought about it that way, but she considered his words. She had underestimated Parag.

Two hours later, after Parag had downed two vile coffees (the milk didn't help, in her opinion) and seemed to be bouncing out of his skin as a result, they fell into a silence. Uma had never had so much to discuss with a mortal before. With anyone.

"You're interesting, Parag," she said, leaning back against the sticky leather of the couch. She tilted her head and regarded him.

"Interesting? That sounds like a bad thing."

If only he knew what she had called mortals in front of the celestial court. The names didn't deserve to be repeated, especially as they had been severe enough to anger Lord Indra. He treasured mortals, or at least, he believed in them.

Parag was the opposite of what she had expected. Kind and considerate. Sharp and witty. Thoughtful.

"It's not," she said.

"Hey, we've been working for hours. I think we deserve a break," Parag said. "Let's do something fun."

"Fun?"

Parag laughed. "Fun."

He took her to a shop that sold churned cream that had been frozen and mixed with different crunchy toppings. Uma was skeptical, until she took her first bite. She would have to bring this iced cream back to the celestial court.

After, he took her to a theater, where they watched a film. She had heard of films from her mother's books and from apsaras who specialized in the performing arts, but a literature apsara like herself, and a young one, didn't qualify for the court's film nights. It was wildly different from what she imagined, especially watching a film alongside others, the whole crowd gasping and cheering at the same time, many hearts synchronized as one.

When they left, Uma was smiling so widely her cheeks hurt.

And so it went, day after day, week after week.

Uma spent her free hours writing or observing humanity with Parag. One weekend, they went to the local fair, where she learned that humans enjoyed hurling themselves through the air and screaming. Uma enjoyed it, only because every time the roller coaster would dip, Parag's face would light up with a thunderous joy.

The week after, they went to the mall, another human invention Uma hadn't understood at first. Then she tasted those cinnamon-specked buns Parag loved, and it began to click into place. Sure, they didn't rival the dishes of the celestial court, but they were very, very close. Something about the gooey, oozy icing and over-the-top sweetness seemed so human. A little too much, too earnest. Imperfect.

And yet, lovely.

A few months passed, and winter had begun to knock at their door before Uma remembered her initial gambit.

The school day was over, and she wandered the halls, searching for Parag's nylon bag and loping gait. They were supposed to try out a new delicacy. Something called ramen that Parag called the noodles of the gods. Uma was ready to be the judge of that, given that she had actually met a few gods.

The hallway near his locker was empty, but she heard voices at the end of the hall. She had grown accustomed to his voice—deep, with a staccato lilt that only intensified when he grew passionate about something. She heard it now and drifted toward the sound.

"This is awesome. Some of your best work yet, Parag. Working with Uma has helped you level up. This novella is some legit MFA-grad-style work."

Uma faintly recognized the older boy who stood across from Parag. His name was Toby, and he was a senior who Parag seemed to worship, as he'd been accepted into some of the top writing programs and was the editor of the school paper. Uma stepped back from the door so they wouldn't see her.

"Working with Uma has been like an MFA, that's for sure,"

Parag said. "And that ending was all hers. She pulled it out of that notebook of hers. It seems like she's been collecting ideas for years."

"A notebook full of ideas? Sounds like the perfect writing partner," Toby said, grinning. "You got something special here, Parag. If you can get two more pieces written, a short story, another novella, you can totally submit them to those summer programs I mentioned. With those on your résumé, you'll be a shoo-in for any creative writing or film school you want. I know that's what you've always wanted."

"Two more pieces? It took me forever just to finish this one." A hint of panic leeched into Parag's voice.

"I get that, but these programs have deadlines. I'm sure you can whip something up," Toby said.

"Sure . . ." Parag's voice was unsteady. "I could push something through, but where do I start?"

"Hey, you said your writing partner has a notebook full of ideas, didn't you? Start there, if you need to."

Parag hesitated. "I guess."

A pause, a beat of silence. "Dude, this is the big leagues. You want to go to the Hyscraft workshop? Or Nightsmith? You've got to produce work. Lean on your writing partner, she seems pretty cool. Ask if you guys could go through some ideas."

"Yeah, but she's really private about that notebook."

Toby made a disbelieving noise. "She's a writer. Probably thinks they aren't good enough. It's just a notebook."

A beat. A pause.

"Maybe she won't mind sharing . . . ," Parag said. "I'll figure something out."

Uma didn't need to be well versed in mortal writing programs to understand that this was a big deal for Parag. It was also obvious that Parag felt unprepared, worried.

Scared.

And fear turned even the best of humans into shadows of themselves. It hadn't escaped Uma that her notebook held interest for Parag. And now? It was only a matter of time before he succumbed to his fear, like all humans did.

What surprised her was the disappointment that pulsed in her chest at the thought of Parag's imminent betrayal. His lack of belief, of trust in himself, would lead to breaking hers.

But wasn't this what Uma had wanted? To show Lord Indra that she was right. Humans could not be trusted.

The thought of winning her argument with Lord Indra no longer warmed her. It only left her cold.

When Parag found her later, on the grass, she had a smile on her face, as if she had not heard a thing. As if she had not seen the shadows in his heart.

Uma hadn't forgotten what she had heard. And as they ate ramen, and worked, and ate more ramen, she kept an eye on Parag, watching for the turn.

She had always known humans were different than

celestials. But somehow, this one had wormed past her defenses. She had set the test to challenge his mettle, to prove a point to Lord Indra and the other apsaras who so loved humanity.

And now her trap, her notebook, might catch a fish.

But the agony of waiting for Parag to spring the trap became too much. Uma knew what was to happen. It was a tale as old as humanity.

The next day, she devised a way to speed things up. She couldn't stand the in-between anymore. If Parag was going to betray her, she would rather get it over with and get back to her old life in the skies.

Somehow the thought didn't have the same luster as it had before.

They went to their coffee shop again, sat on that sticky leather couch next to the window where they had written together.

Parag left to get them their regular order, coffee and something glorious Uma had discovered called chai. The mortals insisted on calling it a chai tea latte, despite the redundancy of the phrase, but still, it was the closest thing to nectar that she had found on Earth.

It was here that she made her move.

Parag turned from the counter, both mugs in hand.

Uma jumped to her feet, expressing her need for the restroom. She bolted away and hid behind the nearby stairs, watching her notebook, alone and unattended. For the few months she had known and worked with Parag, she had never taken her eyes off of it. Never even stepped away for a moment.

At first, Parag did nothing. He drank his coffee and watched the people around him. But then he noticed her notebook.

His head swiveled around, his eyes intent on the notebook. It had taken a few minutes, but still, now that she had left, his eyes were on what wasn't his.

On something she had asked him never to touch.

Uma had known this would happen, and yet it still hurt. Deep in her heart, nestled among the thorns, it pricked the tender core of all she had hoped.

This was why humanity couldn't be trusted. She heard the words she had said in the celestial court.

Humans are fickle, selfish creatures. They change with the wind, and they use all that comes their way, all for a fleeting chance to taste the immortality that is ours. If we let them close, they will burn themselves reaching for us. And they will take all we have. They can never be trusted.

This time, they felt hollow. They gave her no relief, no sense of power, just the deep, deep fall of disappointment.

The smell of honeysuckle and jasmine drifted under her nose with the breeze, drawing her back to memories of her life in the celestial court, staring at the humans from up on high, dancing and playing and laughing with her apsara sisters.

Every memory had a gray wash over it, like it had been

painted over or left out in the sun too long. Because of him.

Still, the celestial court was home. And she would be going back home.

Everything she had wanted, right?

Parag reached forward and—

Uma burst out of her hiding place and rushed away from the coffee shop, away from Parag. Away from his clove-and-orange scent, his sweet smile.

Away from him.

He found her later at the football field.

"You left this," he said. Her notebook was in his hands, his heart on his sleeve. Uma didn't want it.

"Keep it. It's tainted now."

A pause, and then the crunching of leaves beneath a sole. "Tainted?"

"Did you open my notebook, despite what I said? Did you gather up my ideas to pass off as your own? Tell me, how easy was it for you to break my trust?"

Uma's face contorted, her heart unsure whether to express its anger, its fear, its hurt, or its disappointment.

She should've known.

She should've trusted her instincts.

Parag shook his head quickly, and then slowly. "No, I didn't."

The words landed like heavy pebbles in water. She didn't believe him.

Parag's face appeared in front of her own. He crouched down and tipped her chin up.

"You are a treasure, Uma."

She looked up at him in surprise.

"When I first saw you on those steps, flailing about with your backpack, I thought you couldn't possibly be real." He smiled at the memory. "I thought I would be lucky to just be in your presence. I never imagined that you would want to hang out with me. That you might want me too."

"Want you too?" Uma's face scrunched up.

How had he known? That her feelings toward him had been shifting, shifting, changing like a slow, steady stream of water. That this was why her heart felt so heavy at his betrayal.

"At least, I think you do?" Parag's face melted into uncertainty, his smile drooping, his eyebrows knitting together.

"You read my notebook," she said in accusation. "I specifically asked you not to." Her words were sharper, her tone a blade.

"I didn't."

Slowly, she realized what he was saying. *He didn't?* Uma brushed her fingertips over his pulse, checking for the lie.

His heart beat in a steady rhythm. *Thump, thump, thump.* Truth, truth, truth.

Joy pierced her entire body, rays of sun on a dark morning. She had never been so happy to be wrong.

"I wanted to, if I'm being honest," he said, gnawing on the

side of his lip. "But you said not to."

"I did. I made it very clear."

"You did—" Parag paused, understanding washing over his face. "You did that on purpose, didn't you? I thought you were just a private person. Or that you were embarrassed—but you ran out of the coffee shop. Almost like you—Wait, Uma. Were you testing me?"

"Yes." There was no point in denying it.

"Which is kind of messed up," he said slowly.

Uma's head shot up and she stared at Parag. His normally smiling face was twisted in thought, a line of worry running across his forehead.

"Actually, yeah. Pretty messed up," he said.

"Messed up?"

He nodded. "Like, you don't test your friends or, um, your boyfriend. If that's what we are." Parag said the last bit in a swallowed mumble. "It's not really a cool thing to do. Like, sure, I get that it's private and maybe you aren't ready to share your ideas, but you said you wanted to write them together. Also, it's just psychology. The minute you mention not doing something, it makes you kinda . . . want to do it. Right? I know it's not just me. But yeah, it felt like a test. And a bad one. A pop quiz."

Uma was so confused by his words that she didn't even notice the term he used. *Boyfriend.* She would have laughed.

"It was a test," she said. "I know that's not kind of me to admit."

247

"At least you're being honest."

Her cheeks burned as she realized how wrong she had been. She had meant to trick Parag into showing the worst of humanity, and instead, he was revealing the worst in her. She had lashed out, assuming the worst of him.

A question lingered in her mind, the one that had started everything.

"But how else do I know I can trust you?" she whispered.

Or your kind?

To his credit, Parag didn't look offended. He merely looked thoughtful. "Deep question, Uma. I guess, you never know for sure? You only hope. And believe. Humans are imperfect, didn't you say that once? But I also said that we can learn. So hope, believe, and . . . maybe be honest?"

Uma was finally beginning to understand.

"I mean, I really like you, Uma. But I don't feel like I know you? And I want to. Know you. But you have to let me." He drew closer to her, getting down on his knees in front of her. "Let me know you."

Parag's smile was the hint of a new dawn, a hopeful promise. If she would take it.

Maybe humanity did have a lesson to teach her.

"So, trust?" Uma said slowly.

It was a foreign concept, to be honest. She had dealt with tests and bargains, curses and punishments, her whole immortal life. It would be a change. To see the person in front of her for who they were. To put herself in their hands as much as they put themselves in hers.

"Yes," he said.

"You want to . . . know me?"

"Yes."

Her reply was soft. Sad. "But why?"

Still, a part of her was looking for the trick. Old habits died hard.

Parag tucked a lock of her hair behind her ear. "Because I only have one lifetime. What better way to spend it?"

This time, her smile was enough to bring the heavens down.

She nodded, once, twice.

And when his lips touched hers, she thought she smelled honeysuckle and jasmine.

Her queen found her the next day, sitting by a jasmine bush at the edge of a park. She was decked in the finest of celestial clothing and jewelry, silks laced with gold and jewels.

"So you understand now."

Uma immediately fell into a bow.

"My queen?"

"You understand what it is humanity has to offer."

Uma paused. "I am beginning to."

"Lord Indra will be quite pleased to see that you've begun to change your mind. And that you're helping a mortal. He has forgotten most of his ire in the past few months, Uma." Her voice was kind. "If I ask, you might be able to return home sooner. Especially given your progress."

Home. What she had hoped for.

At the start.

"I think I shall remain for the year," Uma said slowly.

Her queen smiled, as if she knew what was in Uma's heart. "And perhaps longer?"

Unspoken words passed between them, and Uma knew she understood. She was not the first apsara to be ensnared by Earth. Or by a mortal.

"Does he know," her queen asked, her voice light, "about who you are?"

"Not yet," Uma said. "But I will tell him soon. When the time is right."

And when she had decided herself.

Her queen placed a gentle hand on Uma. "There will always be a place for you at home." And with that, she vanished in a soft glow of light.

Home would always be home.

But for now, Uma let the fragrance of soft mulch and sweet jasmine envelop her. She had months left on Earth, and months left to discover what made humanity so special.

And to believe.

AUTHOR'S NOTE

I've always been fascinated by the story of Urvashi and Pururavas—a romance between a celestial apsara and a mortal human—which has similarities to the myth of Eros and Psyche. Except Urvashi and Pururavas's ending is more tragic, with the two never reuniting after Pururavas's betrayal. I wanted to reimagine their story in a modern setting, with a more nuanced take on what might have happened if the two of them had tried things differently—and tried a little bit of trust and communication.

ART BY SIBU T.P.

MIRCH, MASALA, AND MAGIC
By Nafiza Azad

"The bhajia is an achievement that marries the salty with the spicy," Daadi says, holding up the bite-size snack in her hand. "It is a simple dish. Gram flour, wrapped around slices of potatoes, spinach, and onions, seasoned with garlic, ginger, mirch, and a dash of magic before being deep-fried. When dipped in tamarind chutney and accompanied by a sip of masala chai, it will make even the most recalcitrant bear loquacious. What I want to know, however," Daadi looks at each of us in turn before pausing on my face, "is which of you thought that adding raisins to the bhajia mixture was a good idea?"

Everyone in the kitchen turns to stare at me.

I admit it, okay? I have made some questionable decisions

where ingredients are concerned in the past. But this time, I'm innocent!

"It wasn't me!" I protest loudly, crossing my arms to address the accusations in the eyes of my sisters, cousins, and grandmother.

Outside, a rooster crows to punctuate my outrage. It is hideously early on a Saturday morning. Too early to be up and in the kitchen, in my opinion, but I'm the youngest Noisy, and no one cares about my opinions. Because our names all begin with N and we're all loud, our family calls us the Noisies.

"If I were you, Daadi," I say, "I would lay the blame squarely on Noor's stinky feet. She's the one with the unhealthy obsession with raisins!"

"My feet aren't stinky!" Noor protests. "Also! Why would the blame be on *my* feet, anyway? In my opinion, the true culprit is Nadia. She was the one wandering around with the raisin jar!"

Nadia, who was discreetly stuffing her mouth with almonds, is startled by Noor's words. She sputters before gulping down some chai to clear her throat. Directing a wounded look at Noor, she says, "I know better than to add raisins to bhajia!"

"Ladies." Daadi's fatigued voice puts an end to our bickering. Chagrined, all four of us stand in a line and wait for judgment. I can hear our mothers talking in the outside kitchen, the birds singing as they make breakfast of the ripe mangoes on the trees, and a kid bleating somewhere. There is no sleeping in on a farm—especially not during harvest season.

254

"Bhajia is usually eaten as a snack during teatime or between meals. The saltiness serves to enhance the flavor of a gathering. When normal people cook it, bhajia has no effect outside of tempting the tongue, but when *we* make it, with the magic within us, the bhajia becomes a way to animate gatherings." Daadi pauses to take a breath. "Adding raisins to the mixture negates the saltiness and thus the magic of it. If your purpose is to deepen the flavor, corn will be a better choice."

"Aha!" Nawal, the eldest Noisy, since Nazneen bubu moved out, claps her hands. "So I wasn't entirely wrong. I just chose the wrong ingredient."

We stare at our shameless sister. I wish Nazneen bubu hadn't left. She was the only one who treated me as though my opinions mattered. Why did she have to get married to someone who lives so far away from us? All the way in Suva, on the side of the island. She is the only one who can control Nawal.

Daadi clears her throat and Nawal grins, thoroughly unrepentant. "Sorry." The lesson continues.

It is not cooking we learn from Daadi. I mean, cooking is a part of it, but cooking alone can't encompass the entirety of the private education we receive. What we learn from our grandmother is an alchemy of spices and flavors. A secret sorcery with which to draw forth the appetite and storm the senses. We learn to riposte with fire. We learn to conjure hunger with the aroma of the dishes we cook. The foods we make are our choice of weapons when waging the different battles that when linked together, make life.

Our paternal grandmother, Hoor Begum, or, as we call her, Daadi, inherited the magic that flutters in all of us. Our fathers have the potential for this magic, but much like recessive genes, they aren't able to utilize it. We have no spell book or written recipes.

Daadi is called Didi by those who can't claim blood relationship to her, the term assigning her the status of an elder as a mark of love and respect. She, who has cooked for presidents, royalty, and religious leaders, teaches us the measure of the saltiness in a sob, the sugar in a smile, and the spice in a squabble. The magic is within us, see, but to infuse this magic into the food we create, we need to learn to understand the materials we are cooking with, and to know exactly what we want to achieve. The intent cannot be ambiguous.

"What do you think the raisin bhajia tastes like?" Noor whispers to me.

"I'm not in a hurry to find out," I mutter, staring at the potato in front of me. It's a remarkably healthy potato. How can it be anything else, growing as it did in Daadi's garden?

"If you've finished communing with the potato, go get me some mint from the front garden," Nawal commands.

"Why should I?" I demand.

"Because you're the youngest," she says, as if that should silence all my protests.

You know the worst thing?

It does.

Grumbling, I leave the potato on the counter, ignore Noor's sympathetic look, and march to the veranda that wraps around the front of the house. I exit the veranda from the right to a stone staircase that forms a path to the lower maidaan. On either side of the staircase are gardens containing a wealth of herbs and flowers. It being harvest season and this being a sugarcane farm, the air is redolent with the smell of sugar. I breathe in deeply and head toward the small clump of mint growing beside the yellow buttercup. The grass is wet with morning dew, and my toes curl around the chill of it. A strangled sob suddenly comes from down the stairs.

Since I don't think murderers and ghosts would frequent their potential victims' houses just to cry, I abandon the mint and, displaying courage I don't possess, inch down the stairs. I come to a standstill when I spy a bedraggled figure curled on up the first stair. The sun isn't out yet but that doesn't stop me from identifying the person as Nazneen, my cousin, and the eldest Noisy.

"Bubu?" I whisper, and she flinches, hunching forward as if she cannot bear to look back and face me. I fly down the stairs and crouch beside her. I reach toward her. When she whimpers, I startle. "Bubu? Are you hurt? What can I do?"

She still doesn't speak. She won't move and I don't know how to get her to follow me inside. I leave her and run to the person who has always been able to fix things: Daadi.

I remember the joy when Nazneen bubu got married only three months ago. We were all but drunk on it. There was a bit of sorrow at the upcoming parting, too, but we mostly celebrated the new journey our sister was embarking on. A new love to explore, a new family to make memories with, and a new life in which to grow happiness from.

Our sister left a starry-eyed girl, and she returned a woman, dressed in a shabby kurta. Her eyes are dark, like the sun within them set when we weren't aware. The only time her stoic expression changes is when she sees Daadi. Then she crumples like the sugarcane plants during a hurricane.

We don't know what she went through, and she won't say. No matter how much the adults beseech her, she maintains a stubborn silence. Or perhaps a protective one. Our parents and our grandmother closet themselves in the small sitting room to discuss the next steps while we, the Noisies, and our brothers take Nazneen bubu to her room, which remains the same even though Nawal has been coveting it. While bubu takes a shower, we make her breakfast, eggs and tava-toast. Nawal makes maleeda using magic, intending the sweetness of the rolled-up balls of parantha to provide comfort.

We may not see any wounds on Nazneen bubu, but we can sense them within her. When Bubu falls asleep, we leave her room, only to find our elders standing outside. They still don't know why Nazneen bubu is home, but all of us understand that the reasons behind her return are anything but happy.

Time passes, and we return to our duties on the farm. After

all, life doesn't care to stop for broken hearts. We coax Nazneen bubu back into the circle of our sisterhood. When she wants to be alone, we leave Sa'ad, our youngest brother, with her. When she's quiet, we curb our tongues and sit silently by her side. When she wants to converse, we talk to her, discussing the newest Bollywood movie or the latest twist in the Indian serials Noor is very fond of.

We don't ask our eldest sister about what she went through or why she returned home. Daadi has my dad make an appointment for her with a therapist in the city. Nazneen bubu attends the first session and returns home with the glacier in her eyes melted. She sits outside under the neem tree for a long time, covered by dappled shadows. We watch her from a distance and ply her with chai when she returns with a smile we thought we'd never see again.

On a crisp Wednesday afternoon, we return home from school to find the entire family seated around the kitchen table. The smell of gunpowder lingers in the air.

Nawal, who is home on a break from university, signals to us with her eyebrows and whispers, "Phone call from the villains. They are coming for dinner on Saturday." Nazneen bubu's dad, my uncle, stares at her with a distressed expression. Daadi and my aunt are seated on either side of Nazneen bubu, giving my uncle the gimlet eye. Our brothers immediately make themselves scarce and I'm torn between doing the same and staying to satisfy my curiosity.

Before I can make up my mind, Nazneen bubu snaps, "What's the point of saying anything? Why should I tell you everything—" She breaks off and breathes deeply. Daadi places a comforting hand on her shoulder. "Why should I say what they did? I tried before. No one believed me. They said I was lying. Overreacting. That Daadi spoiled me."

"If you tell us, *we'll* believe you, chanda," my aunt says, her voice wobbling. My mom squeezes her hand.

Nazneen bubu scrunches up her face, as if trying to endure some hideous pain. In my heart, I skewer her husband. "I know you will, but I don't want to tell you. I'm ashamed, Daadi. You raised me to be strong, and I tried. I tried so hard to be strong, to endure, but in the end, I couldn't. I"—she sobs, and she's not the only one crying at this point—"I ran away. I couldn't stand it anymore. I shamed you."

"Nazneen, child, you didn't shame me by returning home. You respected yourself enough to remove yourself from a situation that was hurting you. You did exactly what you needed to. The rest is up to us." Daadi gives Nazneen a hug.

Half an hour later, Daadi, our mothers, and all of us Noisies, including Nazneen bubu, are still sitting around the kitchen table, which is all but groaning under the weight of scones (yes, with raisins in them), gulgula (also featuring raisins), clotted cream, and large cups full of steaming chai.

"The villains actually want us to *cook* for them?" I swallow my mouthful of buttered scone and ask, "Are they serious?"

Nadia sneers. "*Of course* they are serious."

"Oh yes, we'll cook. We'll serve them a dinner they'll never forget," Nawal says.

"Even if they wish to," Noor adds.

I am very intrigued.

"No," Daadi says suddenly, taking the wind out of our sails. Before we can protest, she holds up a hand. "This time, I will cook."

For a second, we all gape at her. Even Nazneen bubu is shocked.

We want to protest, but Daadi has spoken. And for us, her word is law.

Two and a half days isn't really enough time to prepare all the ingredients we need to cook dinner for the villains, but needs must. With Daadi at the helm, there's nothing to worry about.

The first thing to do, as Daadi always tell us, is to make niyat, *intention*. The clearer we understand what we desire from the food we cook, the greater our chances of succeeding.

"We will have them confess everything they put our sister through," I say. "Let everyone hear them admit the wrongs they've committed." I glance at Nazneen bubu. "Is that okay?"

She bows her head and doesn't reply for a moment. I bite my lip, wondering if I've done something wrong. Then she says, "Will they? Are they capable of it?"

"It doesn't matter whether they're capable of it or not," Daadi says. "When I'm done with them, they won't have a choice."

When the intent has been verbalized, we plan the dishes we'll cook and the ingredients required to make them.

We make fresh mango achaar. The mangoes are picked at noon (Nawal's duty) when the sun is at its peak and everything is illuminated. After the mangoes are quartered, we dry them on the surface of the roof for maximum sun before taking them down to season them with spices, mirch, and magic.

We butcher the rooster that crows the loudest at dawn; its meat is prepped to make curry for the dinner. Freshwater fish caught under the light of the full moon are cleaned and cut into pieces to fry an hour or two before Saturday's dinner. We wash moringa leaves for a stir-fry; the slightly bitter taste will lubricate the tongue and draw forth the feelings hidden inside. We make a variety of chutneys: tamarind, mint, and coconut to coat the tongue and ease the throat.

We also decide to make nimbu sharbat from lemons collected early in the morning, when the air is full of birdsong, and well water drawn at dawn. We collect all the ingredients we will use to cook dinner under full light. Just right for illuminating the secrets the villains are hiding.

I venture out into Daadi's garden at the back of the house on Friday evening, an hour after Maghrib. The fragrance of jasmine is heavy in the air and the chirruping of the crickets is loud. I am on an errand to pick up the dalo leaves we'll make into a dish called saina, where the leaves will be layered with minced lentils and spices, rolled, steamed, then fried crisp. I find Daadi sitting under the starlight on a bench my uncle built for her. The lamp on the post beside the bench illuminates her face and the immeasurable sadness contained within it.

I stand silently, as much part of the night as the darkness, watching as Daadi wipes away tears she is usually so careful not to show anyone. I don't know if I should step forward, or retreat so she can rest assured that no one has witnessed her momentary fragility. However, she notices me before I can make a decision and waves me forward.

I sit down beside her and give her a hug. Daadi smells like cardamom and home.

"Here for the dalo leaves?" she asks.

I nod. "Do you need help picking the mirch?"

Daadi's garden contains almost all the vegetables we eat daily, but the majority of the space is reserved for the various varieties of chilies. See, mirch is essential to marry the intent and the ingredients to the magic innate in us. Even when the dish being cooked is not savory, if it has a purpose beyond filling the stomach, we need to use a bit of mirch. This is why Daadi's garden features chilies ranging from ají dulce, which has a sweet flavor, to 7 Pot Douglah, hot enough to be used as a weapon.

"No." Daadi gestures to the full baskets sitting beside her. "Go pick what you need. We will rest early tonight. Tomorrow is going to be a long day."

We prepare for battle in the kitchen. After breakfast, which we don't linger over as we usually do, we get busy preparing the ingredients we've gathered over the course of the past two and a half days. We'll prep the ingredients to make it easier for Daadi, who is going to magic the dishes as she cooks them.

Nazneen bubu accompanies us. Though her eyes are too bright sometimes and the sparkle in her smile has the brittle nature of glass, she is present. While we busy ourselves in the inside kitchen, our parents are busy in the outside kitchen. They, too, are cooking a dinner, but theirs is meant for the villagers and other relatives Daadi has invited. The food they cook has no purpose but to satisfy hunger.

Soon the air is fragrant with the smell of tarka, the process of adding spices to hot oil to season it before we add the primary ingredients to the pan. We watch Daadi as she adds mirch, masala, and magic to each pot over the crackling flames. Adding magic to the dishes is a simple matter of intent. Knowing how much magic to add is a matter of experience. The rooster is made into curry and the moringa is stir-fried. We use taro leaves and coconut milk to make the Fijian roro. Nawal fries the papad and Nadia the fish, while Noor grates the coconut to make into chutney. Later, we compete over whose rotis are the roundest (mine).

Nazneen bubu makes kalonji, digging out the red heart of the bitter gourd and stuffing it with seasoned minced meat before tying a thread around it and frying it.

"Karela is Taufiq's favorite food," she muses out loud. We freeze. This is the first time she has mentioned her soon-to-be-ex-husband's name. Without thinking, we turn to look at Daadi, who stares back at us without reacting.

I lick my lips, trying to think of a way to say what I want to without offending anyone. "It's not surprising that he's a villain if *karela* is his favorite food."

"I suspect you're discriminating against karela," Nawal says. "What wrong did it ever do to be liked by that man?"

"Bitter things stick together?" Noor offers.

We may not know the specifics of what our sister went through, but we don't need to. We would be on her side no matter what.

"Let's finish up," Daadi says, looking amused.

We clean the kitchen and wash the dishes two hours before the scheduled dinner. The air is full of tantalizing smells. I can't lie. I'm tempted to take a bite of all the dishes Daadi cooked, but I know better than to try. As we sit at the table, enjoying a cup of chai to celebrate a job well done, Nadia suddenly stands up. "Daadi, we didn't make dessert!"

Daadi puts down her cup and smirks. "Our guests won't be staying long enough to eat dessert."

One hour before the guests are supposed to arrive, Nazneen bubu and Nawal take the car and leave for an afternoon of leisure in Lautoka City. Daadi had offered her the choice to either stay and confront her in-laws or take her abbu's bank card and enjoy an afternoon away.

Nazneen bubu had hesitated. "Doesn't it make me weak to run away from them?"

Daadi scoffed. "You are not running away, beta. You are choosing to put yourself first. Why should you have to force yourself to see them when all that will do is hurt you?"

Nadia, Noor, and I decide to stay home instead of accompanying the other two, ~~because we are nosy~~ just in case our help is needed.

Around five in the evening, the villains arrive. We peer at them through the windows, watching as they dawdle in their van for a while before realizing that no one is going to come welcome them in. The guests Daadi invited are all on the veranda, looking curiously at the people coming up the stairs.

There are seven of them. We see them more clearly when they get to the entrance, and I confess, I'm surprised. They hardly look like people who have made my sister cry herself to sleep for the past week.

Noor suddenly hisses, "She's wearing Nazneen bubu's clothes!"

"And her jewelry!" Nadia is equally incensed.

Imagine having the gall to not just steal someone else's belongings but to wear those belongings to their original owner's home. Fury makes breathing difficult for me, but I know better than to rush out at the woman right now.

The in-laws stand at the entrance, looking toward the other side where everyone is sitting. A tense second passes before Daadi gets to her feet. As she rises, so do our fathers, flanking her like two pillars.

"You asked us for a meal. We've cooked you one," Daadi says, not bothering with greetings. "Please seat yourself at the table." She gestures to the dining table arranged in the middle of the veranda.

The in-laws look gobsmacked. Perhaps they expected this dinner to unfold differently. They exchange glances, hesitating, before the eldest of them all, a man with gray hair and a stern face, marches to the head of the table, pulls out a chair, and sits in it. His wife, the grandmother of the family, snorts her displeasure before following him. The others follow without a word, though Taufiq looks around the gathering as if searching for someone.

As soon as they are seated, Daadi signals our brothers to start serving the food. The in-laws hesitate again. Social conventions dictate that a conversation precedes a meal, but no one here will oblige them. Eventually, they succumb to the allure of the dishes in front of them. Few, if any, can resist Daadi's cooking.

At first, the guests pay marked attention to etiquette and decorum and eat with exquisite manners. Then, slowly, the magic catches them unawares. No one can defend themselves against our magic. It is not the illusion of spark and dazzle like Merlin's magic, but the sorcery of quiet afternoons and star-studded tropical skies. It is the kind you consume, with spices, one bite at a time.

As the magic, filled with our intentions, gathers in the villains, they forget everything in their haste to cram the food into their mouths.

"I'm going to be sick," Noor whispers, turning away. I, however, don't move my eyes from the spectacle unfolding in front of us. The guests eat, their finery stained by oil and gravy, their cheeks bulging. They eat until not a single morsel remains. They even drink up the dahl, slurping it up, before belching their satisfaction.

The old man leans back in his chair, his stomach straining against the constraints laid upon it by his no-longer-white shirt.

"Have you had your fill?" Daadi asks gently.

"Is there more?" Taufiq asks, a hopeful expression on his face. Food particles are lodged in his hair and around his mouth.

His mother glares at him before replying to Daadi. "Yes, we're full." Her mouth is still smeared by the food she ate.

"Good," Daadi says. In the next moment, the smile on her face fades and her eyes grow cold. "Now, speak. Tell me what you did to my granddaughter."

As if he has been waiting for the command, Taufiq's brother gets to his feet, pushing his chair so it falls back. "I admit it, all right?" he blubbers. "I peeked at my sister-in-law when she was in the shower. I cornered her in the kitchen and tried to touch her. When she didn't reciprocate, I told everyone she tried to seduce me."

My uncle roars his anger. My dad's hands tighten into fists. Our mothers have fire in their eyes. Our brothers grow still, their anger in the lines of their bodies. Suddenly I'm glad Nazneen bubu is not here.

"I hit her," Taufiq's mom says next. "So what? I dislike her too-beautiful face. I don't like the way she seems to know everything, so I hit her. Whenever I could and always in places no one could see. What are you going to do about it, huh?"

"I kept her separated from my grandson," Taufiq's grandmother says. "I made her sleep in my room in case I woke up and needed her. I made her cook dinner every night, because what else is she good for?"

"I took her clothes and jewelry," Taufiq's sister-in-law says. "What need does she have for these things when she's little more than a servant for the old woman?"

"I made her drop out of school and made her school refund the tuition her parents paid," Taufiq's father says. "I needed the money more than she needs an education."

By this time, Nadia and Noor are holding on to me so I don't throw something at Taufiq and his family. They are all monsters underneath their human skin.

"I cast her out of the house in the middle of the night," Taufiq's grandfather confesses. "I was sure she'd go running back home, weeping, and look, I wasn't wrong. How much will you give us to take her back? The amount can't be low or I won't accept her again."

The only person who hasn't spoken is Taufiq. He is sniffling.

"I failed her. I promised to always be on her side, but when it mattered the most, I chose my family over her. I knew my mother was hitting her but pretended I didn't. I supervised her calls home because I was worried she would tell you what she was going through. I thought if we endured, things would pass. I failed her. Over and over again." He weeps, but no one is impressed with his tears. He should cry forever.

I want to slice him into a thousand pieces. I want to hurt them all as they did our sister.

"Bring the girl out!" Taufiq's grandmother demands. Her spit sprays in the air.

"Hasn't she suffered enough in the months she spent in your house? Do you think us fools that we'd subject her to your presence a second time?" Daadi says. Her voice is even, but her eyes are colder than I've ever seen them.

Taufiq's mom sneers. "It's her luck to marry into our family."

"When I married my granddaughter to your son, Sabra, I did so with the expectation that you would know how to treat the treasure I gifted you. I expected you to respect her." Daadi's eyes narrow to slits. "Alas, it seems I expected too much from you." She nods at my dad.

My dad picks up a document bag that has been lying to the side and removes a stack of paper from it. He hands the papers to Taufiq, who takes one look at them and blanches. He holds the papers with trembling hands and faces Daadi. "Is there no way to reconcile?"

"Stop begging them!" Taufiq's grandmother snaps. "A divorced daughter is a taint on the family name. They will be running after us soon, wanting us to take that slut back!"

Daadi takes two steps forward, the rage in her eyes spilling over, and a second later, the woman's face is thrown to the side, a handprint appearing on her skin.

"In my family, daughters are more precious than sons. The loss of a partner does not make a woman any less. Everyone has bad luck sometimes. However, when you step in mud, you don't stop walking. You simply wash the dirt off before continuing on your way." Daadi sneers at them, making no secret of who she thinks is the dirt.

"We will expect all of Nazneen's belongings, every single piece of clothing and jewelry, to be returned to her. Any attempts to cheat her or any instances of slander and defamation will lead us to take legal action against you. From the confessions you made not a few minutes ago, you all know what the result of such actions will be," my dad says, using his lawyer voice.

"Let me see her," Taufiq begs. "Just once."

"You can either sign the divorce agreement now or wait for the courts to command you to do so," my dad says.

Taufiq's grandfather gets to his feet in a hurry. "What are you waiting for?" he screams at Taufiq. "Sign the papers! You think she's the only woman around?"

Taufiq is unable to resist the urgings of his family and signs the papers. Once he's done, the guests don't even pause to wash their hands and faces. They drag him back into their van and are gone, leaving behind their dirty dishes and a stink in the air.

Daadi sprays some air freshener and I march to her. "Don't you think they got off too easily?" I demand. "We didn't even make them bleed!"

"Nesrine!" my dad rebukes me.

Daadi laughs grimly. "Don't worry, beta. It's not just our family they will be honest with. They are going to spend the time until the food is digested confessing their sins to everyone they have wronged. And tomorrow, the mirch will start working." A rare darkness arrests her face before she says, "I didn't kill them, but before the mirch is done with them, they'll wish I had."

I nod, somewhat mollified. Nazneen and Nawal return while we're praying Maghrib. After the prayer, we set the table again, but this time with the food our mothers cooked: chicken pulau, tamarind chutney, and raita. There is no other magic in these dishes, apart from love, which there is an abundance.

Nazneen bubu doesn't ask us about what happened with the guests, but smiles when she sees the signed divorced papers. Her eyes are full of tears, but her smile has a bit of sunshine in it. She's going to be okay. We're going to be okay.

When we're done eating dinner, Daadi brings out motichoor laddoo she made secretly. I see the chili flecks in them and know these sweets contain magic.

Laddoo are eaten during celebrations, during happy times. Nazneen bubu eats a laddoo and the tears in her eyes disappear.

When my grandmother cooks, she creates magic.

I pick up a laddoo and pop it in my mouth. The taste of the morning on Eid, sweet and full of anticipation. Daadi's magic. The fireworks in the sky.

AUTHOR'S NOTE

My Daadi, Hur Begum, was a great woman. She didn't win any awards and she didn't cook for kings and presidents but, just like Daadi in "Mirch, Masala, and Magic," she made magic every time she cooked. This story pays homage to the woman she was and the women I look up to.

ART BY NEHA KAPIL

DAUGHTER OF THE SUN

By Sayantani DasGupta

*Poets have told it before, poets are telling it now, other poets shall
tell this history on Earth in the future.*
—The Mahabharat, Book 1: The Book of the Beginning

*At the best of times, a story is a slippery thing. Perhaps that was
why it changed with each telling.*
—Chitra Banerjee Divakaruni, *The Palace of Illusions*

There is blood all over the battlefield, the broken bodies of
warriors and weapons. Spirit shadows rise like mist from the
ground, and among the fallen soldiers rides Jōm, the god of
death, upon his mighty buffalo, gathering souls. Dark as a
rain cloud, with eyes of burning flame, he brandishes a noose

and spear in two of his four hands. Newborn babies in Bharat are never given names too early, lest Jōm call them to him. And until they are old enough to protest, mothers mar the cheeks of their sons with black spots of kajol, so the god of death is not tempted by their beauty. Girl babies, considered by many to be a less precious commodity, are not afforded such protections, but instead are too often given to Jōm like gifts of obeisance showered upon an indifferent king.

That is, in fact, why we are here on this battlefield. At least in this lifetime, this version of the oft-told tale. I lead the women's army of one hundred royal Kaurav sisters against my own kin, my own brothers, the Pandavs. We seek revenge for all those girls who could not write their stories. We battle for all those girls' lives cut short, or not allowed to begin at all.

For I am Karna. I fight for justice, a better world for the oppressed, a new ending to this epic tale.

I cannot be distracted from my goal. Not by the calls of Jōm; not by the trickster Krishna, who I know seeks my downfall; not even if Indra, king of the gods, were to charge down on me from the clouds upon his trumpeting elephant. I could not be swayed even if the sun god Shurjo, my own birth father, were to deem me worthy of his attention and bring me into his golden embrace.

I am not afraid, though I have been thrown from my chariot, its wheel stuck in the mud. Even if I could dislodge it, I could not fix its splintered spokes. An ironic end for one adopted and raised by a chariot-wheel maker.

And so I wait for my enemy, Arjun. I wait to kill him or be killed myself.

My lips form, over and over again, the holy words of the mantra I will use. I refuse to forget its magic power. A hundred arrows may fly from his hand, but I do not need such showmanship. I will send from my bow only one arrow, straight and true. The very sun will burn and fire rain down from the sky.

But I am not the hero of this tale. I am an interloper, even in my own life. This much the blue-skinned Krishna has shown me. By my very existence, I have somehow screwed up the mechanics of the universe, broken the spokes of the wheel of life. Unless Arjun kills me, the circle cannot turn, or so the gods say; life cannot go on in its unending cycle of birth and death.

They know this because it has happened before. And it will happen again. They say our lives were already lived out during other ages in other bodies, our joys and sorrows all played out in other times. They say that existence itself is a recurring illusion, veiling us from seeing the truth of the universe.

I never used to buy it. Reincarnation always seemed like a lot of nonsense to me. Made up by the sages and mystics to keep us lower sects scared. Get out of line, and be reborn a cockroach. I never had the patience for that kind of thinking. I knew what I knew. I felt what I felt. This life, right here, right now, was all I had.

Now I realize I'm living a story that's been played out a

hundred thousand times before. But maybe this time, I can kill my enemy rather than be killed. Reverse the way the wheel spins, I don't know. Perhaps this life is the one that alters things for good.

For I've already changed the story. I've already scrambled the plot. Because this time around, I was born a girl.

> *Discontent is the root of fortune.*
> —*The Mahabharat*

The first time I see Arjun, I know nothing of the coming war. I know nothing of gods or chariots, battlefields or death. I have felt the burdens of girlhood, but don't know the depth of the violence against those like me. I know nothing of my true identity, my lost brothers or cruel mother. I don't even know that Arjun is one of the five legendary Pandav princes hiding as monks in the forest with their widowed mother, the queen, barely having escaped being murdered by their Kaurav cousins over the inheritance of Bharat's throne. All I know is that I am poor and hungry, and his family is plentiful with food and weapons.

I do not guess there is something mystical that brings me to his hut that day. I do not even suspect when, instead of just gathering all the unguarded fish and mangoes and sweets I can, I feel so compelled by that dratted bow. It calls to me, a magical voice made audible by the golden earrings I was born with, the ones welded to my very skin.

It's not like I make a habit of stealing things. Well, at least not expensive things, anyway. But the beautiful weapon calls to me, begging me to hold it in my hands. It is like an ancient legend made real, an entire history of Bharat carved into one arching body of silver. I swear it whispers stories to me: stories of gods and demons, princes and sages. It whispers about death, glory, and revenge. And when that is not enough, it promises to reveal the story of my origins, the truth of my mysterious birth.

So I do the only logical thing I can. I take it for my own. The moment I do, of course, the treacherous weapon screams for its master and sends him running. Just my luck.

I run through the forest, chased by Arjun. I am strong and fast, but my magical hearing allows me to track his every quickening footstep, and I know he is swiftly catching up to me. My breath is raw and my foot throbs from twisting it on a banyan root. But I don't have time to feel the pain. I can't afford to get caught and handed over to the patrols, and I certainly don't fancy getting killed. I am young and convinced my story still holds many more chapters. So I run through the humid forest with the stolen weapon on my back. I run, and run, and run.

My shorn hair and patched-up cotton kurta stick to me. My thighs burn. I barely duck in time as Arjun's arrow whizzes past my head and pierces the trunk of a nearby mango tree. The bark splinters like a thundercrack. Despite the fact that the arrow was meant for my skull, I am seriously impressed. *I want to learn how to shoot like that,* I think, even as I push myself to run faster.

"Stop, thief!" Arjun's voice echoes off the thick-leaved trees. "You, boy, stop!"

Stopping is obviously not an option. I know what the patrol does to thieves. And that is nothing compared to what they would do if they found out who I really am. Not a poor village boy, as I am dressed, but a girl. Not just a girl, but an unnatural thing with metal fused into her flesh. The patrol wouldn't just chop off my criminal hand—they'd chop off my head to keep it company.

And I like both my head and my hands. I like them a lot, thank you very much.

So I ignore the boy and keep running with his stolen bow on my back. My vision gets blurry from the sweat dripping into my eyes, but I don't slow down.

Another arrow comes screaming by my sensitive ear, almost slicing a hair from my head.

"Didn't your mother ever tell you it was nice to share? You clearly own more than one bow!" I yell.

"Turn around and speak about my mother to my face!" Arjun's fury leaps from his voice like sparks.

Obviously, I don't. I may be a thief, but unlike people who leave piles of food and gorgeous weapons unguarded outside their forest huts, I'm no fool. And this warrior monk is an amazing shot, even with his target running zigzag through the dense trees. I'm not about to stop and help his aim.

I jump over a fallen branch; leaves and twigs crunch under my injured foot as it reconnects hard with the earth. I bite back a cry of pain and push myself to keep going.

I should have gotten away with it. All that food was sitting on the wide porch of the hut, just asking to be taken. I was careful, listening a long while to the steady breathing of the six sleepers inside the hut; everyone dreaming during their midday nap, the sweltering time of day no sane person stays awake. Had Arjun's bow not called to me, they never would have known. Had his bow not called to me, I would have escaped and made it home to feed my adoptive parents, maybe see some color come into their gray cheeks at my bountiful find.

But that's not the way destiny works, I guess.

Because I don't get away. It is rainy season; the leaves are slick under my feet. I slip on a swath of soggy palm fronds and fall hard. My ankle screams a cracking agony. I can't get up. I have no option but to turn Arjun's own weapon on him as he nears, barreling toward me through the forest like a furious stag.

But I can't kill him. Unlike the rich, who are used to throwing precious things away, I know the value of a life, and I can't bring myself to kill even someone seeking my death. So I aim above Arjun's head, dislodging several bumpy green jackfruit, which come crashing down on him, cracking open on his head in their pungent splendor.

The falling, pummeling jackfruit stop Arjun in his tracks.

My heart is screaming in fear. But instead of turning his weapons on me, he does something totally unexpected. He laughs. He laughs and laughs, jackfruit insides running down his thick hair, over his dark face, and into his pale, silken kurta. The handsome boy doubles over, trying to catch his breath between whoops of laughter. The epic hero Arjun laughs so much, the birds join him, the forest animals dance in play. He laughs so much he makes me start laughing, too, without even knowing if I am laughing from nervousness or in response to his unadulterated joy.

"You bastard," he finally manages with a dazzling grin that shoots across his face like a shaft of silver lightning. "How'd you get to be such a good shot?"

Remedies certainly exist for all curses, but no remedy can avail those cursed by their mother.

—*The Mahabharat*

The world is full of monsters, this I know; monsters with teeth and claws, whose eyes glow wild with hunger for your flesh. But there are other monsters, too, ones who do not feed on flesh, but souls.

My birth mother was such a monster. The day I was born, she left me to drown in the river. Of course, there is a long history of parents in Bharat killing baby girls—for it is boys who house and feed parents in their old age, boys who are able to perform their parents' death rites. It is said that girls, from their birth, do not belong to their parents but to the families of their future husbands. We are expensive mouths to feed, burdens whose births are too often mourned while the arrivals of our brothers are celebrated.

And of course I wasn't *just* a girl, but an abomination, born with metal attached to my flesh—golden earrings and armbands that give me heightened hearing, aim, and strength.

So my birth mother cursed me, threw me into the river. I was found and brought up by a chariot-wheel maker and his wife, poor in everything but love. Yet as I grew up, despite the care of my adoptive parents, there wasn't a day I didn't wonder about the mother who had thrown me away—was she old or young? High- or lowborn? Did I inherit my thick hair from her, or maybe my determination?

Even the most lowly street sweeper of Kuru can recite at least seven generations of his forefather's names, but I can't even remember the first thing about my mother's face. I used to think that the lack of a past was the unluckiest sort of fate. I didn't realize that knowing the truth would be even worse.

When shown the door, take the door, but put no trust in kings.
—The Mahabharat

It is Arjun who first trains me in the ways of war. After that day in the forest with the jackfruit, I return his bow, but only after extracting a promise to have him teach me the warrior arts. The fact that he agrees surprises us both in equal measure. Maybe he feels the same connection between us that I do. Knowing he would never agree to train a girl in battle, I keep up appearances.

The day I first meet him to train, Arjun waits for me in the ancient forest. We are dressed similarly, in loose white cotton kurtas and pajamas. Only mine are threadbare, while his clothes are a heavy, expensive cloth embroidered with silvery thread. The shining white of his garments sets off his dark skin, making me conscious of my fraying, unadorned clothes.

"You came, rich boy. I didn't think you would." My words are like armor, a show of bravado. But I am nervous. I can hear everything—the early morning birdcalls, the waking forest, his breath, his heart beating steady and strong. Arjun's blue eyes seem brighter in the morning light, the color startling in his dark face. They pull me in with their familiarity. I know him. I know him.

"Ready to learn the ways of war?" Arjun smiles in an easy way, making me unsure where to look.

Before I can come up with a response, my stomach gives an earth-shattering grumble.

Arjun laughs, throwing me a green guava—tart and delicious. "Can't have you fainting during training."

"Thank you." I pause mid-bite, feeling an unfamiliar shyness. "So you're really going to teach me the ways of war?"

Arjun is doing some sort of warrior's dance with a long staff, bending and thrusting, blocking and twirling. "I said I would, and a warrior never breaks his word." He flips his staff high in the air, expertly catching it on its way down.

"I'm ready to learn everything you know," I say, hungry for his skill and knowledge.

"It's just the basics." Arjun raises a dark eyebrow at me. "Don't dream of winning any glorious battles just yet."

His words prick my ego. "Bloody hell, I won't. You saw how I hit that jackfruit yesterday."

"A lucky shot," he says. "How old are you anyway, boy? You haven't a bit of hair on your face yet."

"Old enough." I strategically move between Arjun and the vivid rays of the sun so he can't see me clearly. The sun warms my back like a caress, making me feel braver.

Unfortunately, beginner warrior training really isn't the stuff of legends and glory. Mostly it comprises holding Arjun's bow for hours without moving. For days, it is the same. As I stand, bow outstretched, arms trembling, Arjun quizzes me on the ethical rules of war-making.

"During war, when does fighting begin and end?"

"No earlier than sunrise, and it must end exactly at sunset."

"Under what circumstances can two warriors duel?"

"If they have the same weapons and are on the same type of mount," I grit out through clenched teeth. "On foot, horseback, elephant, or chariot."

"Good." Arjun is pacing around me, but I stare straight ahead, eyes fixed, sweat dripping from my hair down my neck. "What are the sixth, seventh, and eighth rules of combat?"

"No warrior may kill or injure an unarmed or unconscious warrior. No warrior may kill or injure an animal or person not taking part in war."

"What are the rules regarding a warrior who has surrendered or turned away?"

"No warrior may kill or injure a warrior who has surrendered. No warrior may kill or injure a warrior whose back is turned."

In that moment, I do not know that I am pointing out the ways that Arjun himself has broken the warrior's code every time our tale has been told.

I do not know I am outlining the dishonorable ways that Arjun will kill me.

It is the righteous upon whom both the past and the future depend.

—*The Mahabharat*

Most epics tell the stories of kings. But I will tell you a story of two queens: one made of iron and will, the other of magic and mantras.

Most say the Kaurav queen Gandhari tied that silken band around her eyes from her marriage day onward to give wifely company to her blind husband, King Dhritarashtra. But I say that Gandhari blindfolded herself because she did not want to see a world where even a king could be dethroned by his brother because of a disability, where girls and women could be treated unjustly and even she, a queen, could do nothing about it.

Queen Gandhari became pregnant. Her belly grew for many years, yet she did not deliver a child. Finally, she commanded her maid to beat her stomach. When Gandhari birthed an iron ball, she ordered that it be cut into one hundred and one pieces and placed in water vessels. One hundred of those iron pieces became the iron-willed Kaurav princesses, and the last, their fierce brother, Durjadhan. With that one fateful pregnancy, Gandhari created the entire Kaurav clan. Which goes to show what a stubborn woman with a will of iron can do.

Gandhari's sister-in-law was Queen Kunti, wife of the younger royal brother, Pandu; and mother of Arjun and the Pandavs. As a young girl, Kunti was given a boon by a mystic sage, a mantra of such power it could call down any god from the heavens to give her a child. When she was still unmarried, Kunti brought this mantra boldly to her lips, drawing Shurjo, god of the sun, to her bed. The child born from that union was powerful and golden, shining with magical earrings and golden armbands. But Kunti, unlike her future sister-in-law, could not bind her eyes to social proprieties. She was ashamed to have given birth out of wedlock, even to a sun-blessed child. She did not have the courage to chop up her reputation like it was nothing more than a ball of iron. So Kunti sent the shining baby down the river, hoping that it wouldn't die, while hoping, on another level, that it would.

> *To save a family, abandon a man; to save the village, abandon a family; to save the country, abandon a village; to save the soul, abandon the earth.*
>
> —*The Mahabharat*

Over our weeks of training, I grow to love Arjun. Not the romantic love of a woman to a man, but something far greater. I love him like a comrade, a sibling, like he is a reflection of my very best self. I do not know, of course, how this love will be betrayed. I do not know yet how this love must be protected.

Before I go to meet Arjun one morning, I head down to the river to fetch water for my family. On the banks, I see a beautiful dark-skinned woman holding a pitcher at her waist. Her sari shimmers like crashing waves and her sleek hair tumbles wetly down her back.

"I am the river Jamuna," she says. "Twin sister to Jōm, the god of death."

I bow in fear and respect. "What do you want with me, O goddess?"

"I love my brother. He is the other half of my soul," Jamuna says. "But still, I must warn you of his plans for you."

"I am to die?" My magical ears hear the life all around me: the fish swimming in the river, cool water gliding over their scales; the birds chittering overhead. The leaves keeping rhythm to their song. Among this plentiful life, death seems like an illusion. "Is there nothing I can do to stop it?"

"A war is coming." Jamuna's voice trips like water over stones. "Which has begun and ended many times already. But in every version of this tale, you are the one who must be sacrificed."

"What if I don't want to die?" My body trembles, but I am more angry than afraid.

"Everyone has their dharma," Jamuna answers. "As the river must run to the sea, your path has always been this: to be killed in the great war by Prince Arjun."

"Arjun?" My steady heart skips wildly like a small animal hunted. "But he's become like a brother to me."

Jamuna studies me, unblinking. "He is like a brother because he *is* your brother. But he is also the one who brings your death."

The goddess tells me of my mother, my five brothers, my royal origins. She tells me how the future queen threw away her firstborn, her golden, sun-kissed baby girl. She tells me about my tragic role in this epic story that goes on and on without change, goes on without end.

My fury at all this unfairness makes me want to become a dam, something strong and unmoving that can change the course of mighty waters. "But this time, you came to warn me, despite the love you declare for your brother. So you must want a different ending. You must know how can I rewrite this story."

Jamuna smiles, then runs her fingers through the river. As she does, I see them. The ghost girls standing in the mist midstream, half submerged and transparent, perched somewhere between life and death, legend and curse. And I know, without having to be told, that they have been sacrificed by their birth parents, just like I was. But unlike me, they were not plucked from the water by kind villagers. Thrown away like so much trash, they went all the way down the river to Jōm's kingdom.

Who will remember our names? the ghost girls ask me. *Who will write epic songs and stories about us?*

I hear all their clamoring voices, all their sad tales. They are the over one hundred million girls and women gone missing in Bharat—girl babies who have been killed, or neglected, or prevented from being born. One hundred million souls robbed of their time on Earth.

Sister, you must avenge us! the ghost girls cry.

Their voices are so jagged with pain, they are weapons that cleave my heart. "But how can I avenge so many deaths?"

You must break the wheel. Kill the hero, they say. *Only then can there be a new ending to this old story.*

"What hero must I kill?" I fear I already know the answer.

Arjun. They name him over and over again. *Arjun. Arjun. Arjun.*

I want to plug my ears. Like Gandhari, I want to bind a cloth around my head and refuse to stand witness to this part of the story. But I cannot refuse to hear. I cannot refuse to see.

This cannot be. I want to scream, run, fight.

I turn to Jamuna, searching for answers, but all trace of divinity is gone.

The ghost girls disappear from sight, too, but their stories have burrowed permanently underneath my skin. I may have been the lucky one, plucked out of the river of my fate, but they are no different from me. We throwaway girls have no one to value the weight of our souls.

From that day on, I no longer train with Arjun. Because there is only one way for a girl to come to terms with the fact that it is her own brother who has always, and will always, end her story. I burn the love I have for him and smear myself with the ashes.

I prepare with all my determination for the battle against not just one, but all my brothers. I make myself ready for war, gripping Arjun's bow tightly in my hands. I will not only defeat him, but defeat him with his own weapon.

"What will you do if Karna is able to kill me?" Arjun asked Krishna.

Krishna smiled and replied, "The sun will fall, the earth shatter into a thousand fragments, and fire lose its heat before he kills you. But if he does, it is a sign that the end of the world has come. As for me, I shall kill him with my bare hands."

—The Mahabharat

The heart of war is upon us, and there is no longer night or day. The sky remains a steely gray as we coat the earth in the reds and browns of death. The gods have abandoned us, children bored of their play—all save Krishna, who drives Arjun's chariot through the bleeding battlefield on the wings of time.

I fight because I fight for something larger than myself.

But my own life and death somersault over the edge of a knife. Pain and victory dance hand in hand. With each arrow released and each sword thrust of this battle, I feel myself inching closer to Jōm's embrace.

I am no longer the Karna I was before. Not daughter, sister, student, or friend. Just warrior. I call on all my teachings, sending divine energies through each and every shower of arrows. But Arjun meets me volley for volley, his arrows hitting mine in midair. When they do so, our weapons melt from the heat of their own power, folding into one another until they become indistinguishable. We murmur mantras of war, our voices falling and rising together in a chorus of death music. He is my brother, he is my friend, he is my enemy. I turn any remaining scrap of love I have in me into hatred, or something like it.

This war is like a machine, grinding us all in its unstoppable gears.

Arjun looks tired. His face is smeared with dirt and blood, his fingers caked with it. His blue eyes, once like lotus-shaped pools, are distraught, aching, numb. He too has changed— for one year, I hear, he traded his princely robes for a silken sari and became the musician and dance teacher Brihannala, neither man nor woman but a third gender altogether. What has he learned from this other self, this other life he has lived while exiled from his kingdom, his gender, his privilege?

We are evenly matched. I can meet Arjun's every volley, but I can't get the advantage. I feel my power ebbing. I want nothing more than to end this here, to lay down my bow and arrow. But I'm not brave enough. I feel the weight of my own soul, its power precious, unlike any other's. There are so many things I have yet to see and do. And I want so desperately to have a chance, to live. At my wit's end, I send Arjun's way the Nagastra, the snake arrow, which shoots through the air with the power of the serpent underworld.

There is no fighting the Nagastra, that I know. Suddenly, with a flash of insight, I realize what I have done.

"No! This will kill him!" I shriek, weeping tears of triumph and sorrow at the death of the great Arjun, my brother.

I leap from my chariot, as if I can somehow stop the flight of the arrow with my own body. But there is no need. Krishna holds up his hand and stops the arrow from piercing Arjun's breast.

The reverberations of Krishna's magic intervention are so great, they shake the atmosphere, making cracks and fissures in the ground upon which we fight. There is a horrible sucking sound, and I don't have to look to know that the greedy earth has claimed my chariot wheel.

There is a crack, as the spokes on my wheel are broken.

"Stop the fighting!" yells Arjun. He raises his hand and stills his weapon as I struggle to dislodge my broken chariot wheel from the earth.

This is what the ancient scrolls foretold—the story of how, in this and every age, I have lost my life.

Arjun tries to descend, but Krishna spins his discus and

prevents the prince from leaving his chariot. "Let me go, Krishna, I would help her."

"That is not the way this story ends, my prince. I have told you that," says the man with 108 names.

The gods are stubborn. Relentless and all-powerful. They are possessive of their stories, and do not want them altered, like writers precious about each and every word they have bled onto the page.

And so I struggle against my own story. My back and arms heave at the wheel, and my feet slip in the mud.

"Release your arrows, sire," I hear Krishna say.

I pull with all my might upon the wheel, but it does not budge. I look up, my brown eyes locking on Arjun's blue ones, bright again in his midnight face.

"No." Arjun's voice is strained. He does not break our gaze. "I will not fire on Karna anymore. Not now that her chariot is broken."

"You must defeat her," says Krishna. "This is the way it has always been and the way it will always be."

My body falls deeper into the soft mud, and I hear those ghost girls all around me again, only this time we are all waist-deep in the river of the earth.

"We have been pushing this wheel all our lives," they whisper. "How much longer must we endure?"

I have failed them. I have failed to change the story, begin the world better and anew. I want to scream. I want to rage. But there is nothing I can do but keep pushing my burden, trying to dislodge the wheel of our future from the mud.

"*Father, help me,*" I cry. But the sky is the color of ash and death. The sun does not answer. I do not even try to call for my mother Kunti's aid. She has made it clear which child she wants to see live, and which to die.

From somewhere, I find the strength to keep fighting against the yawning, hungry earth.

"I won't fire," Arjun argues with his divine charioteer. "Such an act would go against everything I have been taught—more importantly, everything I am." But my brother's determination fails, his voice trembles before the will of the gods.

I flail desperately, calling on my sister warriors, every friend, and every enemy I have ever known. But Krishna has made sure we are alone, trapped in a desolate corner of the same old tale. I call on my very best self, the self I have been growing and cherishing within me, the self I was waiting to become. But my future only sinks further and further away. I choke back a sob. So this is how I will die. Ignominious, muddy, kneeling like an animal on the ground.

In my struggle, I slash my hands open on a broken spoke. Blood rushes down my arms, soaking me. I shut my eyes, wishing the earth could swallow me as she has my chariot.

"Do it, Arjun," I finally say. I open my eyes to see the sky one last time.

"I won't!" cries the prince. But I can see him struggling. The old story has him under its spell.

It's time. I know it. I feel my foremothers and forefathers behind me, whispering my name, gathering me in their arms, preparing me to meet my destiny. I feel the goddess rise above me on her tiger, her ten mighty arms raised in power and protection.

My feet have planted roots, and I cannot move.

"You cannot change this tale," Krishna declares. His smile is sad, but victorious. "It is as it has always been and must always be. There are only two sides—heroes and villains, victors and vanquished."

Arjun is losing the fight just as I am. The old stories rob him just as they rob me. He raises his arm, but he has dropped his weapon. A last attempt to save me. His face is streaked with tears, but his eyes blaze. And in that expression, I see all our selves—prince and pauper, monk and thief, dancer and warrior, man, woman, and all the genders beyond.

I awaken from my battle sleep like the sun rising on a new dawn. I suddenly know what I have to do. I toss my weapon, the bow I stole, the bow we shared, back to him. It screams in betrayal, swearing it will bring about my destruction.

My brother grabs the ancient weapon out of the air, as if against a great wave of water, and breaks it, his arm trembling and straining against so many centuries of oppressive stories.

"Forgive me, sister, for not being stronger in all the times before," cries Arjun, the body of the broken weapon limp in his hands.

The scene of the battlefield disappears and reappears, as if transforming into something new.

"There is a different way," I say, my voice gaining strength with every word. "There are new stories to be told."

> *Love, well made, can lead to liberation.*
> —*The Mahabharat*

Together, we siblings are the sun and moon, the earth and sky, the flowing rivers and unmoving mountains. We are a single banyan tree comprising a mighty forest. We are death, and life, and love, all together. We remember our origins but leave behind the old stories that do not do us all justice. Together, we celebrate new ways of being ourselves. We dream of the new stories we can tell, and the new worlds we can together create.

AUTHOR'S NOTE

Nobel Prize–winning economist Amartya Sen once posited there were approximately 100 million missing girls and women in Asia due to the continent's widespread patterns of son bias. These girls were never born due to sex-selective abortion, or died from infant neglect or femicide. "Daughter of the Sun" imagines what would happen if those girls were to be reborn, seeking revenge. What if Karna, one of the most misunderstood epic heroes of The Mahabharat, *were to return as a warrior woman to lead this vengeful women's army?*

ART BY NEHA KAPIL

WHAT THE WINDS STOLE
By Sabaa Tahir

It began with a sound, small, unnoticeable to the ears of most, but like thunder in the bones of the earth. A *plop*. A stone of lavender glass from a warm tropical sea fell into a mountain lake thousands of miles away. The glass was unremarkable, having languished in the sweaty paw of a small male human child until, enamored by the fish in the waters of the Lake, he'd let it slip.

The sound was unremarkable, too, a sad blip that did not signify the love the child had for the glass, nor the lengths he would go to see it returned.

Hiba, Peri of the Lake, who had lived in the mountains above its shores for eons, perked up at the sound. She lumbered forth to snatch up the precious glass. It took a few tries, but after a moment she grasped it in the clawlike protrusion that served as a hand. There it thrummed, singing of faraway seas shaded in undulating blues and greens, of the *bloooop* of jellyfish dancing in the shoals.

When the child realized he'd lost his bauble, he wailed and turned out his pockets, and perhaps Hiba could have returned it then. But it was a pretty thing full of memory, and the child was a flame to be blown out soon enough. In an hour, he'd be occupied with a kabob or a bowl of fruit chaat and he'd forget all about the sea glass.

While the child's mustachioed father comforted him, Hiba headed north. If she'd had her wings, she'd have shot straight into the sky and flown to her cave. If she'd had her voice, she'd have hissed curses at the old storytellers sitting cross-legged on the shores of the Lake, spinning lies about her. If she'd had solidity or strength to her gelatinous form, she'd have tipped over the rainbow-hued boats plying the water, instead of merely ruffling the clothing of the people within and taking their things.

But wings, voice, and body had been stolen from her. Instead she oozed along the ground, sluglike. If the humans *could* see her, they'd see an oily blob the color of dead roses, much like the shape of an overgrown mole. A far cry from the bright-eyed winged beauty who'd once inspired a prince to abandon a kingdom for her.

Hiba didn't like to think about that. She exited the water and slowly made her way up the scrubby hills to a cave that overlooked the Lake, the valley, and the snowclad behemoth mountains to the north.

Hiba's cave was expansive, meant to house more than one barely substantial peri, even with her treasure hoard. But her sisters, who'd once shared the cave with her, had long since passed on. She had said goodbye to so many of them when they gave up and departed the world. Some were heartbroken, others sick, and others simply ancient and tired. *I cease*, she'd heard, over and again, two words that had torn her world from her. Until only Hiba remained. She'd tried to end it, too. Many times. But because of her curse, when Hiba said *I cease*, nothing happened. So she clung to life, a reluctant and surly barnacle.

She deposited the sea glass in the cave, nestling it amid gold bracelets and silk scarves, a fat black pearl on a silver chain, and a small hillock of car and motorcycle keys. She chuckled nastily at the sight of them. Of all the things she stole, the keys caused the most ruckus. She especially liked it when the humans accused each other of theft. They were desperately attached to their ugly steel chariots, relying on them for freedom of movement. A sad existence.

Though the humans could leave, at least. She, on the other hand, was bound here by that damned curse, laid by a prince who tricked her into giving away her powers and then condemned her to this form for eternity.

Hours later, Hiba inched back to the Lake and wound her way between the boats until she found a particularly vapid-looking human girl admiring her own reflection in the water. The peri submerged herself before surging upward.

She had almost no mass to her form. Enough to thieve small items, and enough to splash a teaspoon's worth of lake into the girl's face. She grinned at the girl's curse of surprise. To humans, Hiba was invisible. No more than a ripple in the air, if that.

"You have angered Hiba, the Peri of the Lake!" the old man rowing the boat chuckled, and Hiba seethed, hearing her name spoken aloud. *Gift*, her name meant. She hated it, for her existence was anything but.

"Hiba has a special hatred for pretty young creatures, for they remind her of her lost love, Shezada Khan, the prince for whom this lake is named."

The peri snarled and slithered toward the shore, cursing her slowness, her useless form. She wanted to see the boy from whom she'd stolen the sea glass, to see if he was still weeping.

Much to her disappointment, the child no longer cried, but he had waded waist-deep into the lake. He plunged his little hands into the water again and again, bringing up gray stones and blue stones and green ones and black ones.

But no lavender.

Hiba twined around him, affectionate as a cat at dawn.

You'll never see it again, she whispered. He wouldn't hear the words—no human had seen or heard her since that crook Shezada Khan had traded her wings and voice and form for power. What a fool she'd been, following him away from her Lake. *I wish to show you my castle—a most wonderful place, dear Hiba.*

Her sisters had warned her not to trust him, but she'd been a vain and stupid peri, convinced they were jealous that, while they pined after shepherds and merchants, she had a prince hanging on her every word.

Of course, there had been no castle. He'd forfeited his kingdom when he went adventuring and didn't return for ten years. Instead, he'd taken Hiba to a cave far in the jungles to the south, where three of the winds were lying in wait. They bound her and stole her wings, her voice, and her body. Then they laid their curse upon her, a curse of three parts: to never leave the Lake; to remain in this blobbish, useless, and invisible form; and to never die.

The curse will only be lifted if you retake your powers, the winds told her. But there was no way to do so. How could she retake her powers if she had none?

She'd begged for mercy. She'd tried to remind Shezada of their love. But he'd laughed at her. *For a eons-old creature, you are remarkably stupid, Hiba. Your powers are wasted on you.*

Shezada Khan had, in exchange for this treachery, used the winds to win back his pathetic little kingdom. There he'd ruled for half a century, fathered a passel of brats, and then died. Within two generations, his kingdom had been absorbed into a neighboring one, his progeny scattered.

He'd traded a few decades of decadence for Hiba's entire

future. Because that was what selfish, vile humans did.

Hiba turned from her thoughts back to the little boy whose stone she'd taken. He, at least, would feel her venom.

It's mine forever, she hissed. *And I shan't give it back.*

"Why?" the boy whispered, and Hiba was so surprised that she froze, just inches from his face. He appeared to look directly at her, his huge brown eyes red-rimmed, dark lashes speckled with tears.

But he couldn't possibly see her. He definitely hadn't heard her.

Because this world takes, Hiba screamed, remembering her sisters, all of whom had left her. *And the sooner you learn that lesson, child, the more prepared you will be to survive it.*

The child didn't hear. He merely turned away from her. So Hiba turned away, too, crawling slowly up the mountains to her clearing, a place where she sought calm and the comfort of the stars.

That night, they seemed cold and angry, as if they disapproved of what she'd done.

After that, she stopped stealing from children quite so much, and turned her attentions more to adults. Over the years, her hoard grew and Hiba buried the sea glass beneath bangles and pashminas and ruby-studded tikkas. She never took it out. She tried to bury the very thought of the glass and the way the child had said *why* and how lost he had looked.

But the boy did not forget.

One winter many years later, Hiba slithered down to her cave after visiting her clearing. The Lake was buried in snow, the glaciers thick and forbidding. She liked mornings like this, when the clouds rolled in over the mountains and the mist lay like a sheepskin over the land. The Lake grew cold and depthless, cloudy as the jade bracelets that littered her hoard. The humans departed, and all was silent.

Sometimes, the snow peris visited from the north, bored in the winter months without any human climbers to torment. Unlike her, her cousins hadn't been stupid enough to fall in love with traitorous human scum, so they still had their wings and voices and bodies. They brought bags of tea from the foothills of Darjeeling, far to the east. They built fires strong enough for even Hiba to feel and steeped the tea for hours so she could inhale the scent even if she couldn't taste it.

The peris of Intihamdimafak, the mountain humans called K2, were her favorite. Intihamdimafak—"Scratches at the Underbelly of the Heavens"—was dangerous largely because its peris made sport of the humans who tried to conquer the mountain.

Though Hiba couldn't communicate with them beyond a few moans and grunts, they visited every year, so when Hiba felt the wind change, she assumed it was her cousins.

She went to greet them, only to find that her visitor was not peri, but human. Alone, hiking over a nearby rise, hardly out of breath despite the climb. He was young—only just come into adulthood, and as he approached, he glanced up, pinning the peri with a dark and strangely familiar gaze.

"Hiba," he said, and she flinched at the name, for time had not lessened her dislike of it. "Peace be upon you. I have waited long years to seek you out."

Hiba stared at the boy, bewildered.

"You must be wondering who I am," he said. "My name is Sule. And I believe you have something that belongs to me."

Then Hiba knew the young man. She remembered how she'd relished his tears. How he'd asked *why*.

"The sea glass," Sule said. "You stole it. I would like it back, please."

Hiba curled in on herself protectively, snarling at him. The fool—as if he had the right to ask her for anything! He'd dropped the glass in *her* Lake. It was hers to claim.

She observed him balefully, narrowing her eyes.

He was thinner than he'd been as a child, all the baby fat gone. His age was hard to determine. Nineteen, perhaps, or twenty—the same age as her peri form, if she'd still had it. Had she been a human, she'd not want to meet him in a dark alley, for though not imposingly tall, he was lean and mus- cled, with a hawkish intensity that made her squirm under his gaze.

"Perhaps you're wondering why I want it," Sule said. "It's worthless, after all. Nothing but glass. If I tell you, will you give it to me?"

Hiba shook her head emphatically enough that Sule

understood. It was his turn to consider her. She was embarrassed of the way she crouched upon the ground, of her flat red eyes and viscous form. Would that he could see her as she was long ago. He would never dare to demand his pathetic little stone then. He would cower in fear.

"May I sit?" He waited for her to nod and then dropped down onto a flat boulder outside her cave, pulling a silver bottle from his pack and drinking from it. The muscles in his throat jumped, a distinctly human movement that reminded her of Shezada Khan. She looked away.

"You weren't always like this," he said after he'd drunk his fill. "And I'm certain it's not how you want to stay. If I help you, if I return what was stolen from you, will you return my stone?"

Hiba laughed, a sharp and bitter thing. The boy raised his eyebrows, astute enough to interpret the shift in her body.

"You're amused? But I ask you, Hiba, do you have any better options? The storytellers say many things. They say that you gave your powers to Shezada Khan. But I don't think that's true. I heard a different story—that your powers were taken from you. By the winds themselves."

Slowly, Hiba nodded.

"Which wind did the stealing? The Wolf of the Far-Northern Desert? The Pillar at the Heart of the Damson Tree? The Snake of the Centerland Jungle?"

For the third time since making his acquaintance, Hiba regarded Sule with astonishment. Only one human had ever known of such Mysteries. Shezada Khan had also known that the winds had multiple directions but separate homes. That there were seven of them, not four. And that their names held power.

"Don't be so astonished," the boy said. "My mother's mother's mother is the Singer of the Azure Seas."

Hiba was skeptical, for this boy had nothing of that bedazzling peri. The Singer was legendary for her beauty, her many lovers—and her aloofness. She ignored her fellow peris and her legions of progeny.

"She didn't much care about me," Sule went on, "but her domain has many libraries." He smiled, and in the flash of his white teeth, Hiba felt her stomach lurch. She wished for fangs then, that she might bite him.

"Right," Sule said. "You can't tell me which wind it is, so I'll guess, and you nod." He repeated the three winds he'd already spoken of, and Hiba remained stubbornly still. But then he spoke a fourth name.

"The Crone Who Reigns over the Five Rivers," he said. Hiba shuddered, remembering the way the Crone had stared greedily at her body. The Crone had wanted it, for she did not have one of her own, and Hiba's had been young and strong.

Sule understood. "Thank you," he said. "I will see you soon."

Hiba scoffed and waved him off. She would go to her clearing. She would speak with the stars and the stream that ran nearby, and she would forget this human.

But even as he headed toward the Lake and out of sight, she watched him, unable to look away.

After Sule left, Hiba resolved not to think of him. The Crone's home was leagues away. There were mountain ranges and rivers and wars in between, and she did not expect to see Sule again for some time, if ever.

But his presence had shaken something loose, and shortly after he left, she found herself wandering through her spoils. She could pretend she didn't know where the lavender sea glass was, but she knew every inch of her trove. It was wrapped in the pink scarf of a Lahori socialite.

The glass appeared simple enough. Quiet. Hiba nosed it into the light. It changed color, depending on which way she turned it, from rose to deep purple to softest lilac.

It was a unique specimen, rounded and softened into the shape of a teardrop. But beautiful as it was, it was still nothing but glass. Why did it matter so much to Sule? Hiba hated that she cared enough to be curious. She cast the glass aside.

Over the next few months, she snuck into the winter homes of the shepherds and perpetrated tiny meannesses: putting out fires and pulling washing down from the line and upsetting breakfast dishes. She pestered sleeping bears and hunting leopards. These were not easy tasks for her. They took time and effort and intention, for her molelike form was limited. But they kept her occupied, and for that, she was grateful.

After a time, the Lake froze and the nearby glacier crept

close. When the days were at their shortest, Hiba found herself slinking slowly along the ice-crusted coastline of the Lake, remembering her long ago humiliation.

She should have realized the winds would try to take her power. Their own was limited. The Sun-Touched Lion of the Western Sea could stop time. But otherwise, they were bound to their own domains. They could not walk among humans. They could speak but not sing or laugh or joke or tell lies.

And so they became thieves. Somehow, they'd roped Shezada Khan into their scheme, and because of that, she would never trust a human again. Not even this boy Sule, with his dark eyes and polite words and—

"Peace be upon you, Hiba."

She turned to find Sule approaching, his curling dark hair a bit longer, his skin sun-darkened to a deep, glowing brown. His clothes were more tattered than they'd been the last time she saw him, with flashes of muscled skin showing through the holes in his shirt.

Over Sule's broad shoulders, he'd slung a large sack. He put it gently on the ground and withdrew what looked like a glowing golden cloth.

"Your body, Peri."

Hiba stared at it, moving with aching slowness toward it until she could touch it. For a moment, she felt nothing. She was as she had been for hundreds of years, a sentient blob, a slug with hands good only for thieving and a body that could barely smell or feel.

And then—then—

She dropped to her knees and buried her fingers in the cold earth, relishing the brush of eyelashes on her cheeks, the freezing wind swirling down off the mountains, the rough scrape of dead grass beneath her legs. The earthy scent of lake ice filled her nostrils, stronger than it had in centuries. She looked down at her hands—*hands*—which shimmered with light. She picked up a stone and squeezed. Long ago, she'd been able to crush rocks in her fingers. No longer.

Disappear, she thought, and her body flickered and was gone before quickly reappearing, her skin unused to obeying her.

No matter. She was weak now, but she would relearn the magic within her own body.

She did not know how long she knelt there, marveling at being able to feel again. When she finally sat up, a jacket had been thrown over her—the tattered remnants of Sule's garb—and night had fallen. The human was curled up against a nearby rock, shivering.

"T-t-tell me," he said through chattering teeth, "which wind is next?"

Again, Sule surprised her. For she was certain he'd demand his sea glass after so momentous a feat. She was, in fact, relishing the opportunity to turn her back on him—to ignore him completely. Then she noticed his lips were blue.

He *had* returned her body. And long ago, when she had still cared, hospitality had been sacred to her.

Come inside, she tried to say, but it came out as an awful rasp, almost a gargle. So instead, she stood and gestured, wrapping the jacket around herself to cover her nakedness—humans were so fussy about that sort of thing—and led the way to her cave.

Her fists bunched as they entered, and she watched him carefully, wondering if he would attempt harm. She would not have feared it if her body did not feel so new. But he merely collapsed before an ever-burning and smokeless fire—a gift from one of the Intihamdimafak peris.

Hiba left him there and went to her stores, finding hand-woven woolen clothing for herself and Sule. He certainly couldn't keep wearing the rags he was in.

After a time, she brought Sule a bucket, a towel, and the clothes. She did not want to hear the crushed-glass grating of her own voice, so she mimed bathing and signaled that she would return with food.

She still did not have her wings, so it was hours before she made her way back with a tureen of goat curry she had stolen from one of the nearby herding settlements. Sule, clean and changed, sat before the fire with his legs folded beneath him, contemplating the dancing flames. He offered her the food first, but she refused—peris ate little, and rarely.

He was looking at her, she noticed then. Intently—almost bemusedly.

"You are . . ." He shook his head and looked away. "You are not what I expected. Where I grew up—in America—there were no stories of peris."

Hiba watched him. America. In Ancient Peri, it was called *Didikinaffisit-suhama*, "Dancing Carpet of Emeralds and Sapphires." It was once green and ancient, filled with peris, for it was endless leagues of river and rock and beauty.

Before humankind ruined it, anyway.

"I didn't learn of your kind until I visited my homeland, Pakistan. My mother is from a village near here," Sule said. "She visits when she can."

Interesting that the Singer had progeny here. Perhaps she had visited long ago, and Hiba, in her fallen state, had not realized.

"My mother told me stories about you," Sule went on. "Ever since I was little."

Stories. Hiba made a snorting sound. They were likely of her thievery. Her malice.

But the human shook his head and his gaze on her was gentle. Careful. "She told me she heard you weeping once, and she thought you must be lonely. She left you flower wreaths sometimes, and when she came back they were always gone."

Hiba did not remember the flower wreaths. She slashed at the earthen ground of her cave with her fingers, drawing a crude lantern. A horizon. An island.

Sule studied the drawing, tracing the sand where her fingers had been moments ago. Then he looked up at her and she found she was caught in his gaze. She saw the Singer in him now. In the way the lamplight was reflected in his eyes and his hair, the way his body moved, easy like flame. He reached toward her, running one finger along her arm, and she closed her eyes.

It had been decades since anyone had touched her. Centuries. She let herself bask in his warmth for one blissful moment before jerking away and pointing to the image she'd drawn.

"The Lantern Who Lights the Skies and Sand Pink," he said. "He stole your powers, too?"

Hiba nodded and made a violent shooing motion. Sule bowed his head, giving her a fleeting, unreadable look before exiting.

Hiba expected Sule to take longer to return this time. A few months instead of a few weeks. But her clearing bloomed with wildflowers, then turned green and springy with moss, before fading to reds and golds and back into stark whites and grays. By the time winter lay its cold touch upon the brow of the Lake, there was no sign of the human, and the peri was certain he would not return.

Part of her wanted to look for him. But though she'd tried to leave the Lake, she could not. The curse that bound her here remained unbroken, and when she pushed against the barrier, her skin smoked and burned.

Sule returned to Hiba at the tail end of winter, well over a year after he left. The glacier had not yet retreated and the human crowds had not returned, but the lake ice had thawed and tiny white flowers had begun blooming on the mountainsides.

She was asleep in her cave when she felt the air stir. She

walked outside and stopped short at the sight of a head of dark, curly hair and sparkling brown eyes. He looked older, as if much more than a year had passed.

The sack he held in his hands twitched. His voice was scratchy and tired.

"Your wings, Hiba."

Her name did not sound as awful to her as it used to, and she managed a nod of thanks before taking the wings from the sack. The purple feathers glittered and gleamed in the late winter light, a bit tattered but beautiful and whole. The moment she shrugged them onto her back, they adhered tightly and she shot into the air. She swooped over the Lake and danced in the air currents, so elated that she forgot to cloak herself until she heard the panicked bleating of a mountain goat running from her.

She flew to the edges of the Lake's valley. But there, she smashed into the same burning barrier that had penned her in for centuries.

By the time she landed, her dark hair was disheveled, her clothing ice-crusted from the clouds. And Sule—Sule smiled.

"You are so beautiful when you fly," he said.

She rustled her wings before tucking them away, but did not respond to his comment, suddenly embarrassed.

"Your voice," he said. "That is the last of what was stolen from you, I think."

Hiba nodded and then drew a sun on the ground, and a lion, a high peak, and storm clouds.

"The Sun-Touched Lion of the Western Sea," Sule said. "A formidable foe. Nonetheless, I will bring you your voice. And when I return it to you, you will give me my sea glass."

Hiba threw up her hands and made a slicing motion across her throat. *You're going to die*, she was trying to say.

Sule chuckled. "I won't die," he said. "I have learned much about these winds, and they are not so clever as they think. Though, the Lion will be expecting me. The other two did not know I was coming. The Crone did not even realize I'd stolen your body until the Lantern came complaining to her of my theft."

Hiba gestured for Sule to sit down in the grass outside the entrance to her cave. She disappeared inside, returning a moment later with a pencil and paper she'd stolen from one of the Lake's visitors.

The peri spoke many languages, having nothing better to do than learn them. But her writing was less skilled. Still, she had enough words to communicate. Sule's eyes lit up when he saw the pencil and paper.

How you beat wind? Hiba wrote, trying not to notice the way Sule watched her hand, her wrist. He smiled and looked up at her. She cocked her head, awaiting his reply, and he shook himself.

"The winds are malevolent. But not especially clever. The Crone lives alone and, in the early spring, leaves every evening to bluster in Punjab. It was easy enough to sneak into her home while she was gone. The Lantern was more difficult. He lives on a lagoon far to the east, and it's difficult to get to. He also has many minions, but fortunately for me, he treats them terribly. I persuaded one to help me get inside his home."

Scared? Hiba wrote.

Sula shook his head quickly, but then sighed. "Not scared." He looked at Hiba, dark eyes pinning her. "Lonely. And perhaps confused. About—" He looked like he wanted to say more and Hiba found herself leaning forward. But then Sule shrugged.

"What of you, Peri? Do you not have family?"

Sisters, she wrote. *Dead. They ceased.*

One after the other, they'd said it. *I cease. I cease. I cease.* Hiba heard the words in her nightmares.

I alone, too, she wrote.

"And yet you abide," Sule said softly.

I cannot cease. Curse. I cannot leave Lake. Curse. Until you take my voice from Lion—curse.

Sule rose. "I will go now," he said. "I will win back your voice."

But Hiba shook her head. *Rest. Sleep,* she wrote. *Lion very powerful.*

She stood and gestured for him to follow her. Then she led him up past her cave and into the mountains. She knew, even as they crunched along the snow-covered paths, that she was sinking too deep into friendship with Sule. She knew she shouldn't reveal so much of her heart. But he had returned her body. Her wings. And he wouldn't yet take his stone. She wanted to repay him somehow. Why not with her favorite place?

They traveled up miles of winding trails, their breath heavy and flocculent by the time they arrived at Hiba's clearing. Sule turned slowly, taking in the perfect circle of brown trees; the pure, untouched snow; the glossy black ribbon of the stream cutting through it. He looked above at a sky so close that Hiba could make out the clouds of supernovas, the dancing arms of distant galaxies.

He could not see it with his human eyes, of course, so she reached out to him, touching his arm for a moment, giving him her sight.

Sule gasped, and Hiba's heart filled at the sheer wonder on his face. She followed his gaze upward until she realized how still he was and found that he was staring at her with the same wonder, and something more that had been simmering beneath the surface from the moment he gave her back her skin, something like want.

She released him quickly then, too aware of their closeness, of how completely human he was.

Hiba nodded to the grass and laid next to him, close but not touching. Together they looked up at the stars until they slept. When dawn came, she stirred, and found herself curled into him, his strong arm wrapped around her, his breath light on her neck.

She extricated herself hastily enough that Sule woke with a start.

Go, she wrote in the earth. *Do not die.*

Then she launched herself into the sky, away from him and all that he awoke within her.

Weeks passed. Seasons.

Years.

Sule did not return.

The peris of Intihamdimafak visited, but Hiba was not as amused by their stories now, seeing only Sule's face when they spoke of the humans they pulled from the mountain. Her thieving interested her no more. Disguising herself, she wandered among the humans to listen for a scrap of news, a story—anything that might tell her if Sule still lived.

In time, she began to return the items she'd stolen over the years, leaving bangles and bags, coins and scarves and jewels in and near the Lake. These items did not, of course, go back to those she had stolen them from. But at least they were in the hands of humans again. Soon, those humans made up their own stories about her generosity. And eventually, the Lake ceased to be called Shezada Khan Lake and instead came to be named for the gifts humans found there.

Lake Hiba.

The peri should have been happy. She had her form, her wings, and something she had not even realized she had lost. Her name.

But she could not forget Sule.

Long years after she had last seen the human, long after it was likely he was dead and gone, Hiba returned to her treasure trove, looking for something else to return to the Lake's shores. But it was empty, for she had given away all that she'd taken. All but the lavender sea glass shaped like a tear.

Hiba grasped it in her hand and wept. She burst out of her cave and flew straight up, wanting to feel anything but the pain in her heart, even if it was the fiery burn of the barrier that kept her here.

She flew and flew—until she was long past where the barrier should have been, until she was deep within the range of mountains called Oorthesfehan, "Touched by the Endless Ether."

It was then that she realized Sule must have stolen back her voice. It did not have to be returned to her to break the curse—only removed from the wind who had stolen it.

Finally, she could leave the Lake. She could go anywhere. Even voiceless, she was free of the curse.

If she wished for it, she could cease.

She stopped midair at the thought, her sisters' voices echoing in her head. Were they waiting for her? Or was it only the endless darkness? Either would be a relief. Either would be better than the torture of this world.

Sule.

She could not abandon him. For she knew now that she loved the human. And that she could not live another day without knowing what had become of him.

Hiba tucked the sea glass into her belt and launched herself into the air, heading toward the setting sun, to the lair of the most fierce of winds, the Sun-Touched Lion of the Western Sea. If Sule yet lived, that was where he would be, languishing in that ill wind's prison.

The Lion's domain was at the top of a sharp peak in a distant wild sea that few humans had seen, let alone survived. The peak rose straight up from the ocean like a dagger, forever shrouded in clouds and mist.

Hiba approached at night, cloaking herself and easily avoiding the small, meddlesome creatures the Lion set to guarding his domain. She penetrated the mountain caves, following the stench of death and torment past the Lion's halls and kitchens and chariots, past his gardens and reflecting pools, down into the deep, noisome dungeons.

She steeled herself as she passed cells filled with skeleton after skeleton. Would she recognize Sule's? There were so many. Would she even know if he made it here?

He could be dead already, her doubt whispered. *He could have died a hundred different ways, and you'll never know.* So much time had passed. Nearly five decades.

She wrapped her fist around the sea glass, which seemed to pulse faintly in her hand. If Sule was gone, she felt certain that somehow, she would know.

Hiba walked silently, moving from shadow to shadow, listening. Until she began to hear the same story again and again. Of a human deep within the mountain, a human the Lion especially enjoyed tormenting.

A human who refused to break.

She followed the whispers underground, until she did not know if it was day or night, until she found the darkest, smallest cell.

And there he was.

Shrunken, chained to a ring in the floor, his hair longer than hers, his body scarred in dozens of places. She knew her heart had not yet been burned out of her, for it broke at the sight of him brought so low.

But he was alive. And that was all that mattered.

Sule. Hiba let out a strangled cry, and he looked up.

"I knew you would come," he whispered. "I knew."

His hair had not silvered and his face remained unlined. Time had no meaning to the Lion, and so here, one did not age

Swiftly, Hiba snapped his chains and lifted him in her arms.

"Your—your voice," he whispered to her. "I—"

But she shook her head. She did not care about her voice. Only Sule.

She wound her way through the mountain as silently as she had come. When she finally broke free of the Lion's domain, she heard a deep, echoing laugh on the air.

"You are a fool, peri." The Lion surrounded her, buffeting her in all directions, clawing at Sule and trying to pull him from her and cast him into the sea. "Even if you escape me, he shall not last. Without the protection of my mountain, he will become an old man. You will lose him."

Hiba felt her wings fail. The cold penetrated her very bones and the Lion laughed again, each chortle echoing with the clap of thunder, the crack of lightning. He had always been the most powerful of the winds. The most cruel. She could not withstand him.

Then she felt a sudden, small warmth at her throat. She looked down to find Sule's hands glowing.

"Your voice," he said, and she felt the tingle of ancient magic flowing through her skin as her voice was finally returned to her. "He told me if I gave it up, he would let me go. But—"

"But you wouldn't," Hiba said. Sule's eyes opened wide at hearing her speak, and Hiba wanted to weep, thinking of all she wanted to say to him, if only they had time.

But she did not weep. Instead, she roared.

The Lion did not expect it. He recoiled at the wrath of the peri, and she raced away from him, spinning high into the clouds, darting this way and that, always one length ahead of him. Until she and Sule had left the Sun-Touched Lion of the Western Seas behind altogether. Hiba did not look down, did not speak. She only knew she had to get home, to the Lake, to her clearing. And so she flew as if the Lion still chased her, until finally, the icy blue waters of the Lake appeared below. Hiba dropped into a spiral until her feet touched the dead grass of her clearing.

And there, finally, she looked down at Sule.

She knew he would age after leaving the Lion's island. But

she hadn't expected it to be so swift. His hair was the purest white, his face lined with the struggle of the past fifty years.

"No, my love," she whispered, and pulled out the sea glass. "No. You cannot leave me, for look, I have your glass."

"The glass was a gift from my peri ancestor to her daughter," he whispered. "Passed down parent to child. When I received it, I had a vision of the Singer. She told me that my world would break, and the stone would make me whole. And so it has."

He smiled and lifted a hand to Hiba's face. Then his gaze went past her, to the great wheeling dance of the stars beyond. He breathed once before letting go. In moments, his bones had faded to dust in Hiba's arms.

There, finally whole again, her body glowing, her wings unfurled, her throat alive with magic, Hiba spoke the words she'd heard so many times before, from sister after sister after sister.

"*I cease.*"

And she, too, felt the sweet relief of surrender as she joined her beloved in the after. Hiba, Peri of the Lake, was no more.

AUTHOR BIOS

TRACEY BAPTISTE is a *New York Times* bestselling author. She writes middle grade fantasy (the Jumbies series), non-fiction (*African Icons: Ten People Who Shaped History*), picture books (*Because Claudette*), and young adult (*Angel's Grace*). You can find Tracey online at traceybaptiste.com and Instagram @traceybaptistewrites.

NIKITA GILL is a Kashmiri Irish poet and writer who currently lives in the south of England. She has written seven volumes of poetry and one novel in verse. Her work has been featured on BBC R4 and in the *New York Times*, the *Guardian*, the *Times* (UK), and others and her novel in verse was recently optioned for TV by Peephole Films and Boatrocker Productions.

TANAZ BHATHENA is an award-winning author of young adult fiction. Her books include *Of Light and Shadow, Hunted by the Sky,* which won the White Pine Award and the Bapsi Sidhwa Literary Prize, and *The Beauty of the Moment,* which won the Nautilus Award. Her acclaimed debut, *A Girl Like That,* was named a Best Book of the Year by numerous outlets including the *Globe and Mail, Seventeen,* and the *Times of India.* Born in India and raised in Saudi Arabia and Canada, Tanaz lives in Mississauga, Ontario, with her family. You can visit her at tanazbhathena.com or on Instagram @bhathenatanaz.

OLIVIA CHADHA is the author of the adult literary novel *Balance of Fragile Things.* Her debut young adult novel, *Rise of the Red Hand,* was the winner of the Colorado Book Award for Young Adult Literature and is followed by the sequel, *Fall of the Iron Gods.* She writes speculative fiction and comic books for middle grade, young adult, and adult audiences. She has a PhD from Binghamton University's creative writing program, and her research centers on the history of exile, India's Partition, global folklore and fairy tales, and the relationship between humans and the environment. She lives in Colorado with her family. Find her online at oliviachadha.com.

SANGU MANDANNA was four years old when an elephant chased her family's car down a forest road and she decided to write her first story about it. Seventeen years and many, many manuscripts later, she signed her first book deal. Sangu now lives in Norwich, a city in the east of England, with her husband and kids. She is the author of *The Very Secret Society of Irregular Witches*, the Celestial Trilogy, and more. Find her online at sangumandanna.com or on Instagram @sangumandanna.

TAHIR ABRAR (they/he) is a writer from a Muslim Indian immigrant family. Their baba's stories are the source of their love for Indian storytelling in all forms: everything from Premchand to Akbar Birbal, from family jinn to Vikram Betaal, and from masala films to OTT releases.

SONA CHARAIPOTRA is the author of *Symptoms of a Heartbreak* and *How Maya Got Fierce* and coauthor of *The Rumor Game* and *Tiny Pretty Things*, now a Netflix original series. She earned a master's degree in screenwriting from NYU and an MFA in creative writing from the New School. A working journalist, Sona has held editorial roles at *People*, *Teen People*, ABCNews.com, MSN, several parenting publications, the Barnes & Noble Teen Blog (RIP), and, most recently, as senior editor of trends and features at Parents. com. She has contributed to publications from the *New York Times* to *Teen Vogue*. She is a former We Need Diverse Books board member, and she cofounded Cake Literary, a boutique book packager focused on high-concept diverse titles. Find her on the web talking about books, Bollywood movies, and chai at sonacharaipotra.com.

Hailing from Atlanta, Georgia, **PREETI CHHIBBER** is an author living the dream and writing her favorite characters. The first book in her Peter Parker trilogy, *Spider-Man's Social Dilemma*, came out in 2022. She's also a speaker and freelancer. She's written for *SYFY*, *Polygon*, and *Elle*, among others. Find her cohosting the podcasts *Desi Geek Girls* and *Tar Valon or Bust*. You might recognize her from one of several BuzzFeed "look at these tweets" lists. Find out more at preetichhibber.com or follow her on social media @runwithskizzers.

SHREYA ILA ANASUYA (she/they) is a writer and researcher from Calcutta, India. Her fiction has appeared in the *Magazine of Fantasy & Science Fiction* and *Strange Horizons*, among others, and has been recognized by the Otherwise Fellowship, the Sangam House Residency, the Toto Award for Creative Writing, and the British Science Fiction Association Awards long list. She is currently a PhD candidate at King's College London. For more about Shreya's work, please visit shreyailaanasuya.com or find her on Twitter @thresholdrose.

NAZ KUTUB was born and raised in Singapore and currently lives in Los Angeles with his partner, Benson, and his two furry garbage collectors—Alex and Raffe. He will forever be grateful to fried chicken for being a primary motivator in his early years, and also for preventing him from becoming a fitness model because writing is much more fulfilling. He can be reached at @nazkutub on all social media and at nazkutub.com.

SWATI TEERDHALA is the author of the Tiger at Midnight trilogy. She's passionate about many things, including how to make a proper cup of chai and the right ratio of curd-to-crust in a lemon tart. You can find her on the streets of New York City, dreaming up her next story as well as online @swati-teerdhala.

NAFIZA AZAD is a self-identified island girl. She has hurricanes in her blood and dreams of a time she can exist solely on mangoes and pineapple. Born in Lautoka, Fiji, she currently resides in British Columbia, Canada, where she reads too many books, watches too many K-dramas, and writes stories about girls taking over the world. Nafiza is the author of *The Candle and the Flame*, which was nominated for the William C. Morris Award, *The Wild Ones*, and *Road of the Lost*. Learn more at nafizaazad.com.

SAYANTANI DASGUPTA is the *New York Times* bestselling author of the critically acclaimed Bengali folktale and string theory–inspired Kiranmala and the Kingdom Beyond books, the first of which—*The Serpent's Secret*—was a Bank Street Best Book of the Year, a Booklist Best Middle Grade Novel of the 21st Century, and an E. B. White Read Aloud Honor Book. She is also the author of two other series set in the Kingdom Beyond multiverse, the anticolonial and Indian revolution–inspired Fire Queen series and the younger middle grade, environmentally themed adventures Secrets of the Sky. She is also the author of *She Persisted: Virginia Apgar* as well as two multicultural Jane Austen–inspired contemporary young adult novels *Debating Darcy* and *Rosewood: A Midsummer Meet Cute*. Sayantani is a pediatrician by training but now teaches at Columbia University. When she's not writing or reading, Sayantani spends time protecting her black Labrador retriever, Khushi, from the many things that scare him, including plastic bags. She is a team member of We Need Diverse Books and can be found online at sayantanidasgupta. com, on Twitter at @sayantani16, and on Instagram.

SABAA TAHIR is a former newspaper editor who grew up in California's Mojave Desert at her family's eighteen-room motel. There, she spent her time devouring fantasy novels, listening to thunderous indie rock, and playing guitar and piano badly. Her #1 *New York Times* bestselling An Ember in the Ashes series has been translated into more than thirty-five languages, and her most recent novel, *All My Rage*, won the National Book Award for Young People's Literature and the Michael L. Printz Award. Visit Sabaa online at sabaatahir. com and follow her on Instagram and Twitter @SabaaTahir.

ARTIST BIOS

TARA ANAND is an illustrator from Bombay, India, based in New York City. Tara loves to work in bright colors and organic textures to make paintings that feel sensitive, tense, and nuanced. She draws on her love of history and her surroundings to bring her images to life. Tara is currently illustrating her debut graphic novel, *Fitting Indian*, by Jyoti Chand. Visit her online at taraanandart.com.

NEHA KAPIL is an Indian American visual artist and fashion designer currently based in Los Angeles. She is a creator whose work uses a range of diverse mediums to celebrate South Asian culture and women of color. From painting and illustration to clothing and graphic design, Neha's work centers around feminism, storytelling, and amplifying cultural narratives.

Drawn to detail and tradition, Neha's art is a modern take on classical realism and art nouveau styles. A self-proclaimed maximalist, her designs are a representation of beauty and self-empowerment. Visit Neha at nehakapilart.com.

Kohla is the personal work of **MIRA F. MALHOTRA**, a Mumbai-based visual artist and illustrator and the founder of Studio Kohl.

Mira is known for her memorable, colorful illustrations that incorporate pop-culture references, feminist themes for a modern India, odd animals, and playful characters. She is heavily influenced by DIY, alternative culture, and the punk rock ethos. Nominated as one of the top thirty illustrators in India by *Creative Gaga* magazine, her clients have included WhatsApp, Nike, Penguin Random House India, Adobe, Godrej, Meta, Sony Music, British Council, AIGA, Kulture Shop, Apple, Facebook, Snapchat, Grazia India, Adidas, and many more.

By day she is the principal designer and founder of Studio Kohl India since 2013. She served as a jury member for the Drum Awards for Design in 2021 and 2022. Mira is a cofounding member of the South Asian feminist collective Kadak. Visit her at studiokohl.com.

NIMALI is a Sri Lankan American illustrator residing in the Midwest. When not drawing, she can be found indulging in various fandoms and watering her indoor plants. View her work online at nimali.org.

CYNTHIA PAUL is a writer and illustrator with a deep love for wild and whimsical desi stories. After a long career of doodling in the margins of her homework, she decided to jump into children's illustration and has loved it ever since. She has worked on graphic novels, picture books, book covers, and more. She currently lives in Los Angeles. To see more of her work, go to thebrightagency.com/us/childrens-illustration/artists/cynthia-paul.

CHAAYA PRABHAT is an illustrator and lettering artist from Chennai, India, currently working out of Goa. She has worked on a number of picture books, including *The Culture of Clothes*, written by Giovanna Alessio, *The Best Diwali Ever*, written by Sonali Shah, *Bracelets for Bina's Brothers*, written by Rajani LaRocca, and *Anni Dreams of Biryani*, written by Namita Moolani Mehra. Visit Chaaya at chaayaprabhat.com.

NEHA SHETTY is a freelance illustrator from India. Her work involves using bold colors and copy in an attempt to bridge the gap of underrepresentation of South Asian creative prowess in the global arena. Her unique experience of the world around her heavily inspires the approach to her artworks' own authenticity as well. Find more of her work at behance.net/thatzanymartian.

SIBU T.P. was born and raised in New York, from parents who immigrated from Kerala, India. He is an illustrator and writer who works in a space somewhere between magic and memory. He received his BA in English literature from Stony Brook University and his MFA in illustration from the Hartford Art School. Find Sibu at sibudraws.com and @sibutp on social media.

ACKNOWLEDGMENTS

Sona Charaipotra and I first discussed the possibility of this anthology years ago at the Kweli Color of Children's Literature Conference. There, as we sat with a small table of other desi kidlit writers, we imagined bringing together diverse voices from the South Asian diaspora to tell new tales. We are a people of infinite variety, and our distinct experiences—all of them still South Asian—are rarely fully recognized. While it would be impossible to pull together an anthology that represented every unique aspect and individual of the desi experience, we wanted to draw together a sampling of the gorgeous diaspora talent that would, at least, hint at the complexity and beauty of all that we are.

This book that you are holding in your hands is very much a dream come true, and for that I give endless thanks to:

All our brilliant authors who trusted us with their stellar

stories—Tracey, Sabaa, Naz, Shreya, Swati, Nikita, Tahir, Nafiza, Preeti, Sayantani, Sangu, Olivia, Tanaz. Your stories are all that we hoped for and so much more. I'm honored that you shared your voices with us. Simply, this anthology is in the world and in the hands of so many kids because of you.

The truly remarkable artists who helped make these stories come to life: Jyotirmayee Patra for our stunning cover. And for the interior art: Neha Kapil, Cynthia Paul, Chaaya Prabhat, Mira Malhotra, Nimali, Neha Shetty, Sibu T.P., and Tara Anand.

Fantastic agents and incredible advocates, Joanna Volpe and Suzie Townsend, and to the entire fabulous team at New Leaf Literary, especially Jordan Hill, Sophia Ramos, Jenniea Carter, and Lindsay Howard: You are all simply the best, and I am forever grateful for your incredible support and grace.

Our brilliant editor Megan Ilnitzki, who believed in the vision of this book and worked tirelessly and enthusiastically to make it real. And to all the amazing folks at HarperTeen and Epic Reads who put so much heart and support into this anthology, especially Parrish Turner, Erin DeSalvatore, Joel Tippie, Michael D'Angelo, Katie Boni, and Patty Rosati and the entire School & Library team!

To my family, the ones who kept me fed and told jinn stories that kept me up at night and captivated me with tales of peris and the wonders "back home."

To Thomas, Lena, and Noah, you are the ones that inspire the stories I tell. You are my home. To me, you are everything.

And big love to you, dear reader, for going with us on this wondrous journey into the heart of the magic we grew up with and the spirit of the home we all come from.

Finally, to all the desi kids, you are the heroes of your own stories. Let your light shine. This one's for you.

—Samira Ahmed

Samira Ahmed and I first cooked up the idea for this anthology of magical and mythological South Asian stories—lore and legend twisted and reimagined—more than five years ago. So I have to thank her, first and foremost, for humoring me over the course of many years as I brought it up time and time again, until it was finally time to make the vision a reality.

And while any book bears the author's name on it, it takes the effort of many. That is especially true for an anthology of voices like this. So first and foremost, thank you to the contributors to *Magic Has No Borders*. The writers: Tahir Abrar, Nafiza Azad, Tracey Baptiste, Tanaz Bhathena, Preeti Chhibber, Sayantani Dasgupta, Nikita Gill, Shreya Ila Anasuya, Naz Kutub, Sangu Mandanna, Olivia Chadha, Sabaa Tahir, and Swati Teerdhala. And the illustrators: Jyotirmayee Patra, Neha Kapil, Cynthia Paul, Chaaya Prabhat, Mira Malhotra, Nirnali, Neha Shetty, Sibu T.P., and Tara Anand.

Thank you to my publishing team at HarperTeen—the brilliant Megan Ilnitzki, Parrish Turner, Erin DeSalvatore, Joel Tippie, Michael D'Angelo, Katie Boni, Patty Rosati, and the rest of the Harper crew, who all work so hard. Thank you, too, to the awesome team at New Leaf Literary, especially agents Joanna Volpe and Suzie Townsend, Jordan Hill, Sophia

Ramos, Jenniea Carter, and Lindsay Howard. You guys are far more amazing than I could ever actually express in words.

And last but certainly not least: To my heart and soul, my family. The Charaipotras, the Dhillons, the Bhambris. You are my favorites, and so very loved.

To Navdeep, Kavya, and Shaiyar, my beloved little band of storytellers: Thank you for always being patient, always being present, and reminding me to do the same. I can't wait to see the stories you will share with the world. And to Mommy and Papa: I know my path wasn't exactly the one you were hoping I'd take. But everything you've taught me has led me here. Thank you for believing in dreams, and in me, no matter what direction I went off in. I hope I can make you proud.

And perhaps most importantly, to all the little brown kids—the dreamers, the schemers, the overachievers, and especially the underachievers: I see you. This story is for you. I write so that maybe you can see yourself, too. To all of you: You can be whatever you want to be. It's okay. Thank you for chasing your dreams and changing the world.

—Sona Charaipotra